CARMEN

LOVING A WINSTON SERIES
BOOK FIVE

STACY EATON

CHAPTER ONE

CARMEN

"I can't believe I'm going to be thirty-seven soon," I mumbled as I stared sightlessly out the window to the parking lot in front of my sister's café.

"You're getting old," my sister Candy commented with a smirk.

"You aren't that far behind me," I commented dryly.

"No, I'm not, but at least I am engaged to be married and have a kid."

"Harley is not officially your child," I reminded her.

"Yes, but he might as well be. He calls me Mom, and once Mike and I get married, I will adopt him officially."

"Are you sure you want to do that?" I asked.

She blinked. "Are you trying to tell me that you don't think it's a good idea?"

I shook my head. "I didn't say that. I'm just saying that you need to be sure you want to do that. What if things don't work out for you and Mike? What would you do then?"

Candy barked out a laugh, shifted in her seat, and glanced around momentarily as if thinking about her response. "Why are you being all doom and gloom about my relationship? I have no plans on my marriage to Mike not working out. Why would you even say that?"

"Nobody goes into marriage believing it won't work."

She pursed her lips at me. "When did you leave child psychology and become a marriage counselor?"

"Funny," I replied and shook my head, crossing my arms over the table and sighing. "I'm sorry, I'm just stuck in my head right now. With my birthday approaching, I thought I would have achieved more by this point in my life."

"Carmen, you are turning thirty-seven, not seventy."

"I know, but now I'm past the safe age of bearing children. You know I wanted several children."

"Doesn't Chad have two kids?"

I forced myself not to react. "Yes, he does." I wasn't a big fan of his kids. I know that wasn't nice to say, but truth be told, they were spoiled brats. Although not Chad's fault, his ex-wife doted on the kids to the extreme and gave them anything and everything they asked for.

"Then you will probably end up with at least two."

"Candy, I want my own kids," I whined. "His kids are a handful, and I disagree with their behavior. It has caused more than a few arguments between Chad and me."

"I'm sorry to hear that," Candy replied.

"I'm sorry I feel that way," I stated. "It's hard because I really like Chad and thought I saw a future for us. A real one, but then I met his kids and ex-wife, and I'm not sure I want a ringside seat to that circus."

Candy chuckled. "Then why don't you break up with him?"

"Because I like him. It's easy, as long as we don't have to deal with his children or ex." I stared out the window again, watching a car drive past. "Besides, it's not like anyone else is waiting in the wings."

"You could sign up for those dating sites again." She hiked a brow with a lopsided grin.

"Thanks, but no thanks. I never found anyone on those, and trust me, I looked."

"You could try a different one." She sipped from her iced mocha.

I gave her an exasperated look. "I was on five sites, and so were the same men. If I am not interested in them on one site, why would I be interested in them on another?"

Her lips parted. "Five? You were on five different dating sites?"

"Yes, so shut up. I tried that, and it didn't work."

Candy began to laugh, and then our sister Coral joined us. "What is so funny over here?"

"Did you know that Carmen was on five different dating sites?" Candy said between laughs.

Coral sank into a chair. "Really? Damn, I guess I'm glad I never signed up for one of them. I'd hate to be competing with you."

"Trust me, Coral; there was nothing to compete with. Besides, you are already married to your business." I took a drink of my coffee.

"Yeah, well, there are days I want a divorce," she huffed.

"You could try a separation," I suggested.

"Excuse me?" she asked in a puzzled tone.

"You know, take a few days off. Go on vacation. Let someone else do the work."

"I can't do that. You know what happened the last time I took a few days off. I came back and almost had to close my doors."

"Exaggerate much," Candy muttered.

"I'm not exaggerating, Candy. Chantel nearly cleaned me out while I was on vacation. How she thought I would not notice several thousand dollars missing is beyond me."

"Didn't she recently get sentenced?" I asked.

"Yeah, she got three years behind bars and three more on

3

probation."

"Monica is not Chantel," Candy stated.

"No, she's not, but I still don't know if I can trust her."

"Well, you need to find someone to trust, or just close the place down for a week and go on vacation."

"I can't close the place, Carmen. I barely make enough to pay the lease on this place. The landlord just raised it—again!"

"Then you need to learn to depend on your assistant manager because you look like hell and need a vacation," Candy stated.

"Do I really look that bad?" she asked in a weary voice.

I touched her arm. "You look like you could sleep for a week, and it's obvious you aren't eating enough too."

She rubbed her hands over her face. "How did we get on the topic of me looking like shit? I thought we were talking about your love life."

"We were, but let's talk about yours instead," I said with a chuckle.

"What love life?"

"Exactly!" Candy and I repeated at the same time and snickered.

"If I don't have time to take off, how could I date?"

"You're going to need to figure it out sooner or later, or you're going to end up an old spinster like Carmen," Candy said seriously, and I tossed a balled-up napkin at her.

"That's enough from you," I told her as someone at the front counter called for Coral.

"I'll see you guys later." She quickly disappeared, and Candy glanced at her watch.

"I should probably think about going too," she said as my phone rang.

"Sorry, I need to take this."

"Fine, you take that. I'm going to use the restroom before I get going."

I acknowledged her with a slight wave as I put the phone to my ear. "Hello, Ingrid. How are you today?"

"I'm doing well. How are you?"

"I'm all right. Did you need me at the office?"

"No, where are you?"

"I'm having coffee with my sister. Why? Is there an emergency someplace?"

"Not exactly an emergency, but you are supposed to be at a meeting at the middle school right now."

The moment she spoke, the conversation with Tammy exploded into my mind, and I began to gather all my stuff. "Holy crap, okay, I'm on my way." My phone started to beep, and I saw Tammy's name on the screen.

"Ingrid, please call Tammy back and tell her I am on my way."

"I'll tell her you had an emergency, which took you longer than expected."

"Thank you!" I gushed into the phone, shoved it into my purse as I collected my trash, and rushed to the container to push it in. My coffee cup was only half-empty, and the brew sloshed toward me and all down the front of my cream-colored pants. "No!"

Coral came around the counter. "Carmen, what's wrong?"

"I am late for a meeting I completely forgot about, and now I just poured coffee down my pants."

"Isn't Candy wearing brown pants?"

"Yes," I replied as Candy approached, and I got Coral's drift. "Hurry back to the bathroom. I need your pants."

"What?" She eyed me like a crazy person.

I pushed her toward the bathroom. "I need your pants! My assistant just called and reminded me I am supposed to be at the middle school right now. I can't go into a meeting covered in coffee. They will know where I was."

"Don't you drink coffee at your office?" she said as I shoved her into the bathroom and locked the door.

"Yes, but that doesn't matter. Change pants with me. You can go home and change. You already told me you don't have an appointment until eleven."

She huffed, but she began to take her pants off. "Come on, come on!" I waved my pants in the air as she took her time removing her slacks. Finally, I shoved mine at her and grabbed the ones she had removed. They were a little long on me, but I had bone-colored pumps in the car that I could change into that would help with that. I barely had the pants fastened when I collected my purse and tore open the door. Outside, a young woman with a small child stared at me in surprise. Her gaze slipped past me as I rushed down the hallway with a quick, "Excuse me."

"You could at least have waited until I was covered," I heard my sister yell behind me.

"Sorry! I love you, sis! Thank you!" I shouted over my shoulder as I ran toward the exit.

I started my car and put it into reverse faster than I ever had, and then I heard my brother's voice in my head. *Never get into a car in a mad rush. Always think before you begin to drive and slow down. You will get to your location when you get there. If you rush, you will get in an accident, and you will be even later. It is easier to apologize for your delay than never to say anything again.*

I closed my eyes, inhaled, exhaled a couple of times, and then checked to ensure it was safe to drive.

I made sure to drive *almost* the speed limit—praying I didn't get pulled over—and arrived at the middle school in nine minutes. I grabbed the first parking spot I saw, collected my work bag and purse, and exited the car, dropping my handbag to the ground after it got hooked on the corner of my door. I bent down and began to shove all the little things that had spilled out back into it, then burst up and started rushing for the school door, only to stop a few feet away from my car.

Crap! I needed to change my shoes! I did an abrupt about-face and returned to my car, popping the trunk and digging around the mess to find the ones I wanted. A sweatshirt flew out and landed on the asphalt, and I had to retrieve it, but then I saw one of the shoes. I growled to myself as I dug more, swearing that I would clean out my trunk, and finally found the second shoe. I quickly traded them for the ones I was wearing and discarded my other footwear into the trunk before slamming it closed.

I spun around and started to rush toward the front of the school. Out of the corner of my eye, I noticed someone standing about forty feet away watching me, and I pretended I didn't see them. I knew I must have looked like a madwoman the way I was behaving. Hopefully, it wasn't anyone I knew—okay, I knew everyone. Let's make that not someone I wanted to impress.

Right before I entered the school, I glanced back toward the parking lot. The person was a man, and he was climbing into his car, a smile on his face that stopped me in my tracks for a second—that smile. Holy crap, I would know that smile anywhere, but I had to be wrong. It couldn't be him. He had moved away long ago, and he had no reason to return.

I yanked my head around so I wasn't caught staring at the stranger as he drove away and put one foot in front of the other to avoid the ghostly memories of my past.

CHAPTER TWO

TIM

What were the odds that my company would open a warehouse in the same area where I had lived in my childhood? I had lived out west for the last twenty years, and now I was moving back.

Until recently, I hadn't thought much about where I'd spent the first chunk of my life. I moved to Millerstown in fourth grade and left again seven years later as a junior in high school. It had been challenging to move when I was seventeen.

About six months after I'd left Millerstown, my new friends were badgering me to stop pining away for a girl I would never see again. There were way too many things to see and experience in California, and I needed to get a move on. I had taken their advice, and I didn't regret it.

However, here I was, moving back to the area after my company expanded this way and built a new warehouse. I took a few days off to fly into town, look for a place to live, and get all three kids registered in school.

Being back here and seeing how much it had grown since I was a teenager was odd. I drove down the main street of Millerstown and remembered small shops along the roadway, but now about half of those shop buildings were gone and replaced with taller office buildings or strip malls. Apartment complexes were everywhere you looked, and cookie-cutter homes replaced the fields that once were in abundance.

I wondered briefly if my old house would be on the market, and I had even driven by it and pulled to the side of the street to study it. The two-story sprawling house looked smaller than I remembered, but the exterior was still the same —only aged. It would need new shutters, paint, and a roof; the grass my father had painstakingly worked on every weekend was patchy and brown. The driveway also required to be dug up and relaid, as it had gaping holes, and the asphalt was almost white with age instead of black as it should be.

I was almost relieved it wasn't available since I knew I wouldn't have the time to handle repairs and manage the new warehouse opening. I would have to settle for one of those generic homes. I had already anticipated this situation as I had researched the housing market before contacting an agent.

Ironically, as I had searched for a Realtor, I came across a name I remembered well from high school, Kayley Young. Only she went by Kayley Sexton now. I was pretty sure it was the same person as I hadn't met too many Kayleys in my lifetime, and with a quick search, I located a picture of her and confirmed. I tried to reach out to her but learned she was on vacation this week, so I settled for someone else in her office.

Eventually, I would run into her again, and Kayley would be a great person to speak with to learn about the status of others we had known—like Carmen Winston. They had been very close friends, and we had gone out on more than a few double dates.

In the meantime, Brianna, a young woman who worked for the same agency, showed me those not so wonderfully made all-look-alike homes. I hated them, but that was pretty much all that was available in quick rentals.

Once we moved and got settled, and my house in California sold, I would begin searching for another home—one with more character. At least I found one in a great price range with four bedrooms. The kids wouldn't have to share, which had been their number one priority request for leaving behind their friends and moving here.

I remembered that feeling well. When my parents told us we were moving, my world shook. I had been irritated with my parents for doing that to me in my junior year. It broke my heart to leave the school I loved, the life I was building, my friends, and Carmen—especially Carmen. We had been inseparable for years, and I had even imagined us going off to college together, getting married, and having babies.

Since I had been back in town, I'd had one eye open as I drove around. Wouldn't it be great if we ran into each other? What would she think of me moving back to town?

I wonder who she was married to now and how many children she had. Perhaps I should look her up on social media and see what I could learn. It had been at least twelve years since I had done that. I hadn't found much then, but some pictures were on Wesley Young's account. Over the years, Wes and I had distantly kept in touch on social media.

It had given me enough to know that she was still beautiful and appeared to be doing well. Since I had learned I was moving back here, I had continually wondered how she would react to me being back. Each time I thought about it, I pushed the thoughts aside. I wasn't ready to be thinking about another relationship—not that we would have any type of relationship. I had a new job and kids to worry about.

I had already checked in at the jobsite where the new warehouse was being erected. Everything was on target and would be operational in about five weeks.

Initially, I was supposed to have stayed in California and run the main warehouse out there, but Charlie, the guy to take this one, learned his wife had cancer, and they didn't want to leave the medical care they had in place. So, I accepted the position.

How could I say no? I got a bonus and a raise, and I was moving to a smaller, more laid-back community where my kids would be safer than the big cities in California. It was a win-win situation.

Since I had been able to find a house so quickly, I changed my flight, and I was heading back to California later today. The only thing I had left to do was to get the kids registered for school.

I had already dealt with the elementary school for Savannah and the high school for Tripp, and I had just finished at the middle school for Dean. With all that accomplished, I could head to the airport early without stressing about rushing.

I was walking to my car at the middle school when a small gray sedan zipped into the lot and parked haphazardly. Thank God no kids were around because the driver was a maniac.

Suddenly, the door opened, and a woman popped out. I got a flash of wild blond hair before she disappeared from view between two cars. I kept walking toward my rental car but kept one eye in her direction to ensure she was okay and wasn't lying on the ground, calling for help.

A moment later, she popped up and began hustling toward the school, mumbling something I couldn't make out. I had just reached my car when she spun around and moved back toward her car, and I stopped in my tracks with my hand frozen a few inches from the door handle.

Holy shit! That was Carmen Winston! She still had the same wavy bright-blond hair and thin but curvy frame that she'd had as a teenager. She rushed around to the back of her car and popped the trunk, and I started to chuckle as I watched her dig around inside it.

Obviously, she wasn't any tidier than she had been when she was sixteen. I imagined her trunk looked about as neat as her closet had when I had last known her. It was a war zone.

I continued to observe her animated display in searching for something and leaned back against the car, crossing my arms lightly over my chest as I grinned. She hadn't changed much in her mannerisms, and I soaked them up.

Carmen still tucked her hair behind her ear and stomped her foot when frustrated. I bet she didn't even realize she did that. She bent over and retrieved a sweatshirt that had flown over her head and onto the parking lot, and I couldn't help but stare at the way those brown slacks accentuated her ass.

Just then, she pulled out two shoes and quickly changed. The higher heels kept the pants from touching the ground, and she collected her bags, slammed the trunk lid, and began to run toward the front of the school.

I watched until she was almost there. Had she not seemed to be in such a rush, I might have tried to stop her and say hello. However, it was obvious that she had somewhere to be, and she was late. That was something she had been as a teenager too. Not that she was late, but she always seemed hurried and arrived everywhere at the last second.

So what was she late for today? Was she a teacher or perhaps a parent rushing in for a meeting? I hoped everything was all right as I climbed into the car and got on the road.

On the way to the airport, my mind was swirling with memories. Not just of the town and growing up, but of Carmen too. She had been such a massive part of my life, and most of my middle and high school memories revolved around her.

Then I thought about her brothers and wondered if they were still in the area, and her sisters too. As I drove through town one last time, I spotted a coffee shop and decided to pop in and grab a cup for the road.

It wasn't until I was inside that I put two and two together when I saw Carmen's younger sister, Coral, behind the counter. Her sister owned the coffee shop, or at least I assumed that since it was called Coral's Coffee Café.

I watched her as she hurried around the small space behind the counter. Her eyes darted this way and that, but she kept a smile plastered on her face. She had been pretty as a teen but had grown into a beautiful woman, although she looked tired now. Her long dirty-blond hair was pulled back in a ponytail at the back of her neck, and she wore small diamond studs in her ears.

As I approached the counter, I looked forward to saying hello to her and wondered if she would recognize me, but as I stepped up to place my order, she spoke to someone off to the side and then disappeared into the back. Another woman took my order, and I was out the door before Coral returned.

Well, I'd have time to catch up with her later too. At least I knew where to find her.

I was at the airport an hour later, and it took thirty minutes to get through security. Once at my gate, I pulled out my laptop and signed into one of my social media accounts. I searched Carmen Winston, and it wasn't hard to find her profile, but there wasn't much to see as she had it set to private. The profile picture was that of a sunset, and not even her.

However, there were a few businesses that she liked that showed up on her profile page. One was her sister's coffee shop, and I clicked on that and then scanned through the pictures. It took a while, but finally, I hit pay dirt. There was a picture of Coral, Carmen, Candy, Evan, and Ethan together around a table.

I zeroed in on Carmen. She looked even more beautiful than she had as a teenager. Her eyes sparkled with light, her face shone with pleasure, and her smile made my heart beat faster. It had always done that. Anytime she looked up at me and smiled widely, I felt it to my toes. As I sat here staring at her image, a

14

whirlwind of emotion spun through me. There was regret at losing touch, happiness that she looked like she was doing well, and perhaps a bit of residual love that had long since been buried. All of those and more bubbled to the surface.

I studied the other people in the photograph. They all looked really good, too, but where was Cara? Maybe she couldn't make it that day. I hoped that was the case and something terrible hadn't happened to her. I knew too well what bad things could happen and didn't wish them on anyone.

After skimming more photos, I returned to Carmen's page and clicked on the Millerstown Tavern she had also liked. One of the first photographs caught my eye. Candy Winston was in it with a guy who had intense eyes. Obviously, they were together, as the way Candy leaned against him said it all. The protective arm around her finished the story without even reading the caption. Interesting. He looked more like the kind of guy Cara would have dated, not Candy.

I skimmed through the pictures and found more of Carmen and her siblings, but most were of the food and other people in the community. As I was about to close the page, I saw another picture of Candy and the man from earlier. I read the post and found that Candy was engaged to Michael Bollard, the owner of Millerstown Tavern.

Michael Bollard? The name didn't ring a bell, but as I stared into his direct eyes, I felt I never wanted to be on the wrong side of that man. I laughed, not sure why I would even think that. I guess it was just the bad-boy vibe he gave off.

I skimmed down one more picture and stopped, surprised at who was in the picture. Candy and her fiancé were there, but also Evan Winston, who had his arm wrapped possessively around Alaina Marshall-Buckworth, the owner of the company I worked for.

"Holy shit!" I murmured as I suddenly remembered that Alaina had recently been married, and that is why she moved here and was opening a new warehouse. I opened another browser and searched Alaina Marshall-Buckworth's marriage; the search results populated, and I chuckled as I clicked on the first link. There was a picture of Evan Winston with the owner of my company. Talk about a small world.

CHAPTER THREE

CARMEN

I t had been almost four weeks since that meeting at the middle school, and I remembered it as if it were yesterday. Not because the meeting was anything special. It was just another meeting on the new risk assessment strategies we were starting to use for kids in trouble.

No, I could recall every minute of that day because the man in the parking lot had sparked many long-buried memories.

I knew some sights and scents were deeply ingrained into our minds, and those memories could surface if they were touched. Well, my memories hadn't just been touched; they had been squeezed from every squiggle of my brain.

All because of one single smile from over a hundred feet away, and the damn smile hadn't even been directed at me. The man had been climbing into a car. The car was dark blue. The man was tall, and his hair was brown. Those were the only things I could tell you about that moment.

All other thoughts had vanished and were replaced by snippets of memories of when I was young, carefree, happy, and in love—in love with a young man who broke my heart after he moved away and stopped communicating with me.

For about the tenth time, I thought about that day and what happened after seeing him in the parking lot.

I walked through the maze of hallways from the office to the conference area; my mind was going a million miles an hour. Every time I tried to shove a memory aside, another would burst forth, and I felt like I was being bombarded with emotional baggage stuffed into a closet, and the latch had finally given way.

When I neared the conference room, I detoured into the restroom and locked myself in a stall, putting my head against the cold metal. There was no way it was Tim Kohl. It had been a random man who just looked like Tim had. That was all it was. Tim lived in California. He had no family here and no reason to come back to town. It was just a man who looked like him.

Why was I physically reacting to seeing this man if that was the case? Because I had been dwelling over my lack of love life and talking to my sister about it this morning? That's the only reason. My subconscious must have pulled a happier time forward and manifested a smile on that man. That was it.

The man wasn't even smiling because of me. He must have been smiling at someone I hadn't noticed in the car.

Get a grip on yourself, Carmen! I hissed inside my head, shook my hair back, lifted my chin, and unlocked the stall. I stepped out and hurried out of the bathroom and down the hallway as I shoved all thoughts of Tim into an area of my mind that I could close off.

The meeting was already in progress, and I slipped into an empty seat as quietly as possible. The other seven occupants glanced at me and then back to Mike Brooks, who spoke.

He finished his sentence and leaned back in his seat, saying dryly, "Nice of you to make it, Carmen."

"I'm sorry, I had an emergency I needed to deal with." I felt my cheeks pinken slightly, but then I fanned my face and laughed. "Sorry, I'm a little flustered. I ran in here from the parking lot."

A few people chuckled, but Mike stared at me for a moment longer. His gaze drifted over my features. Our eyes locked again, and I forced myself not to shift. I wasn't sure what it was about him, but he made me uncomfortable sometimes when he studied me so carefully. Perhaps it was because he had asked me out once, and I had turned him down. I hadn't been interested in dating at that time. Shortly after, I met Chad, and after running into Mike one night while out with Chad, Mike remained aloof with me.

The meeting continued, and forty-five minutes later, we adjourned and went our separate ways. As I entered the main office, I had stopped to chat with a few of the ladies who worked there, and Anna, one of the administrative assistants, had stepped up to the front counter, a folder in her hands as we laughed over a story she was sharing with me. Her phone rang on her desk, and she set the folder down and returned to the desk.

My gaze dropped to the folder without thought and began to shift away, but something caught my eye, and my eyes slammed back to the folder. There was a name and a date written on the edge: Kohl, Dean, Feb 12th, transfer from Santa Ana, California.

The world around me vanished, and my heart thudded in my chest, filling my ears with the sound of a drum as I lifted my head, spun toward the door, and raced out in an utter panic.

Now, I sat at my desk, staring at my calendar. The date had arrived, and if all had gone well, Dean, Tim's son, was starting his first day of school today. That meant his father was in town. Which also meant his mother was here too. That also meant that I would eventually run into them. I dreaded that day.

I had thought about this so many times over the last few weeks. Why would Tim come back now after all this time? What was he going to say when he saw me? Had Tim seen me that day in the parking lot, or had his wife been in the car, and Tim was talking to her? I couldn't imagine he could have missed me, but why hadn't he said anything if he had seen me? Because his wife was with him? What was he going to do when they bumped into me around town? Ignore me? Tell her we dated way back when, but it was no big deal?

It had been a big deal. The thought of running into them made me very anxious, and I wasn't the type to be anxious. I hoped that the first time we came face-to-face was while we were alone. That would make it easier.

Maybe he had seen me that day but decided not to say anything because he couldn't care less. I was someone from his past and no one he cared to associate with anymore. Or he thought I wouldn't be interested in speaking with him after how we broke up or—more correctly—how he broke up with me.

I had been pretty upset the last time we spoke. It had been brief, and I asked him why he never called or emailed me anymore. Tim had told me he was busy and maybe things wouldn't work out—but he wasn't sure and needed time to think about it. Then he said he had to go, and I never spoke with him again after that, and the only other communication I had from him was a week later in a short email.

That email said he was sorry, but he had too much going on and couldn't deal with something else. He wished me well and signed it, love always, Tim. I didn't respond, and I never heard from him again. I was that 'something else' he couldn't deal with. Me, the girl he had vowed to love to death do us part—without the actual vows. The girl whose virginity he had taken. The girl he spent every moment he could with for four years.

I sighed and then sipped my coffee. I was supposed to be planning for a therapy session and reviewing my notes from our previous ones, but my mind was stuck on the fact that Tim was back in town.

How long would it take for Tim and me to run into one another? What would we say? Would he pretend that everything was perfect? Would he introduce me to his wife and act like we had never dated? Would his wife know who I was? How long had they been married? How many kids did he have? What did he do for a living? Why had he moved here? The questions kept falling like water from a waterfall.

Would Tim apologize for how things ended? For never reaching out again? Would he say he missed me and wished he had never stopped communicating with me? Would he say that he cherished the memories of us for years? That he secretly pined for me and thought about returning and sweeping me off my feet?

I frowned. Of course, he didn't. He moved on, forgot about me, fell in love with at least one other woman, and had a family. I was the last thing he probably ever thought about. The day he saw me in the parking lot—if he even noticed me—he probably laughed and thought, thank God he left. He undoubtedly thought I was ugly now, too thin, too short. Or my hair was frizzy—which it was most days.

Geez, he had probably watched me dig through the trunk of my car. I closed my eyes and shook my head.

I had to forget about Tim. It had turned into an almost obsession to know what would happen and when it would occur. I wasn't even able to sleep well, and I generally never had a problem sleeping. I was dreaming about him if I wasn't lying there in bed dwelling over him.

I glanced at the clock on the far side of the room. My appointment would be here any moment. I once again shoved thoughts of Tim out of my mind and pulled Missy's folder a little closer. Missy needed my attention. Tim did not.

No sooner had I done that than my assistant buzzed into my office. "Your ten o'clock is here."

"Send her in. Thank you, Ingrid."

I closed my folders, stacking them neatly on the corner of my desk. My trunk might be a mess, but my office was meticulous. The door opened as I stood, and I smiled brightly at Missy.

"Good morning, Missy. How are you today?" She gave me a tight smile and closed the door. Missy was wearing her traditional clothing options of black pants and black boots. Her usual black tank top was missing and replaced with a dark charcoal gray. The only hint of color on her was the bright blue added to her eyelids. The shade was so vivid that it was hard to look away from it.

"I'm okay," she replied as she got seated in the side chair and threw her leg over the arm to get comfortable. She had a choice of four different seats to sit in, and she always chose that particular one and sat the exact same way.

She had initially come to me after trying to commit suicide. While no attempt was good, her attempt was more of a cry for help than an actual attempt to kill herself.

She had cut her wrists so that she would bleed and make a mess, but it would have taken a very long time to bleed to death that way. In fact, it might have even scabbed over before she could have bled out.

I was thankful for that because now I would have the opportunity to work with her and hopefully help her find the answers she needed to move on and grow from this experience. We were digging into why she felt the way she did and how she had gotten to where she was now.

"Do you have anything new you want to share with me?" I asked after I got seated.

She thought momentarily, then shook her head. "No, I don't think so." She paused and said, "I told my mom I wanted a bullring."

"You mean you wanted to get your septum pierced?"

She pointed to the end of her nose. "I don't know what that is, but I want to pierce this here and put a ring there."

"It's called a septum piercing. What did your mom say about that?"

"What do you think she said?"

"Let me guess. She said no."

"Of course, she said no. She never understands me or what I want. I need to be able to express myself properly."

"And you think having a bullring will express you properly?"

She shrugged. "Yeah, why not?"

"Or it could just be adding a hole to your body," I stated, and she frowned. "Don't get me wrong, Missy. I know a lot of kids have them and like them. I think they are interesting. I don't know if I would have had the courage to get one at your age."

"Do you want one?" she asked almost excitedly.

"Um, no. I don't think it would be very professional of me."

She rolled her eyes. "Kids would think it was cool."

"Maybe, but the parents might not."

"I thought you worked for the kids." She rolled her eyes again. If I had a dollar for every time a teenager rolled their eyes in my office, I would be almost as rich as my sister-in-law.

"Have you thought about getting a different kind of piercing? Like a nostril piercing? I think those can be pretty, and they seem very popular. Perhaps your mother would go for something like that. My sister was actually thinking of getting one."

She thought about that for a moment. "Maybe."

"Might be worth talking to Mom about it."

"Yeah, maybe."

"Anything else going on? Have you been writing in your journal?"

"I wrote a few times this last week, but mostly I just drew pictures of how I felt."

"And how is that?"

She stared at her hands, picking at her nails as the room grew quiet. A few seconds later, she said softly, "Lonely."

That one word described so much about her life. Her mother worked all the time to afford everything they needed, and her father disappeared when she was little. She only had a couple of friends, but from what I understood, she didn't spend much time with them outside of school.

Her cellphone vibrated, and she pulled it out of her back pocket. I usually let them keep their phones on them while we were in session, but if they didn't give me their attention, I would ask them to put them away. Missy rarely looked at hers, but this time she did.

"Huh, looks like we got a new kid in my English Lit class."

I froze; Missy was in high school. What were the odds of two new students starting in the district simultaneously and unrelatedly? Probably not very high.

"That's nice," I stated, not knowing what else to say.

"Kat said he's cute, but she thinks almost every guy is cute."

"Did she say what his name was?"

She shook her head, and her fingers flew over the keyboard. I realized just as she received a reply that I was holding my breath. I released it as she replied, "Tripp. His name is Tripp. Cool name, huh?" She laughed a moment later as she leaned closer to her screen. "She sent me a picture of him. He is cute."

I leaned forward, forcing myself not to grab the phone from her hand. "Can I see?"

She turned the phone around, and I swear the room began to spin. The young man's face on the screen could have been Tim when he was seventeen.

CHAPTER FOUR

TIM

"Come on, Tripp, give me a damn break here."

"I can't believe you are making me take the bus. It's my first day."

"What are you afraid of? This school is a quarter of the size of your old one. You aren't going to have any trouble finding anything."

"I'm not scared, and I'm not stupid enough to get lost, Dad. What kind of an image does it give me if I show up on the school bus? Only the nerds and losers do that."

"Hey! Watch your mouth, Tripp."

"No! I don't get why Dean and Savannah are getting special treatment. You are taking them to school. Why can't you at least drop me off on my first day? It's not fair that they don't have to take the bus."

"Tripp, they are not as mature as you are. Although, with how you act, you should be the one in elementary school, not your sister."

"Whatever, Dad. This sucks. This whole thing sucks! I want to go back to California!"

My blood pressure went sky-high, and I almost lost my cool,

but then I closed my eyes, braced my hands on my hips, and hung my head for a moment, reminding myself of how I had felt the first day at a new school.

I went to stand in front of him. "Tripp, I'm sorry. I forgot how hard this is on you. I remember what it felt like to attend a new school at your age. It is scary." He opened his mouth to dispute that, but I held my hand up and continued. "Yes, it is scary. Wondering where you are supposed to go and who you will meet is very scary. I get it, especially when you don't know how people will respond to you. I remember what it was like, although I was a junior and not a sophomore, when I had to change schools. If you want me to drive you today, I can."

Immediate relief flashed through his eyes, but he would never admit that. Instead, he shrugged one shoulder and turned away from me. "Fine. Let me know when we have to leave."

I glanced at my watch. "Be ready to go in five minutes." He didn't respond, and I turned to Dean and Savannah sitting at the kitchen table watching me.

"How are you guys doing? Are you excited about your new schools?"

"I am!" Savannah said. She was an eternal optimist, just like her mother. "I can't wait to see my teacher again! I'm so glad I got the chance to meet her. Laura said she was super nice, and I think she's right."

Laura was a neighbor's child who happened to be the same age. When we moved in, the mother, Megan, had stopped to introduce herself and her two kids. She also had a son, Will, a year older than Dean, and they seemed to have hit it off pretty quickly too.

Megan was friendly and somewhat surprised when she learned it was just me and the three kids. She offered to help with before or after-school care if I needed it since she worked from home. I appreciated that more than she knew and said I would probably take her up on that offer since I didn't know anyone in town—well, no one I had stayed in contact with—except Wes—but that wasn't really in touch.

"Yeah, I guess," Dean replied. "Will said the teachers were pretty cool there."

"Good to know. I hope Will is right." I glanced at my watch again. "You guys need to finish your breakfast since I need to drop your brother off too."

In a hustle of kids and backpacks, we rushed out of the house seven minutes later and climbed into my SUV. As we neared the high school, Tripp started to shift nervously in his seat, and I again remembered the first day of my new school.

I had gotten lost more than once and had been late to almost every class. The school there had over five thousand students, but my entire school district back here hadn't even had half of that. It was overwhelming.

The other day, I had offered to take Tripp around the school so he could see it first, but he'd taken one look at the building and laughed. "You're kidding? This is the high school? That is all of it? What a joke!"

"It's not a joke, Tripp, and yes, that is all of it, but I promise it will be all you need."

"Yeah, right. I'll be lucky to get an education here. They probably still write on paper instead of using computers. What a dump. So much for getting a good education and getting into a good college."

I sighed as the flashback from a few days ago ended, and I glanced at Tripp again. He looked tense, but that was to be expected. The school might be smaller and easier to maneuver, but he was still new, which would be the biggest obstacle.

"I assume you don't want me to come in with you."

He turned to me, eyes wide and a horrified expression on his face as he shook his head. "No!" I forced myself not to laugh.

Tripp sat with his hand on the handle for a moment. "You're going to do great. Just head into the office, and they will give you your schedule. The office is through those front doors." I pointed, and he followed my hand and nodded. "Do you want me to pick you up today after school?"

"Um, no. I'll find a way home."

"You sure? I mean, you can take the bus."

His face flipped back to mine, his features screwed up like he had tasted something bad. "I am not taking the bus. I'll walk if I have to."

Before I could say anything else, Tripp shoved open the door and bolted from the car, slamming the door behind him. I sighed and took my foot off the brake to move down the lane.

"Tripp sure is grumpy," Savannah stated.

"Yes, he is," I agreed.

When we got to the middle school, it was not as busy. The buses wouldn't start rolling in for another twenty minutes as they had to finish with the high school students, then pick up all the middle school kids.

"You're coming in, right, Dad?" Dean asked from the back seat.

I peered at him in the mirror, noting his wide eyes. I smiled. "You bet I am. Savannah and I are both going to come in with you."

"Does she have to come?"

"Hey!" Savannah whined. "I can't stay in the car by myself."

"Dean, be nice to your sister. Yes, she has to come in."

"Fine," he muttered.

I shook my head as I found a parking spot. Dean and Savannah usually got along pretty well. I had a feeling that this was coming from what he had witnessed with his older brother and not a dislike for his sister.

I told Savannah to leave her backpack in the car, and we headed into the school. Both of the kids were looking everywhere and checking everything out. As we headed toward the front door, I glanced toward the sports fields in the back and noted that the bleachers were different.

I found myself smiling as I remembered that Carmen and I had shared our first kiss under those bleachers during a football game. I wasn't a football fan but I went to the games to see her.

We entered the school, and my mind shifted back over two decades, like the last time I had been here. The paint was all different, but the building itself was the same. Even the smell brought me back to a time filled with laughter and fun.

I glanced at my son as he looked around curiously. I sure hoped that he found his footing soon and found a way to embrace his new school. I knew he would enjoy it as much as I did if he could.

We entered the office as a woman walked in from a back hallway. "Can I help you?"

"Hi, my son, Dean Kohl, is starting classes today."

Looking slightly annoyed, she glanced at the clock. "School doesn't start for another forty minutes."

"I had to drop his brother off at the high school first. Figured I'd just come by here a bit early since I was here."

She gave me a tight-lipped smile. "Have a seat. I don't think Anna is here yet, but I'll see if I can find her."

"Thank you," I replied and turned to find both kids already taking a seat. Dean situated himself to have a good view out the glass window to the hall.

We sat for about five minutes before Anna, the woman I had spoken with previously, entered the office with her arms full. "Hi!" she said brightly to me and then directed her attention toward Dean. "You must be Dean. Welcome to Millerstown Middle School."

"Hi," Dean said with a slight wave.

She grinned widely at him and then shifted her focus to me. "Give me just a minute, and I'll get you guys all checked in. Then I can take Dean to the lunchroom to wait with the arriving

29

students." She glanced at the clock. "Mr. Henry will have the rock wall out this morning. Maybe you will get a chance to try it out."

"You have a rock wall?" Dean asked as he burst to his feet like a jack-in-the-box.

"We do. Do you know how to use one?"

"Yeah! I always went rock climbing at a place back home—I mean in California. I even made it to the top, one hundred feet up. I got to ring the bell!"

"Wow! How exciting that must have been. Our wall isn't quite that big, but I bet you will still enjoy it. You might even be able to help some of the other kids do it."

"Cool!" Dean grinned.

After excusing herself, she disappeared through another door, and Dean made a beeline for me. "Did you hear that? They have a rock wall, Dad!"

"That's pretty awesome."

"Did they have one when you went here?"

"Nope."

"That is so cool! I get to do stuff that you didn't." Dean shifted from foot to foot, obviously excited to check it out.

"I want to go on the rock wall," Savannah said.

Dean turned to her. "Sorry, you're going to have to wait until next year."

"We will see if they have a rock-climbing place nearby and take you there, Savannah."

"Okay," she said with a bright smile that melted my heart. It was so much like her mother's.

Anna returned with a folder and a computer. "Dean, this is your computer. Dad, I need you to sign this. Did you bring the rest of his forms?"

"I did them online last night," I told her as we went to the counter.

"Okay, great, I'll print them out and put them in his folder."

"I get my own computer?" Dean asked with a frown.

"Yep, you sure do. Did you not have a computer at your old school?"

"Yeah, I did, but I didn't think I'd get one here."

"Why not?"

"Because Tripp said these schools are dumps, and it was going to suck to go here."

I sighed. "Older brother. Be happy he is at the high school, and you missed his gloriously positive attitude."

She chuckled and then addressed Dean. "Well, we might be small, but we have a lot of things for our students. I hope you keep an open mind about us and enjoy your time here."

"Probably," he said with a shrug.

"Do you need anything else from me?"

"No, I think that's it. Is Dean riding the bus home, or will you pick him up?"

"I want to take the bus, Dad. Will said he'd make sure I got off at the right place."

"Then the bus it is."

Savannah and I watched Dean and Anna head down the far hallway, and I knew that Dean would be all right in his new school. He might have some growing pains, but he was already asking a million questions about things they had here and seemed excited about the answers.

"Come on, sweetheart. Let's go find your school."

I had already taken Savannah to see her school, and she had even briefly met her teacher, so I wasn't surprised when we pulled up, and she told me that she could go in by herself. She was more mature than both her brothers put together these days.

"Are you nervous?"

"No. I'm excited to meet new people."

"Did you want me to pick you up?"

"Nope. Laura said she would help me get home, and if you aren't there, I can go to her house for a snack."

"Okay, well, I hope you have a great day."

Savannah leaned between the seats and kissed my cheek. "I will, Daddy. I hope you have a good day too."

With that, she climbed carefully out of the car. I remained there as I watched her head toward the school. Another little boy came running from a car behind me, and then an adult opened the doors as they approached. The woman waved in my direction, and Savannah and the little boy disappeared behind closed doors.

I grinned and was about to drive away when I checked for traffic around me and saw a woman about to cross in front of my car. Our eyes met, and it took a second, but then we recognized one another, and she came around to the door.

"Holy shit! Tim Kohl? Is that really you?"

"Riley Young, wow. You might be the last person I expected to run into at the elementary school."

She laughed. "I know, right? I hated school as a kid, and now I teach these little monsters. What are you doing here?"

"I just dropped my daughter off."

"Wait! Hold the damn phone! You live here now?"

"Just moved back last weekend."

Her eyes popped wide. "Holy hell! Does Carmen know? Has she seen you?" She stuck her head into the window, and I pulled back so our heads didn't collide. She looked me over. "Man, she's going to freak out. You look pretty good for an old guy."

I shook my head as I laughed at her. "Thanks for calling me old, but we are almost the same age, and no, I haven't talked to her. I didn't even know if she lived around here." Which was a lie, but she didn't need to know I had stalked Carmen online.

Riley threw her head back and laughed. "She will die when she finds out you are back! That is awesome, and of course, she still lives here. Almost everyone is still here."

Someone called Riley's name, and she twisted to wave at them before turning back and putting her hand on the door. I noticed the wedding ring on her left hand immediately. "Hey, I gotta go, but it is so nice to see you again, Tim. I can't wait to catch up with you."

"You too, Riley."

I watched as she walked away, looking just as gorgeous as she had twenty years ago. I wondered who had put a ring on that beautiful wildcat and pondered if Carmen was also wearing one on her finger as I drove away.

CHAPTER FIVE

CARMEN

It had been a busy week as the school district began to put the new risk assessment program into play. We had been discussing it for months and training teachers and other staff on what to look for and how to report things. Last week it went live.

There hadn't been much the first week, but three cases came to our attention this week.

This program wasn't for kids at risk of failing school but for failing to thrive and showing signs of heading down the wrong path. By that, I meant kids who might show signs of violence— to themselves or others.

In today's climate, when people were shooting up schools, places of business, medical facilities, and places of worship, we had to find ways to get on top of these things.

It was shown repeatedly that had people paid closer attention to someone when they were younger, they might have been able to stop the tragedy that later occurred. We mainly heard about that in school shootings or where the shooters were in their early twenties.

These young people had been showing signs, even if those

signs were minor, for years, and people didn't stop and put the pieces together. I had read case after case of an active shooter after-action reports where they dissected the young person's life and found signs from years previous. Had each piece been identified earlier, thought about, and put together with others, perhaps those tragedies could have been averted.

That is what the risk assessment was for. The purpose was for anyone who saw something that didn't look or feel right to say something. When a report came in, a team would look closer and see if more research was needed.

We didn't just look at the information that was submitted but also family life and friends. We even reached out to law enforcement to see if they had any contact with the juvenile, and then, of course, we spoke to the child in question.

Now we have three related cases in the high school. We hadn't been sure if the threat was real or not. Someone had heard three children discussing a previous school shooting, which alarmed the person who overheard the conversation.

I was on the assessment team, and the minute the teacher entered the threat notification, I had been running nonstop. We had expected to get maybe one or two in the first couple of weeks and expected those to be more like cries for help. We never expected it to be something of such alarm.

Within an hour of that notification, the six-person team was in the high school's conference room. We pulled every bit of information on the children involved and tried to figure out who else to pull in to assist us with the process.

Each child would be interviewed separately. We would need to speak with the family and attempt to get consent to search their lockers and possibly their rooms at home.

Our team had a guidance counselor for that school, the vice principal, a psychologist, two teachers, and an officer from our local police department. I was the psychologist, and Cameron

Sexton, Kayley Young's husband, was the officer. The other people on the teams changed depending on the school.

It was overwhelming to deal with three assessments at once, but it was also an excellent way to learn.

The assessment was received on Wednesday, and by Friday afternoon, we had determined that while the teacher had a warranted reason for the alert, there was no cause for alarm.

The students had been discussing ideas for a class project for social studies. None of the kids turned out to be suicidal or angry with society. They were from steady families with good relationships in and out of school.

We breathed easier that afternoon when we closed the cases for good. We knew the day would come when we needed to keep a case open and watch the student and the circumstances to ensure it didn't proceed to a bad place. This was not the case for these three students.

Word had gotten out around the school about the assessment, and we received positive comments. The kids thought it was a great idea. Some parents had been concerned that something horrible was about to happen in the schools, and we emailed all the parents to ensure all was well and that the new assessment protocols had worked as they were intended to.

My fingers were crossed that this would be our last assessment for a while. I yawned as the buzzer on my desk went off. "Missy is here for her appointment," Ingrid said.

"Okay, send her in."

I stood and shook my head to try and wake up. Since Wednesday, I hadn't gotten much sleep, and the hours my eyes were closed filled my mind with images of children dying.

Missy bounded into the room dressed in her usual black, but her eye makeup was slightly less garish today. In fact, the shading on her eyes was rather complimentary. "You look very nice today."

She smiled at me and slightly turned her face toward me, pointing at the side of her nose. "I got it done!"

"Wow! Your mom went for it?"

She nodded excitedly as she sat. "Not only did she let me get one, but she got one too."

I laughed. "How did that happen?"

"I showed her a bunch of pictures, and she finally agreed. She took me because she had to sign for it, and after Mom saw mine, she decided to get it too because she said it looked cute."

"Well, look at that." I grinned at her.

She was sitting as usual, but today she was swinging her legs back and forth like she was happy. "Is there anything else new?"

"Maybe," she said shyly, peering at me from under her tinted black bangs.

"Maybe, huh? What does that mean?"

"Do you remember that new student I told you about last week?"

"Yes, you said his name was Tripp, right?"

"Yeah, Tripp." She grinned, her eyes sparkling in a way I had never seen coming from her. "He asked me out," she squealed and kicked her feet high.

I chuckled at her excitement. Ah, the joys of teenage love. "When did he do that?"

"Yesterday before we left school. He asked if I wanted to see a movie this weekend."

"And you said no, right?" I perked a brow.

She looked aghast. "Why would I say no? Of course, I said yes. He's so cute."

"Is he nice?"

She shrugged a shoulder. "I guess so."

"You guess so? You don't know?"

"Not really. We haven't spoken much."

"Ah, I guess it would be hard to talk in class."

"Yes, and Mr. Moron is a pain."

I fought not to respond negatively to her depiction of her teacher. It wasn't the first time I had heard him referred to by that name. "You mean, Mr. Monroe?"

"Yeah, as I said, Mr. Moron."

I could correct her, but that would defeat what I was trying to do. I needed the kids I counseled to trust me and feel that they could say anything to me, and I would not judge. I worked hard to keep my features consistent. It was something that I had to work hard to do in the early years.

Now it was mainly second nature. I spent so much time trying not to react to things people said that many times, people had told me that I must be made of stone because I didn't respond to surprising things. Outside I remained neutral, but inside I was an agitated mess.

Like right now, I wanted Missy to tell me every little thing she knew about Tripp and if he had ever mentioned his father.

"When are you going out with Tripp?"

"Tomorrow night. We wanted to go tonight, but he has to stay home and watch his brother and sister."

Brother *and* sister? So, Tim had three kids. I thought it was just two boys. It must be date night, and Tripp was the lucky babysitter.

"And you guys are going to the movies?"

"Yep."

"I hope you have a great time."

"I think we will. At least, I hope we will." She drew her brows closer in reflection. "I wonder if he will kiss me."

I almost laughed. If Tripp were anything like his father, he would. My first kiss with Tim had been under the bleachers at a football game. I wasn't old enough to date, but we had met there and called it our first date. I decided that probably wasn't something to mention and changed the subject.

"Maybe he will. Have you been writing in your journal?"

Missy excitedly jumped into the new conversation, but as

different as it was, it still revolved around Tripp. All of her entries since I had last seen her were about him. I should be happy that she had something good to write about and wasn't resorting to writing morbid poems about death and suicide— which I learned about after she first started seeing me.

Once her session was over, I had one more session, and then I could go home for the day. It was a brutal session, as the eight-year-old was dealing with losing his father. He had gone on a business trip and never returned. He wasn't dead, which might have been easier to deal with. The mother told me that he had been seeing another woman and decided to start a new family with that woman.

It was a kick in the gut for both the woman and child—especially the child. Eventually, the woman would get over it, but would the child ever accept that his father left him for another family?

By the time that session was over, all I could think about was heading to my brother's house and downing a bottle of wine— or two. I even thought about stopping at my house and picking up an overnight bag so I could drink as much as I wanted and sleep in one of their guest rooms. It wouldn't be the first time I did such a thing.

Going to my brother's for dinner once a month was something we started after Alaina and Evan got married. We still went to my father's on Sunday, but once a month, the siblings and spouses got together at Evan's house. It wasn't just my family, but the Young family too. They were like our adopted siblings because our families had grown up together and even shared holidays and vacations.

I was about to leave when I received a parent's call needing guidance. I ended up being on the phone with them for over thirty minutes and arriving late at my brother's. It wouldn't be surprising to anyone at the house. They were used to me being late. As I pulled down their driveway, another car pulled in behind me. We parked, and I saw Henley and Roxy Young exiting their vehicle.

We said our hellos and headed into the house together. "I'm surprised you got off tonight, Hen."

"Yeah, me too. I almost didn't make it." He grinned at me. "You're a little late yourself."

"Late call from a worried parent."

"I get it." He squeezed my shoulder as we headed toward the back of the house and the incredible backyard. I glanced down from the main floor to the area below. Everyone was there, happily eating and drinking around the glorious garden area.

The men were near the outdoor kitchen, where the barbeque was smoking something delicious, and the women sat in the garden, around the fire pit on luxuriously comfortable couches. Above them, the twinkling lights were coming on, and the calming babble of a stream was heard as I passed over the small footbridge. This is what I needed after a long week.

Candy and Riley popped off their seats and said something to each other before Riley rushed around me with a quick hello. Candy hugged me while Coral and Kayley looked at me expectantly. An air of tension rippled around the women as Alaina came to say hello. When she stepped back, she said softly, "Blame it on your brother."

"Blame what on my brother?"

"All I can say is I hope he's right." She put her hands on my shoulders and spun me around, and I came face-to-face with the man who had broken my heart and haunted my dreams for years. My jaw dropped as I stared up into his blue eyes.

"Hey, Carmen. It's good to see you again."

I gaped at him. I had known he was in town. I had seen a picture of his son and his other son's name on the folder, yet it was still a shock to see him standing two feet away from me. Riley bounced at his side, grinning like a fool while waiting for my reaction.

My training kicked in, and I stared back at Tim with clinical interest as I responded with only one word. "Tim." Inside, a maelstrom of emotion had begun to whip into a frenzy.

Neither of us said anything else as we gauged one another, and then Evan stepped into the group. "Surprise! Isn't this great, Carmen? I bet you never thought you'd see this guy again, did you?"

The emotional uproar of the week was taking its toll, and my calm demeanor was about to crack like an egg dropped on a stone floor. The past, the present, and the future all began to collide, and for the first time in my life, I thought I might have a panic attack. "Evan, may I speak with you, please?" Before he could respond, I spun around and returned to the house. My entire body shook, and my chest felt tight. I wondered how long it would be before I collapsed into a heap.

"Carmen, what's wrong?" Evan called, and I heard a few people following me. I also heard someone say something about how it would be all right once I overcame the shock.

The hell it would! I wasn't just shaking; I was seething angrily. How many of my siblings knew he was in town? How many knew he would be here tonight? Why hadn't any of them warned me? Why hadn't any of them broached the subject about seeing him again?

I went into the downstairs area and began walking around the pool table as Evan strolled in, looking disappointed in me. "What the hell is wrong with you? I thought you would be excited to see him."

I walked up to my brother and smacked him across the face. Coral gasped, and Ethan grabbed me as I hissed at Evan, "What the hell is wrong with you? How could you do that to me, Evan?"

He snapped back, shocked, "Why are you smacking me?"

"Do you not remember what he did to me? Do you not remember how he broke my heart?"

"I told him this would be a bad idea," Coral said as she put her arm around me, but I shook it off.

"Come on, Carmen, that was like twenty years ago. You can't possibly tell me that you never got over the guy." Evan laughed.

"Excuse me! Of course, I did, but that's not the point! Obviously, you do not remember what you said you would do if he ever stepped foot in town again?" To my own ears, I sounded like a completely deranged person, but I couldn't stop myself.

He cocked his head as if searching his mind, then shrugged. "No, what?"

"You said you would knock him out for breaking my heart." My voice cracked, and my eyes filled with tears. Suddenly the weariness from the week descended over me like a torrential downpour, and the tears streamed down my cheeks. I had no chance in hell of stopping them.

"Ah, Carmen, I'm sorry." Evan rushed forward. "I'm sorry. Don't cry. I'll go out there right now and kick his ass. I swear."

I snorted loudly and pulled back. "No, I'm sorry. It's been a horrible week, and I can't deal with this tonight. Please give him my apologies. I'm going to leave."

"What? You can't leave." Evan grabbed hold of my arms.

"No, I need to." I wiped my face. "I'm a wreck! It has been a horrible week, and I just need to go home, take a long hot bath, and sleep. I never should have come tonight in the first place. It has nothing to do with him. It really doesn't. I'm just exhausted from work. Please tell him I'm sorry."

I quickly spun around and rushed from the room as more tears filled my eyes. I was doing the one thing that I never did. I ran away because I couldn't imagine facing Tim right now with all the emotions erupting inside me. I just couldn't.

CHAPTER SIX

TIM

We had survived the first two days of school and work. Savannah was thrilled with her teacher and was quickly making friends. She even had a play-date on Saturday. Dean talked nonstop about everything the school had that his old one didn't. He was also making friends and settling quickly into his new home.

Tripp was an entirely different story. He was moody and sullen—not that it was much different from his typical teenage mood—but it was a bit worse. He helped with dinner because that was his responsibility but excused himself when he could and returned to his room and worked on homework—or whatever else he was doing. I doubted he was throwing himself passionately into his studies. Knowing him, he was texting, video chatting, playing a game with a friend from California, or sulking—most likely the last one.

All three kids had chores, and Savannah was responsible for setting and clearing the table. Tripp helped cook, and Dean cleaned up. Dean said he got the worst of the deal, but I told him he would soon graduate to cooking with me. Their mother and I had agreed that the boys should know how to cook as well, if not better, than any girls in the family.

I started working early on Thursday morning because Dean and Savannah went to the neighbor's house to hang out before school. Megan would make sure they got on the bus with her kids.

I pulled into the busy parking lot at Coral's Coffee Café and found a spot. This was the first time I had been here since I'd moved back, and I hoped that Coral was working so I could finally say hello.

What I didn't expect when I stepped inside was to practically get run over by Evan Winston. "Sorry, man," he paused and did a double take. "Tim? Tim freaking Kohl!"

"Evan! Hey, man, how are you?" We clasped hands and did a shoulder hug and bump.

"I'm good, how are you? What the hell are you doing in Millerstown?"

"I just moved back to town."

"Seriously? Why?"

"For work."

"Where are you working?"

I chuckled. "Strange that you should ask. I'm working for your wife."

He scoffed and then laughed loudly. "Get the hell out? You're working at Buckworth Industries? What are you doing there?"

"I'm the warehouse and logistics manager for the new warehouse she just built."

I stepped to the side and held the door open for a woman carrying two cups of coffee. She smiled sweetly at me, letting her gaze drift over my face and chest.

Evan seemed to notice. "Seems like you haven't lost your magic. How does it feel to be back?"

"Strange." We laughed. "No, it's nice to be back—I think."

"Hey, what are you doing tomorrow night?"

"I don't have any plans. Why?"

"Why don't you come over for dinner? I would love to catch up with you, and I'm sure it is already on Alaina's list to do. She invites her management teams over for dinner every other month." He paused. "Speaking of catching up, have you spoken to Carmen yet? Does she know you're back in town?"

"No, I haven't had the chance to speak with her. I doubt she knows that I'm here. Why would she?" I laughed again.

He smirked. "You never know. Should I tell Alaina that you and your wife will be there? Six work for you?"

"Um, just me, and yeah. I should be able to make it. Let me get your number, and I can confirm with you later today."

"Sure." We traded numbers, and then he rushed out the door dressed in medical scrubs after telling me it was great to see me again.

Evan was a few years younger than me, but he enjoyed playing baseball, and more than once, we played together on a Saturday afternoon with our friends. It would be nice to see him and Alaina again. Perhaps Evan could fill in the gaps of the people I once knew—starting with his sister.

I made sure to speak with Tripp when I got home, and even though he wasn't thrilled with it, he agreed to watch his siblings on Friday.

Thursday evening, Tripp was in a better mood and even cracked a few jokes at the dinner table. I wasn't sure what had changed, but I was happy to see it. He even helped his little brother clean up by putting away the leftovers before disappearing into his room. As I went by his door later, I heard him talking, and I paused, wondering if he was talking to an old friend or a new one. I had a feeling it was a new friend, and it was of the female persuasion.

I smiled as I moved away from his door and headed to Savannah's to tuck her in. Things were going to work out.

I WAS a bit nervous Friday evening and wasn't exactly sure why. Having dinner with an old friend and my boss was no big deal. Typically, it would be proper to bring a gift to the host, but I was pretty sure any twenty-dollar bottle of wine wouldn't be to her taste and would either get tossed out or shoved into the back of a cupboard.

That didn't mean I should arrive empty-handed, though, so I stopped at the florist and picked up an arrangement of flowers. Women liked flowers—I just hoped she didn't have an allergy.

When I arrived, I found a few more cars than I expected in the driveway and wondered if other people from work would be there for dinner. I knocked at the door, and a few moments later, a woman with light-brown hair pulled back into a ponytail answered the door. It sure wasn't Alaina. Did I have the correct address? Maybe I didn't.

"Hi, can I help you?" the woman asked sweetly as she looked over the flowers and grinned.

"Hi, I'm looking for Evan and Alaina. Maybe I have the wrong address."

She grinned. "Nope, you have the correct address."

"Oh, okay, I was invited for dinner."

She opened the door wider. "Then come on in. Guests are always welcome. I'm Nolan Young, and you are?"

I stepped in and looked past her. Heading toward us was Evan. "You made it!"

"I did," I replied, realizing I heard several other voices in the distance. "I didn't realize you were having a party."

"Not a party. We just get together every couple of weeks. It's a nice evening so we are out back. Come on in, and I'll introduce you to those you don't know, although you probably know most people. I see you met Nolan."

I nodded to her. "I did, but I didn't get to introduce myself. I'm Tim Kohl, an old friend of Evan's."

Evan slapped me on the back. "No, he's an old friend of Carmen's from high school."

"Nice to meet you, Tim. If you knew Carmen in high school, you also knew the Youngs?"

"I did. Which one of them did you marry? Huntley? Henley?"

She laughed. "No, Bradley."

Wow, Brad had good taste. I wonder what happened to his high school sweetheart. "That's great. It's really nice to meet you, Nolan."

"Come on in and say hi to the others. Carmen isn't here yet, but damn, wait till she gets here. She is going to be so surprised."

Suddenly butterflies exploded through my gut. The last thing I expected was to see Carmen tonight. "Are you sure you want to surprise her? If I recall, she wasn't one for big surprises."

"Nah, it will be great. Carmen will be really excited to see you again. I can't believe you haven't run into her. How long did you say you have been in town?"

"Only about a week. Although I was here about a month ago house hunting. I thought I saw her from a distance but didn't get a chance to say anything to her, and she didn't see me."

We walked further into the house, following behind Nolan, who had gone ahead and out onto a deck. I paused as I glanced around. My boss sure didn't need my puny flower arrangement. Her backyard could have supplied the florist where I had purchased my bouquet. It wasn't even springtime yet. How the hell did all those flowers grow in the cold? "Is that a stream?"

"Yeah, there is a small waterfall over there that Alaina just added. Come on down."

As we went down, my gaze slipped over the people below. I immediately recognized Carmen's brother, Ethan, and Riley standing beside him. Huntley was there with a woman I didn't know. Beside them was Candy with her fiancé, Mike Bollard, whom I had learned about on social media. Wes Young was also there, and he raised his eyes as we descended the stairs.

"Holy shit! There is no way that could be Tim Kohl!" He broke out in a broad smile and came to meet us at the bottom of the stairs. "What hole did you climb out of?"

"Wes." I laughed as I hugged him. "You forget where the barber shop is?" I joked as I took in his ponytail and beard.

"Very funny. What the hell are you doing here?"

"I just moved back to town," I stated, and Alaina slipped up to the conversation and put her arm around Evan.

"Tim, I am so glad you could come tonight. Evan told me that you guys all know each other."

Wes replied, "Oh, yeah. We used to play baseball together, and he dated…" He paused. "Carmen, right?"

"Yeah, Carmen." I nodded.

"Does she know you are back in town?" Wes asked.

"I don't think so unless someone told her. I haven't run into her yet." I turned to Alaina. "These are for you. Thank you for having me over."

"Aw, thank you so much." She sniffed the arrangement, smiling brightly.

"If I had known you had your own garden, I might have thought of something else."

She chuckled. "Flowers are perfect! I will take all I can get."

Evan laughed. "Yes, she will. Seriously, you can never go wrong with flowers for this woman."

"Carmen will be here tonight," Alaina said. "I am sure it will be a nice surprise for her to see you. At least, that's what Evan says."

I could only hope, but unfortunately, it didn't turn out that way.

I was in the basement, having just used the restroom, and

was now checking out the pool table when I saw Carmen arrive. I watched her through the glass doors, noting that she was even more beautiful than she had been when she was younger.

I stepped onto the back patio, and Riley tugged me toward Carmen. When Carmen saw me, her face went pale, her eyes wide, and her jaw dropped. I hoped she would get over the shock quickly, but instead of relaxing, she bristled and rushed away, and a few people followed her.

I instantly thought of leaving. I should never have come here. I should have waited until I ran into her naturally. Eventually, in this small town, we would have. Or I could have found a way to get her number and then called her to let her know I was in town, so it wasn't a shock.

Wes spoke from beside me. "Don't worry about it. Carmen is under a lot of stress right now. She's probably just tired. I'm sure everything will be all right in a few minutes."

"I hope so. I didn't mean to ruin the evening."

"You didn't ruin anything. This group lives for drama. So, what have you been up to? Where have you been living? Last I saw on social media, you were in California."

"I was in California, moved here to oversee one of the new warehouses at Alaina's company."

"Really? Small world. Did you ever think you'd be back in this area?"

"No. Never." I laughed. "You never left?"

"I did, but not far. I live in Summersville. I'm a pediatric emergency doctor at the hospital."

"You always said you wanted to be a doctor after your friend died in that motorcycle accident."

"I did, and I accomplished that."

Evan joined our group, the side of his face red. "Sorry about that."

Wes laughed. "Did your sister smack you?"

"Oh, yeah, she did. Then she yelled at me for inviting Tim

here and not kicking his ass. I guess I told her when we were kids that if I ever saw you again, I would do that for hurting her."

I felt instantly horrible. "Shit, I'm sorry, man. I should have contacted her on my own first. I didn't realize that she would be so upset to see me."

"I don't think it was all you. Carmen said she has been having a rough week, and I think the shock of seeing you just put her over the edge."

"Where is she? I will go talk to her."

"She left. She broke into tears, said she was exhausted and wanted a bath and bed."

Now I felt even worse. The last thing I wanted was to upset Carmen. I had hoped that we could speak, perhaps rekindle our friendship. I never expected her to be so upset to see me.

Someone called Wes' name, and he shifted away, leaving Evan and me alone. "I honestly forgot how upset she was after you two broke up."

"You know I never meant to hurt her, right?"

"Yeah, of course. We were kids, but what happened?"

"Time, man. I was in a new place, doing new things. We were two thousand miles apart, and I couldn't promise her what she wanted." I sighed. "I had also met someone else, and I knew it wasn't fair to lead Carmen on."

Evan frowned. "Was it worth it? That other woman?"

I smiled sadly. "Yeah, it was. Emily gave me three wonderful children."

"If she was so great, where is she? Why didn't you bring her tonight?"

I sighed. "She's not here because Emily died two years ago."

CHAPTER SEVEN

CARMEN

I sniveled all the way home, feeling like I did when I was seventeen all over again. Which was absolutely idiotic, and I knew it. Tim and I had been apart for over twenty years, so why was I such a basket case just because he returned to town?

It had to be because I was so tired, and this week had been hell. Or perhaps it was that I officially knew, twenty years later, that he had indeed moved on and now had a wife and kids. I had nothing. I didn't even have a dog.

Suddenly I had an overwhelming realization and understanding of how my sixteen-year-old client felt: utterly alone. Yes, there were people around me, and I had five siblings, all the Youngs, all the spouses, and my father—yet I felt so very alone at this moment.

I dragged myself into the house and dropped everything in the foyer. Then I located the first bottle of wine, broke open the twist cap, and took a drink straight from the bottle. I started to turn away, but then I reached into a cabinet and collected my largest wineglass before climbing the steps. In my room, I filled my glass, then went into the bathroom and turned on the tub. I guzzled the first glass and undressed while the steamy water filled the old-fashioned claw-foot tub.

I wouldn't admit it to anyone, but that tub was why I purchased this house. The moment I saw it in this room, I knew this house was meant to be mine.

I stared into the mirror, a memory shimmering into focus as I did.

"Are you serious? We are going to take a bubble bath in your mom's tub?" I giggled as Tim pulled me into his parents' room.

"Yep, I know you said you liked baths. So, we could share one while they are out of town."

"That's why you wanted me to wear my bathing suit over?" I giggled again.

"Yeah." He shrugged. "I thought it might be weird to take a bath together naked, so I figured we could wear our bathing suits."

He had been right; it was weird thinking of taking a bath with him. I was only sixteen at the time, and even though we'd had sex twice, it wasn't like we were totally naked with the lights on.

But when I entered the room, Tim had candles flickering on every surface and it didn't seem so strange after all. The bath was practically overflowing with bubbles, and I was overwhelmed by his thoughtfulness.

We had climbed into the big claw-foot tub, sitting at opposite ends and staring at one another. He rubbed my feet, and it did strange things to my insides. Odd enough that I got the idea that maybe we should try something new.

I made a big show of slipping the strap of my bathing suit off. His eyes widened, and Tim shifted my foot under the water between his legs, where he was already hard. It made me gasp and fueled me with the confidence to move forward. Slowly, I shifted in the tub and sat on his lap, wrapping my arms around his neck and kissing him.

A sound in the other room snapped me back to the present, and I rushed to the tub to turn it off before it overflowed. I had no idea what made the noise, but I was glad something brought me back. Otherwise, I would have had a mess to clean up, and I could picture myself sobbing on the floor as I sopped up the soapy water.

I had just turned the faucet off when I heard the sound again, and this time, I knew what it was—my doorbell.

Which one of my siblings was here? Candy? Coral? It better not be Evan! It was going to be a while before I forgave him for this. How could he not remember how heartbroken I had been after Tim broke it off? And how could he invite Tim to our dinner without telling me? That was a shitty thing to do, even for him.

I wrapped myself in my robe, grabbed my wine bottle and glass, and trekked down the stairs toward the door. The bell rang one more time before I got there, and I set the glass and bottle on the entrance table so I had my hands prepared to battle if it were my brother.

When I yanked back the door, I was ready to launch a tirade at Evan about getting lost or inviting my sisters in to get drunk with me. However, it wasn't any of them. There on my doorstep was the last man that I wanted to see.

"How the hell do you know where I live?"

"Alaina gave me your address. She thought we might want to talk."

"I don't think tonight is the right time for us to talk." I started to close the door.

"Come on, Carmen. Let me come in for a few minutes."

I stared at him. "What would your wife say if she knew you were here?"

He shrugged. "I don't know."

"Did you bring her tonight? I didn't even notice." I tried to remember if I had seen anyone at Evan's that I hadn't recognized but couldn't remember seeing anyone as I bolted.

"No."

"Why wouldn't you bring your wife to dinner? I don't think

that behavior is appropriate for a married man." I lifted my chin in a defiant gesture.

He sighed and put his hands on his hips as he looked around. "I'm not married, Carmen. Not anymore. My wife is dead. I'm a widower."

It was a sucker punch delivered to my gut, as that was the last thing I had expected. The painful raw emotions were evident in his haunted blue eyes as he lifted them back to mine.

Without thought, I stepped back and held the door open for him to enter. My heart broke a little as I watched him step over the threshold. How much had he loved her? Was it cancer? Did she have an accident? Did he mourn for her every day?

Then my thoughts shifted as I remembered he had children. How were the kids doing with the loss of their mother? How long had it been? Did they go to counseling? Did they need counseling? Did I know someone else who was good enough for his kids to see if they needed help?

He turned once he was inside and stared at me. I closed the door and retrieved the wine bottle from the foyer table where I had set it. "Do you want a glass of wine?"

"That would be nice."

I walked past him into the living room and then moved into the kitchen, where I collected another wineglass and filled it.

"I am sure you have a lot of questions," Tim said as I pushed the stemware his way.

"I do. Why are you back in town?"

"Because my company opened a new office and warehouse here. I manage the warehouse and the logistics of it."

"What company?"

"Buckworth Industries," he said with a hint of a smile.

I barked out a quick laugh. "Ironic."

"Yes, very."

I stared at him, noting that he had gotten a little taller—or I had gotten shorter—and his hair was cut differently. I liked that it was slightly longer in the back, and I was suddenly tempted to see if it felt as silky as it did when we were teens.

He was even more attractive than I remembered him being. His blue eyes were still bright, and his face showed signs of maturity, which only made him more handsome. He stared back at me, and I wondered what he was thinking. Did he think I looked old now? Was I fat to him? Were the laugh lines around my eyes unwelcomed?

As if knowing what I was thinking, Tim spoke. "You look fantastic, Carmen. Even better than you did when you were in high school."

I felt a blush creeping up my neck and grabbed the lapels of my robe as I suddenly realized that was all I was wearing. I didn't even have underwear on. "Um, would you excuse me? I should probably put something else on."

I hustled away before he could respond and quickly went up the steps and into my room. Holy crap! Tim Kohl was in my house! Tim Kohl! How many times had I dreamed of him showing up at my door?

I quickly put on a bra and panties, pulled out leggings and a T-shirt, but threw them to the side and went to find something better. I stood in my closet, staring at all my clothes and wondering what would be best. What color would convey that I didn't care that he was here but was still flattering? What style would be the most appropriate to say it's nice to see you again, but I'm not interested—even though I might slightly be?

I hung my head. What the hell would he think of me if I came down wearing a freaking pants suit and heels? I sighed and rubbed my temples. That I was overcompensating? That I was trying to show him I was in control of the situation? God, I really wished I could have climbed into my bathtub.

I pulled a pair of jeans off a hanger, tugged them on, and then found a short-sleeved polo to pull over. I didn't bother putting on my shoes and glanced at the mirror to see that my makeup was a mess. I took a moment to clean up the mascara under my eyes but didn't bother to put any new makeup on. He'd already seen me looking like hell, and he said I looked great.

Why? Why had he said that? What did he want? Why was he here?

"You're not going to find the answers hiding in your room, Carmen. Go down there and face him!" I mumbled to my reflection.

I approached the tub, staring longingly at the bubbles floating on top, and I reached down and released the drain with a sigh. What a waste of good bubbles.

Finally, I descended the stairs to confront the man who had broken my heart so badly pieces of it had yet to recover fully. Was I being overly dramatic? Maybe, but I didn't care right now.

Tim stood in the living room, glancing over the pictures I had on the wall. One of the walls had over eighty square tiles that hung with double-sided tape. I kept adding to it whenever I got a new picture I liked.

He glanced at me, his eyes slipping to my feet and back up approvingly before turning to the pictures again. "I like these. I've thought of getting them before."

"They are nice. It shows a timeline of my life in a way."

He shifted to look toward the left and then appeared to be searching for something. "What happened to Cara? I don't see her up here after a certain point and I didn't see any recent pictures of her online."

"You searched for Cara online?"

He turned. "No, I was looking for you, actually."

"Me? Why would you be looking for me?"

"I came here about a month ago and was registering my kids in school. I saw you at the middle school, and I was going to say something, but you looked like you were late for something. I didn't want to bother you. I figured I would see you soon enough, and I decided to look you up while I was at the airport."

"But why would you want to look me up, Tim? You broke up with me over twenty years ago."

He studied me and then sighed as he glanced at the couch. "Mind if I sit?"

"No, I don't mind," I stated and sat at the other end of the sofa from him. I didn't have many different choices. The only other chair in the room was an uncomfortable chair that had been my grandmother's. I never sat in it, but I couldn't get rid of it either.

"I looked because coming back here reminded me of when I was growing up, and of course, you too. I guess I wanted to see that you were happy."

I frowned. "You never wondered that over the last two decades?"

"Of course I did, Carmen. I thought of you often over the years, but I never thought to look you up. I mean, I was married, and then Emily died, and I was busy with the kids. It wasn't until I was back here and saw you that I wanted, more like needed to know more about you, but your profile was private, so I looked at Coral's Coffee Café and found a picture of you and your siblings, only Cara wasn't in it." He paused. "Did something happen to her?"

"She's fine. She moved away and lives with her husband and son in another state."

He looked relieved, which I thought was odd. I tilted my head to the side. "Why do you seem so relieved that she's okay?"

"Because I understand your bond with your siblings, and I know what it feels like to lose someone you care about. I didn't want to imagine you going through that."

CHAPTER EIGHT

TIM

Regret weighed heavy as I stood amidst Carmen's friends and family. I never would have come if I had known it would become such a dramatic affair. Evan assured me it wasn't a big deal and that Carmen would eventually move past it, but I knew her well enough from our high school days to understand that her anger wouldn't easily dissipate. Perhaps the best course of action was approaching her, apologizing, and addressing the elephant in the room—my reappearance in her life.

Lost in my thoughts, Alaina joined me on the patio's side. "I'm sorry about all this. I should have said no to Evan."

"How could you have known?" I replied, trying to ease her guilt.

She shrugged, looking genuinely apologetic. "He mentioned you were his sister's ex, but I didn't think much of it. I failed to consider how upset I would have been in the same situation."

She handed me a piece of paper, curiosity evident as I asked, "What's this?"

She glanced around, ensuring no one was eavesdropping before answering. "Carmen's address." She smiled wider. "I had a feeling you'd want to know. Before you go, how are things going at the warehouse?"

As much as I wanted to rush to Carmen's, I owed Alaina a few minutes of conversation. After all, she owned the company I worked for and provided me with Carmen's address.

"Things are going well, a few minor hiccups, but nothing major. Last week, we had trucks at the docks every day, and this week we're expecting even more deliveries. By Thursday, we should have about seventy-five to eighty percent of the stock ready to fulfill orders."

"Excellent news," she replied. "It's good to know everything will be ready to start shipping on time."

"Yes, it is."

She touched my arm gently, signaling our conversation's end. "Now, I don't want to keep you from where you need to be."

"Thank you, Alaina. I hope we can reschedule dinner sometime."

"Absolutely, and next time, bring the kids. I'd love to meet them."

I chuckled, entertained by the idea. "Maybe I'll see what kind of moods they're in. Tripp has been quite moody lately, adjusting to a new school."

"That is to be expected. Good luck with Carmen." She winked and then directed me out of the house.

I slipped into the basement and ascended the stairs she had pointed out, ensuring my exit would go unnoticed amidst the ongoing festivities.

Nervously, I made my way to Carmen's house, uncertain if she would even open the door. My heart raced as I approached, contemplating the possibilities that lay ahead.

To my surprise, she answered the door, her expression a mixture of shock and disbelief. It was evident that my unexpected presence caught her off guard.

Her beauty struck me with renewed force. Although I had seen her picture online previously and briefly tonight, I couldn't help but be captivated by her again. Her cascading blond waves danced around her face, and her piercing blue eyes shimmered against her flawless complexion.

It was also not lost on me that she wore a robe and little else. My mind went to places it hadn't been in a long time, and I fought to control the tide of desire that was fighting to rise.

As I shared the devastating news of my wife's passing, a wave of sadness washed over her features, and any feelings of desire from me vanished. Perhaps it was the grief that compelled her to invite me inside. Sympathy seemed to be the driving force, as many had pitied me after Emily's death, especially considering the challenge of raising our three children alone.

As she excused herself to get dressed, I took in the surroundings of her living room. It perfectly matched my image of her—a comfortable suede couch, a well-sized coffee table covered with magazines and coasters. The walls were adorned with pictures, forming a timeline of her life. They started in her early twenties, then progressed, featuring her siblings, friends, and scenic views through the years.

Carmen returned wearing jeans and a shirt, and we settled on the couch, discussing her sister, Cara.

"Why do you seem so relieved that she's okay?" she inquired.

"Because I understand your bond with your siblings, and I know what it feels like to lose someone you care about. I didn't want to imagine you going through that," I replied, her gaze fixed on me.

She nodded, acknowledging my words. "You're talking about your late wife, aren't you?"

Carmen's gaze intensified as I nodded back. "Yes."

"How long has it been since she passed away?"

"Almost two years," I responded, the pain still fresh in my

heart. "It wasn't an illness; she was tragically killed during a grocery store robbery. Wrong place, wrong time."

Carmen gasped, her eyes filled with empathy. "I'm so sorry, Tim. I can't even imagine what you've been through."

Reluctant to dwell on the painful memories of her death, I changed the subject. "If Cara simply moved away, why don't you have pictures of her and her family?"

Carmen hesitated, her expression growing guarded. "It's a long story I can't share with you. But I assure you she's safe and happy, and that's all that matters."

"Okay, if you say so," I replied, respecting her boundaries. "Do you at least get to see her?"

"Occasionally, but let's steer the conversation away from my sister if you don't mind," Carmen redirected.

"Fair enough," I agreed, seeking a new topic. "What would you like to talk about that doesn't involve your sister or my late wife?"

Carmen stared at me, seemingly unfazed by my statement, before finally speaking. "Why are you here, Tim?"

"Here? In Millerstown or here at your house?" I asked, seeking clarification.

"You already explained why you are in Millerstown. So why are you at my house," she clarified, her tone slightly distant.

"I came here to apologize," I admitted, my voice tinged with sincerity.

Carmen arched an eyebrow elegantly, clearly surprised. "Apologize? What exactly are you apologizing for?"

I furrowed my brow, taken aback. "For what happened tonight. What else would I need to apologize for?"

She opened her mouth in disbelief, her eyes fixed on me. "Seriously, Tim?"

"I'm at a loss here, Carmen. I genuinely don't know what else I should apologize for. Tell me, and we can move past this." Her scoff echoed in the room, and she shifted on the couch, readying herself to stand. Instinctively, I reached for her arm, hoping to halt her movement. "Carmen, what do you think I need to apologize for?"

"Quite a few things, Tim," she replied, her voice tinged with frustration. She glanced at my hand on her arm, promptly pulling away before rising from the couch.

"Please enlighten me," I urged, my voice filled with earnestness.

"For starters," she began, pacing around the living room, "how about the fact that you stopped communicating with me? You never officially ended things between us, but it was clear that we were no longer together. Or what about the promises you made? You said you'd come back to take me to my high school prom, that we would attend college together and build a future."

Stunned, I sat there, trying to process her words. Was she still upset about our breakup twenty years ago? I understood if she had been hurt then, but two decades had passed. "Carmen, we were just kids."

Her gaze turned piercing as she met my eyes head-on. "We were old enough to have a physical relationship, so I wouldn't exactly call us kids."

"We were teenagers fueled by hormones," I argued, recalling the intensity of those emotions. "I know teenagers well; I have one and two more on the horizon."

She shifted her focus, seemingly unsurprised by what I had said. "That's right; you have three children."

Resting my arm on the side of the couch, I couldn't help but wonder how she knew about my kids. "Yes, three. How did you know?"

Carmen crossed her arms defensively. "You mentioned being at the middle school, and I have a client who knows your son, Tripp. She showed me his picture, and it was obvious he was your child. He looks just like you did at that age."

"You know my son's name? Who's your client? What do you do? Wait, you already knew I was in town."

She lifted her chin, her expression guarded. "I'm a child psychologist." Ignoring my other questions, she continued. "And yes, I knew you were in town."

I leaned back, absorbing the new information. "I see. So, one of your clients told you about my son?"

Carmen shifted uncomfortably. "Yes, she mentioned a new boy in her class."

I wondered who had taken Tripp's picture, though it didn't surprise me. He was a good-looking kid, and being new in a small town, he would naturally attract attention.

"I have two boys and one girl. Savannah is in fifth grade, and Dean is in middle school," I disclosed, observing Carmen's pensive nod. "Did you ever get married?"

Her face turned away, and her eyes darted to the side. "We're not discussing me, Tim. You came here to apologize." She took a few steps away. "Perhaps it's time for you to go."

I let out a sigh, following her to the foyer. She stood there, staring at the floor, preparing to bid me farewell. Stepping in front of her, I gently lifted her chin, cradling her face in the palm of my hand as I locked eyes with her.

"I'm sorry for hurting you, Carmen. Truly, I am. I never intended for any of that to happen. When I left here, I intended to return and build a life with you, but..." I trailed off, a mix of regret and acceptance in my voice. "But life had a different path in store for me."

Her eyes glistened with unshed tears, and I studied her face intently—the length of her eyelashes, the curve of her nose, the shape of her lips. Memories of kissing those lips flooded my mind, and I unconsciously leaned closer, drawn to her, as the desire I had felt earlier began to flow through me again.

She pushed against my chest, interrupting the moment. "Oh, no, you don't. You can't just waltz in here after twenty years, apologize, and expect me to jump into bed with you. That's not happening, Tim."

Raising my hands in surrender, I backtracked, realizing the line I had unintentionally crossed. "I'm sorry, Carmen. That wasn't my intention." I paused and thought about what I wanted to say. "I got caught up in the desire I felt for you. It's been a while since I've been with someone or felt that."

She stepped away, heading toward the front door, but not before I saw that same feeling flash in her eyes. I grabbed her arm, turning her back to face me as I cradled her face again, my eyes locked on hers. A memory of a long time ago surfaced, reminding me how much she loved being touched this way.

"You feel it too."

She stared back at me but didn't pull away, which was a good sign. We remained right where we were for a few seconds, and I watched her eyes drop to my lips. I couldn't help myself as I began to lean forward again. Right before my lips touched hers, she sucked in a sharp breath.

I kissed her tenderly, and at first, she didn't respond, but after a few seconds, she shifted her head to the side, and I curled my fingers around her neck and deepened the kiss.

A few seconds later, she abruptly pulled back and stepped away from me, looking slightly dazed and confused.

"I didn't mean for this to happen, Carmen. I'm sorry if that was inappropriate."

She pursed her lips as a mask fell over her face, blocking all signs of the kiss from view, and she turned toward the door. "Good night, Tim."

I sighed, stepping away and respecting her space. She might have shut down that kiss, but I wouldn't let her off that easy. "Can we have coffee this weekend?"

"Why would you want that?" she questioned, her tone guarded.

"Because if we're going to be living in the same town, occasionally crossing paths, it's better if we can at least try to be friends," I suggested.

She scoffed again, shaking her head. "Fine. Tomorrow at ten, at Coral's Coffee Café. I assume you know where that is?"

"Yes, I do. I'll see you tomorrow," I confirmed, stepping out of the house. Turning back, I added, "And Carmen, I never meant to hurt you. I truly loved you."

She blinked rapidly, her silence speaking volumes, before closing the door without uttering a word.

I stared at the closed door and thought, oh, shit! What did I just do?

CHAPTER NINE

CARMEN

I rested my forehead on the closed door, a tear slipping down my cheek as I whispered, "I loved you too."

The problem wasn't that I had loved him, but that I knew somewhere inside me I still loved him and always would.

I was tempted to peek through the peephole to watch him, but I didn't. Instead, I stood there for a moment, reliving the feel of his mouth on mine, and then I turned and walked into my living room, staring at his discarded wineglass for a couple of seconds. I collected it and washed the glass before refilling mine, turning off the lights, and heading up the stairs.

I debated filling the tub, but I was too tired to do that now, so I slipped into soft pajamas and under the covers. With the television on, I flipped the channels to find something to watch, but the only thing I could see was the replay of the scene downstairs where we had stared at one another, and then Tim had put his lips to mine.

It had been like the first time all over again—the excitement of a first kiss. There had been tingling in my fingertips, my heart had been racing, and my palms were slightly sweaty.

Why had I stopped him? Why had he wanted to kiss me? Had he been caught up in the moment like I had? Was he reliving an old memory, wondering if there was anything there? Was he hoping that we could rekindle our past relationship?

There was way too much water under the bridge for that to occur, plus there was Chad.

I winced. Shit. I was going to have to tell Chad that I kissed another man. What was he going to say? Would he break up with me? If he did, I could date Tim then.

I squeezed my eyes shut. I didn't want to date Tim, but did I want to continue to date Chad? While Tim was here, I hadn't even thought about Chad. What did that say about my relationship with him?

But what if we did break up, and I did want to date Tim? Would I go out with him if he asked? Didn't I already agree to go out with him? I mean, we did plan to meet for coffee. Was that a date?

What if, while we were having coffee, he said that he had secretly pined for me all these years and was so glad to see me again?

Gah! The man had been married with three children; he probably never thought twice about me. Maybe in a passing moment, he remembered a brief time between us or shared a short story with a friend about when he had been with this girl and done something interesting.

How often had I thought of Tim over the years? If I was honest with myself, I thought about him a lot in the years after he left, but eventually, I didn't dwell on him very often. When I did think of him, it was more of a bittersweet reminiscence than a dwelling over the pain of missing someone.

Although it had taken years for me to get to that point, I was in my second year of college before I felt ready to date someone again, and I dated the next guy for nine months before he transferred to another college down south for his master's degree.

My third relationship was a year later, which lasted until I graduated from college. We separated amicably and went about our new careers.

During the next few years, I dated on and off, but no one with any regularity. I had been too focused on building my career, and it wasn't until I was thirty-four that I started wondering where my life went.

A year later, I met Chad, and he had just started his divorce process. I had been dating him for about a year and a half, although I wasn't sure how serious it was to either of us. We had never spoken of a future.

During that time, how often had I thought of Tim? I couldn't say what regularity it had been, but recently, since I had learned he was returning to town, he had been constantly on my mind.

My phone interrupted my musings, and I glanced at the screen. It was Cara. She was probably the only one I would talk to right now because she wouldn't have had anything to do with what happened today.

"Hey, Cara. How are you?"

"How many glasses of wine have you had?" she asked without answering my question.

"Glasses? Don't you mean bottles?" I laughed slightly. Even though Cara hadn't been here, that didn't mean she wouldn't already know that my life was turned upside down. "Who called you?"

"Believe it or not, Candy."

I barked a laugh. "Yeah, I didn't see that. Especially since she was so eager to see my reaction."

"How was it?"

"Brutal, Cara, absolutely brutal. If I had known he would be there, I could have prepared myself, but I had no clue. It's always just us or the Youngs. No one outside the family is ever there unless we are dating them. How Evan thought that was going to be okay is beyond me."

"Evan is an asshole for doing that." She paused. "But how was it? How did it feel?"

"I don't even know how to explain it. I couldn't think or breathe for a few seconds, and then all I could do was run away. I didn't even speak to Tim then."

"Then?"

I sighed heavily. "It has been a shitty week, and I just couldn't deal with the extra drama, so I left and came home. Alaina gave him my address, and he stopped by."

"Oh, boy! Tell me everything that he did! Did he kiss you?"

"Cara! Why would you ask that?" I laughed nervously because I wasn't sure I should tell her.

Cara's laughter filled my ear. "Because I know how you feel about him. Candy sent me a picture of him. He is so damn handsome, Carmen. If I had been you, I might have jumped his bones."

"Did you forget that I am dating Chad?"

"I don't like Chad," she stated.

"You don't know Chad."

"I don't care. I don't like Chad. You should break up with him and go out with Tim."

"What if Tim doesn't want to go out with me?"

"Why wouldn't he? Wait, what did he say when he came over?" I explained some of what we talked about and paused when I got to the point where he kissed me at the door. "What happened then? Did you just let him walk out?"

"No, we were standing there staring at one another, and—"

"And what?" she squeaked. "Don't leave me in suspense. Did he kiss you?"

"Yes, he did."

Cara squealed on the other end of the line. "I knew it! I knew he would."

"How could you possibly know that?"

"Because I remember the chemistry the two of you had

together quite well. When I heard he was back in town, I knew it was only a matter of time before you two got together."

"How long have you known he was in town?"

"I just learned tonight. That's why I had to call you."

"What am I supposed to do now?"

"When are you going to see him again?"

"We are having coffee tomorrow."

"Then have coffee and see where it goes."

"What about Chad?"

"What about him? I already told you I didn't like him; get rid of him. If there is any chance for you and Tim to rekindle what you once had, you need to ditch the finance guy."

AFTER SPEAKING TO CARA, I felt better and eventually drifted off to sleep. I was up early on Saturday but was generally an early riser. Last night before we hung up, I started second-guessing my coffee date with Tim, but Cara talked me into going.

The thought of sitting across the table from him made me somewhat nervous. I would have a coffee with him and see what he wanted to say. At least if we were in public, there wouldn't be any chance of falling into another kiss with him. Was I happy or disappointed in that?

I still wasn't sure what I would do with Chad, but that might depend on what happened with Tim today. If Tim only intended to be friends, I could tell Chad what happened and assure him it wouldn't happen again.

Tim and I could be friends. We were adults, and a lot of time had passed since we had last seen each other. We would undoubtedly bump into one another around town. We had known shared friends, and many of them were still friends of mine.

My goal today would be to have a pleasant and friendly

conversation with him and perhaps get an idea of what he wanted. I was good at asking questions and figuring out what someone was saying without them saying it. Then we could decide how to deal with anything else.

I dressed in slacks and a blouse because I had to go into the office after coffee. Saturdays were for family appointments or new intakes, and I had three today.

So, coffee this morning would work, and if things weren't going well, I could use work as an excuse to get out of there sooner—rather than later.

I was already seated and had my coffee before me a few minutes before ten. I sat so I could see out the window, and I waited, watching every car as it pulled into the parking lot. Finally, a black SUV parked, and I recognized Tim behind the wheel. Butterflies exploded through my stomach, and I shifted in my seat as anxiety—or excitement—began to flood my system.

Instead of coming straight into the café, Tim opened the back door, and a moment later, a young lady exited. She had a bright smile and long blond hair pulled back into a ponytail.

Why did he bring his daughter? Was he trying to pull at my heartstrings? Or did he bring her as a buffer? Did he think if she were here, it would keep us from getting too deep in conversation? Did he regret kissing me last night? Did he bring his daughter here to remind him that he was still grieving for another woman? My psychological mind was going a mile a minute.

They entered the café, and he led her to the counter. Coral was there, and she smiled at him and then peered my way before giving her attention to his daughter. I heard the child say hello and order a mint hot chocolate and a chocolate croissant. Tim ordered a coffee and peered my way, lifting his chin in greeting. I gave him a tight-lipped smile.

His daughter glanced around, then spoke to her father for a

moment. He pointed me out to her, and she gave me a wider smile and waved. I had no choice but to return the gesture or appear rude.

Once they had their items, they approached the table. "Good morning, Carmen. This is my daughter, Savannah. Savannah, this is my friend, Carmen Winston."

"Hello," Savannah said as she took a seat. "Sorry I had to be here for your date with my dad, but my playdate got canceled."

"Oh," I said, surprised by her comment. "Well, it's not a date. It's just coffee."

"Yeah, that's what he said. It was a coffee date." She looked at me seriously. "We call them playdates, but that doesn't mean we are dating our friends either."

I snickered. "Okay, I hadn't thought of it like that. That is a brilliant way to look at it." Savannah shrugged a shoulder as she dug into her croissant as if she already knew this.

Tim laughed. "Please excuse my daughter. She is smarter than she should be and sometimes likes us to know that."

I smiled and spoke to Savannah. "Never apologize for being intelligent. It's good that you can keep people on their toes."

She grinned at me, asking, "You knew my dad when he was a kid?"

"I did. We were good friends in middle and high school, but I guess we met in…" I paused, thinking back.

"You were in third grade," Tim responded. "That's when my parents moved here from Summersville."

"Ah, that's right. You were in fourth grade, and we met on field day."

"Was my dad ever your boyfriend?" Savannah asked the innocent question.

My eyes snapped to Tim's. How did I answer that? If I said yes, would she be upset that her father was talking to me? If I said no, would I be all right with lying to a child? What if she found out later that we had dated? Would she be upset that I hadn't admitted it?

Luckily, I didn't have to respond because Tim replied to her. "We did date in middle school and high school. Carmen was my girlfriend before I moved to California."

"Is she going to be your girlfriend again?" she asked, nibbling on her treat.

"Um, no." I quickly jumped into the conversation. "Your father and I are just friends. You don't need to worry about me dating your father."

She shrugged a slim shoulder. "I'm not worried. My dad can date whoever he wants."

"Whomever he wants," Tim corrected her, and she rolled her eyes.

"Whomever he wants," she parroted back at him.

I was impressed. A lot of times, if a child was corrected that way in public, they would feel embarrassed. She seemed to take it in stride and accept it for what it was.

"Carmen and I are friends." He paused. "At least, I hope we can be friends."

"Why do you hope?" Savannah asked. "Do you still like her?"

Oh, this would be interesting. I waited patiently to hear what Tim had to say.

He laughed nervously as he glanced at me, then focused on his daughter. "It's not quite that easy, Savannah Bee. Carmen and I haven't seen each other in twenty years. We are different people than we once were, but I hope we can get to know one another and become friends again."

She peered my way. "Do you want to be friends with my father again?"

I wasn't exactly sure what I wanted from Tim, but I couldn't come out and say what I was thinking. Instead, I chose the noncommittal response. "You can never have too many friends."

Tim smirked at my comment and said, "Sorry to bring

Savannah, but we were going to her friend's house when we got a call that the girl had just thrown up."

"That's too bad."

"Yeah, Shelby is really nice, and we were going to play Barbies."

"You like Barbies?"

She nodded excitedly. "I have over a hundred."

I grinned at her. "A girl after my own heart. I still have mine from when I was a child. I think I had that many that I played with, but I have collected quite a few more over the years."

"How many do you have?" she asked with genuine interest.

I nibbled on my bottom lip, momentarily peering at Tim before answering her. "Let's just say I have a lot more than a hundred."

Her eyes grew wide. "Are they still in the boxes?"

I nodded. "Yep, many of them are."

Tim chuckled. "I can't believe you still collect them."

"Can I see them sometime?" Savannah asked.

"Maybe you can," I replied, not committing one way or the other.

Tim glanced over my blouse, changing the subject. "You're pretty dressed up for a Saturday morning."

"I have to work after our coffee."

"You said you were a child psychologist?"

"Yes, I am. I do a lot of work for the school district and am on the school board of directors. That day you saw me at the middle school, I was late for a meeting about a new program we are implementing in the schools."

"What kind of program?"

"The kind to keep kids safe. It's a risk assessment program that will help us monitor kids who are in trouble or are starting to show signs of violence."

He frowned slightly. "That's pretty scary to think about."

I nodded. "I agree."

"Has there been a problem around here with that?"

"No, not particularly, but it can happen anywhere. Look at the news on any given day, and you will see new stories about it. We hope that this kind of program will help us continue to remain safe."

"I sure hope it does too," he replied.

CHAPTER TEN

TIM

I wasn't too excited to bring Savannah, but I had no choice. With Savannah here, Carmen and I couldn't talk about what happened last night and what it might mean. However, having Savannah here might make getting to know one another easier.

I had thought a lot about Carmen after seeing her at her house last night. I hated leaving her when she was so close to tears, but our shared kiss had rocked me too. How could it have been so familiar and yet so incredibly different?

It brought back many memories of my younger years, and I had lain awake for hours reliving memories of my time with her. Then I unconsciously began to compare Carmen to Emily.

I didn't want to compare the two women, and I had no real reason to do so, but while my mind was drifting around, trying to find sleep, I found that I didn't have too much control over what I was thinking about.

Emily was two years older than me. I had met her at a college party during the summer before my senior year of high school, and we hit it off immediately. It had not been lost on me that Emily was short, with wild blond hair and blue eyes—just like Carmen. Perhaps that was my type, or maybe I was only initially interested in Emily because she had reminded me of Carmen and I missed her.

Whatever the reason, I pursued Emily, and pretty soon, we were a couple. I went to college with her, and when she was a junior, she had an off-campus apartment where I spent most of my time.

Emily found a job after graduating and helped me land mine before I had my diploma. We would be working for the same company but in different departments.

Emily was a happy person, just like Carmen had been. She was a thoughtful person who believed in family, and while hers was not as large as Carmen's, she did have two siblings.

Both women were driven; at least, I assumed Carmen was still driven. She had been in high school, and if she was a psychologist now, she had to be focused and determined to finish her schooling and build a clientele.

Carmen had a lot of love to give when she was younger and had been passionate and open to public displays of affection, just like Emily had been.

Had Carmen ever been married? She didn't want to speak about it last night, but perhaps in the light of day in a different atmosphere, she would. That was my hope today as we entered the café. I wanted to learn more about Carmen without the emotionally charged energy from last night.

As Savannah and I ordered, I was acutely aware of Carmen watching us. What was she thinking? How was she feeling today? Had she gotten over the shock of seeing me? Had she thought about the kiss at all? If we had the chance, would she want to kiss me again?

Carmen was tense as Savannah asked questions about knowing me and having dated me. I tried to alleviate the tension and was glad when Savannah and Carmen began to speak about Barbies. I hadn't remembered it until then, but

Carmen had quite the collection as a teenager. I wondered how many she had now.

Finally, the conversation changed to more about her and her career. I hated to think that school violence could be happening here. It was an almost daily occurrence in California, but luckily there had not been any school shootings where we had lived. The thought of my children having to deal with that was not something I wanted to consider.

We had already lost one person in our lives to violence. We didn't need to lose anymore.

Carmen glanced at my daughter, who was observing her. "Perhaps we should lighten the conversation."

Yeah, probably not the right time to discuss such profound things. Just because I worried about my kids and violence didn't mean they needed to worry about it too. "How long have you been a psychologist?"

"Officially, for about four years. I did a lot of schooling and intern work before finally graduating with the official title Doctor."

"Do you work for someone?" I asked as Savannah commented too.

"Oh, cool! You're a doctor!"

"I did, and I am." She directed that last one to Savannah before continuing. "But then I decided to open my own practice, and now I do a lot of work with the schools. Many times, they refer the kids to my practice."

"Is it just you, or do others work for you?"

"I have two other therapists in my practice and two administrative support team members. I am the only licensed psychologist there, but I am considering bringing another one onboard. My workload has gotten a bit overwhelming lately."

I nodded. "That's pretty impressive."

She shrugged as if to make light of it. "How long have you been working for Aliana?"

"I got hired by Buckworth Industries as soon as I graduated from college."

Savannah popped into the conversation, proudly announcing, "My mom got him the job."

"Oh, she did?" Carmen replied casually to her, but her eyes slipped to mine, and I saw something in them that I didn't quite understand.

"Yep, she was already working for them and helped him get hired. She used to tell us the story about it all the time. She told him he wouldn't be anywhere if it weren't for her."

I chuckled. "She said that jokingly, by the way."

Savannah grinned as Carmen commented, "Well, that worked out nicely, didn't it?" Was that a bit of sarcasm in her voice? "How did your mom and dad meet?"

I opened my mouth to speak, wanting to move away from the subject of Emily, but my daughter beat me to a response. "They met at a party."

Carmen nodded, a polite smile pasted on her lips that I knew all too well meant she was faking it. Was it odd that I could read Carmen so well after so many years? "Well, how nice."

"Emily was two years older than me," I supplied.

She raised a brow. "Older woman, huh?"

I chuckled slightly. "Yeah, I guess so."

Carmen glanced back at Savannah. "I'm sorry to hear about your mother."

Savannah nibbled on her croissant for a moment, then set it down. "I miss her a lot."

"I bet you do."

"We all do," I added, and Carmen lifted her eyes to mine. In them, I saw empathy. God, I hated that look. I had gotten so sick of seeing that after Emily died.

"I am sure that it has been challenging. Especially raising three children on your own."

"It has had its moments," I replied but tried to smile to lighten the conversation.

She focused on Savannah. "My mother passed away not too long ago too. I know it's not the same thing since you are young, but I understand what it feels like to lose your mom."

"I'm so sorry, Carmen. What happened?"

She shifted slightly in her seat. "She had cancer, but it was sudden. In fact, she learned about it, and a couple of weeks later, she passed away. None of us even knew about it. She had been waiting to tell us until we were all there, but the day she was going to tell us was when she died."

"I'm so sorry. I know how difficult that must have been. You were very close to your mom. How is your father doing?"

"He was rough for a while but seems to be improving." She pursed her lips as if contemplating something, and then her features relaxed as if she was putting the thought to the side.

Carmen asked my daughter, "Do you like your new school?"

"I do!" she said excitedly. "I love my teacher, and I have made a lot of new friends."

Carmen smiled happily at her answer. "I am glad to hear that. What about your brothers? Do they like their schools too?"

"I don't know. I think Dean does."

I jumped in. "Dean is thrilled with all the new things he has at the school, like the rock wall, and that they are putting in a pool. He was on the swim team last year, and I think he was most disappointed to be leaving that and his friends, but he seems really excited about the new pool they are building."

"Ah, yes, the pool." Carmen smiled. "Thanks to your boss."

"Alaina is building that?"

"Alaina donated several million dollars to the school district and promised several more over the next few years. All the updates are thanks to her."

"That's nice to know. How did Evan meet her?"

"She came here to escape the company for a little while. She

83

told me she needed to find herself, and she was working for the domestic violence center. Evan met her at the hospital. He's a nurse, in case you didn't know that. They hit it off, although things almost fell apart when he learned she wasn't who she originally said she was."

"I don't understand."

"She didn't tell anyone who she was. She used the name Alaina Marshall and kept her real identity a secret. Thankfully, she and Evan fixed things, and now they are very happy together."

I chuckled. "I bet he is enjoying all the money."

Carmen grinned. "I can't say that he complains much, but I do know that he enjoys the Maserati she gave him."

"Whoa, nice ride."

"Yes, it is." The two of us stared at one another for a long time, and I flashed back to a memory of the two of us riding in my old Ford pickup. She would slide into the middle seat and hold my hand as I drove. I wondered if she was remembering those times too.

Finally, she looked away, cleared her throat, and glanced at her small silver wristwatch.

"You have someplace you need to be?"

"I do. I already told you that I have to work. I have several patients today."

"Do you routinely work on Saturday?"

She nodded. "Yes, usually I do intakes to have both parents present. It's hard to do them with their work schedules during the week, and I don't want to add stress into their lives that way."

"How long do you have to work today?"

"A few hours." She glanced around the café momentarily to avoid any other mention of work. "So, how is Tripp doing? He's the oldest, correct?"

I frowned; she already knew that from her patient. "Yes, he is the oldest."

"He hates it here," Savannah supplied.

"Hate is a strong word," I commented. "I would say that Tripp is having the hardest time getting settled. Although he seems to be in a better mood the last couple of days."

Carmen chuckled. "That might have something to do with a certain female. I believe they are going to the movies tonight."

I shifted back and blinked. "My son has a date, and you know about it before me?"

"Relax, Tim. I only know about it because my client was so excited and shared it with me."

"I thought you weren't supposed to share what your clients say?"

"Typically, I'm not, but this isn't a secret, and it does involve your son. I doubt she would be upset that I said anything about it."

"Is she a nice girl?" I asked. If she was seeing a psychologist, did I want her around my son?

"She is, and she's had a hard time, but your son seems to be having a good effect on her."

"Well, that's good, I guess. Anything I should worry about?"

"I think you should worry about Tripp, not the young lady."

"What does that mean?" I asked, slightly bothered by her comment.

"It means that boys sometimes have a harder time adjusting to changes." She paused. "Although you seem to have adjusted well. I would keep an eye on him and make sure he finds his place. Moving at his age is difficult."

I bristled. "I am aware of that, Carmen. I don't need you to tell me that."

She stared at me momentarily before shifting to the edge of her seat. "No, I'm sure you don't. Well, it was nice seeing you again, and it was great meeting you, Savannah, but I need to get going."

"It was nice to meet you too," Savannah said as Carmen stood.

"I am sure we will bump into each other again." She smiled at my daughter, then the smile disappeared as she turned to me. "Tim, I hope you enjoy your new job. We will no doubt run into each other again."

Before I could say anything else, she walked away, and I turned to stare after her. She better believe that we were going to see each other again.

I had hoped we could find an equal footing and possibly be friends again, but I almost felt we had taken a step back. I frowned as I faced my daughter again.

"I like her, Dad. She reminds me of Mom."

"Why do you say that?"

"Because she looks kinda like her, and she isn't afraid to say things to make you angry." She grinned.

I chuckled. "You think she looks like your mom?"

She rolled her eyes dramatically. "Yes! She has the same color hair, the same color eyes. She's even short like Mom was."

I already knew this because I had noted it as well. I wondered if I should be worried that my daughter had also. "I guess she does kind of look like your mom."

I glanced out the window to see Carmen nearing a blue SUV. "I'll be right back. You stay here." Before thinking about my actions, I rushed out the door and toward her car. When I reached her passenger window and knocked on the glass, she was putting it into reverse.

She rolled the window down. "Yes?"

"Open the door for a moment," I said as I peered inside.

She put the vehicle back in park and then unlocked the door. Before she could do or say anything else, I pulled it open and slipped into the passenger seat.

She glanced around me as I closed the door. "Where is Savannah?"

"She's still inside. She will be fine."

"What do you need?" she asked, staring at me with a hiked brow.

"I need to know when I can see you again."

She shifted to face me better. "Why do you want to see me again, Tim?"

"Are you trying to tell me you don't want to see me?"

"I didn't say that. I asked you a question."

I reached forward and touched her face, stroking my thumb over her cheek as I leaned closer until we were only a few inches apart. "I don't know why exactly I want to see you, but I do. I feel like we have unfinished business. Can you tell me that you don't feel it?"

"Quite honestly, I'm not sure what I feel, Tim."

"Then go out with me, on a date, with no kids and no work appointments that you have to run off to, and let's see what this is."

An array of emotions slipped over her face. "I can't."

"Why?"

"Because I can't, Tim."

"Give me one good reason why you can't."

"I'm seeing someone."

"You're seeing someone?"

She nodded.

"Is it serious?"

Her features shifted just enough to give me the answer, and my gaze dropped to her lips. I wasn't the type of man to get in the way of a relationship, but I couldn't help myself as I curled my hand around her neck and pulled her lips to mine. She didn't resist me. It only lasted a few seconds, but it was enough to know that she felt the same thing I did.

She looked dazed when I pulled back. "Does his kiss do that

to you, Carmen? Because if it doesn't, he's not the right man for you."

I climbed out of the vehicle and bent down, searching her face. She looked shocked—as if my words had rocked her as much as the kiss had. "Think about that. I'll see you again soon, Carmen."

Without another word, I closed the door and headed back inside, wondering when I could find a reason to show up on her doorstep again to get the answer to my question. I had a pretty good idea of the answer, but I wanted to hear her say it.

CHAPTER ELEVEN

CARMEN

Oh my God! What just happened? I stared at the closed door for a few seconds and then watched him walk back into the café from the side mirror. Did he really kiss me again? Did he just ask me if Chad made me feel that way when he kissed me?

Holy shit, he did to both of those!

I pulled myself together and reversed out of my spot, quickly getting on the road.

"Oh my God, I'm a cheater," I whispered to the empty car. Not only did I kiss the man once, but I let him kiss me again, and I kissed him back. I hadn't even hesitated to do so the second time!

There was no question about whether Chad's kisses made me feel like Tim's did. That was a big fat no! Chad didn't make my heart pound, and he didn't make me weak in the knees. His kisses didn't make me crave more, but Tim's sure did.

"Holy hell!" I muttered as I turned onto another street to take me to my office. I really needed to talk to Chad now and tell him what had happened. No man wanted to be with a woman who cheated on him. After work, I would call him and see if he could meet me for a drink.

As I went into the office, turned on the lights, and set things up for my first appointment, I thought about meeting Savannah. She was very mature for her age, and I appreciated it. She reminded me of myself at that age.

It was not lost on me that her hair color was very similar to mine and that her eyes were blue. Had Tim unconsciously found another woman identical to me to replace me?

That thought bothered me. Tim hadn't just moved on and started a new life, but he had replaced me with someone very similar, and that woman had taken over the life that I was supposed to have. It was stupid to be bothered by it, but irrationally, I was.

Perhaps I was grasping at straws here. Maybe Tim's wife looked nothing like me, and the blond hair and blue eyes were from someone else in their family. I had known Tim's family well, and none of them had blond hair, but what about her family?

That could be it. It could just be a coincidence. I glanced at my watch to see that I still had a few more minutes before my session, so I pulled out my phone and retrieved Chad's number. It rang four times, then went to voicemail. Damn, I forgot he was coaching.

"Hey, Chad, it's Carmen. Are you busy later today? I was thinking maybe a drink at the tavern this afternoon. Let me know if that works for you. I'm about to go into session, so you can text me and let me know if that's okay."

I hung up without saying anything else, then set my phone down and stared out the window. While Chad and I had been dating for a while, we weren't serious, so I doubted he would be upset if I broke it off.

But did I want to break it off with him? Did I want to see

what could happen with Tim? It didn't take long to come up with an answer to that one.

WHEN I CHECKED my phone later, I had several text messages. One was from my brother asking if I forgave him. Another was from Cara, asking how coffee went. A third was from Chad, saying he could meet me around five; the last was a number I didn't know. My finger hovered over it for a few seconds before I touched it. I had no doubt who it was going to be from.

Only when I opened the message I started to laugh. There wasn't a message, only a picture. The picture was of Savannah with all her Barbie dolls around her—some in boxes, some not.

I typed a reply: *That's an impressive collection.*

It was a few minutes before I got a response: *Sorry, she begged me to send it to you. I hope I didn't interrupt work.*

No, my phone is on silent during my sessions. I just finished.

I hope they went well.

Thank you. I wrote, and then I paused. I wanted nothing more than to keep talking to him, but I needed to finish my notes, run a few errands, and meet Chad for a drink. *Have a good evening, Tim. Tell Savannah I will send her a picture of some of mine later.*

She will be thrilled to see them. Have a good night.

I stared at the message for a long time, then set my phone down and forced myself to focus on my work. Two hours later, I was pulling up to the tavern, and I was not sure what exactly I would say.

I had never been one to beat around the bush, but I also didn't know exactly how you told someone you were dating that you had kissed another person. My only hope was that he would understand and not cause a scene.

Mike was at the hostess stand looking over something when I stepped in. "Hey, Mike."

"Carmen, I didn't expect to see you, but I should have expected it since Chad entered the bar. I assume you are meeting him?"

"Yes, I am. Where is Candy?"

"Harley and Candy are at your dad's."

"Oh, okay." The phone rang beside the hostess station, and he reached for it as I said goodbye.

Inside the bar, I found Chad seated at a tall table on the side of the room. He was on his phone, smiling at something. "Hey," I said as I approached the table and hung my coat on the back of the tall stool.

"Oh, hey." He set his phone down and leaned forward, capturing my lips as I took a seat. I shouldn't have been surprised, but I was. Not because he kissed me but because I felt absolutely nothing when he did. "How was work today?"

"Good, how was coaching?"

"Pretty good. The kids are doing really well. We have our first meet next week, and I think they will do a great job."

"I'm glad to hear that." Veronica, one of the waitresses, showed up at the table with a glass of white wine for me. I came here so often, I didn't need to tell them my order. "Thanks," I told her as she placed it on the table.

I took a long sip of my wine and then set it down. "I need to tell you something, Chad."

"What's that?"

"I kissed another man."

He studied me briefly and then laughed. "You did?"

"Yes, I knew I needed to tell you about it."

"Did you sleep with him?"

"No, I only kissed him—twice."

He nodded and glanced around, a smirk on his face that

confused me. He shrugged. "Okay, you planning on doing it again?"

I blinked and blinked again. Was he not upset? "Um—" I wasn't sure how to answer that. I had been expecting to have to explain myself, not thinking about doing it again.

"Don't worry if you do. I get it. You and I aren't that serious, and I'm glad you said something because I wanted to tell you that I have been seeing someone else too."

I shifted back slightly. "You have?"

"Yeah, in fact, I was with her last night."

I let his words shift through my mind. "With her, as in *with her*? You slept with her?"

He shrugged. "Yeah, it's no big deal. If you want to sleep with whoever it is that you kissed, I'm okay with that."

"You're okay with that," I repeated, and he nodded and then took a long slug of his beer.

"In fact, we could all get together."

My jaw dropped open. "As in, we could all get together and have sex? As in sharing partners?"

"Yeah." He laughed.

"I didn't know you were into that."

"Courtney and I used to do that kind of thing all the time. It's what screwed up our marriage, though."

I stared at him, wondering how I could have been so wrong about this man. It's no wonder he never wanted to commit. "I didn't know you enjoyed that lifestyle, Chad."

"Does it bother you?"

"Personally?" I hesitated. "I'm not into that. I'm sorry, and had I known you were, I could have told you sooner. Why didn't you mention it before?"

"I wasn't sure you'd be into it."

"No, I'm not, but I have no problem if you are. I just don't think things would work out for us now that I know."

"I get it." He didn't seem upset, and it surprised me when he said, "But I'm sorry to hear that. I really thought you and I had something. The kids were just starting to warm up to you."

I almost burst out laughing. His kids were never going to warm up to me. "Well, I'm sorry too." I pushed my wineglass back. "I appreciate you meeting me."

"Who is the guy?"

"What?"

"Who is the guy you kissed?"

"Um, an old friend I ran into."

"Are you going to see him again?"

"I don't know." Well, that was a bald-faced lie. I was already wondering when the next time that I could see Tim would be.

"I hope you find what you're looking for, Carmen, but you can always call me again if you don't."

I slipped off my stool, collecting my jacket. "I'll keep that in mind, Chad. You take care of yourself."

"You too, and the offer is always open if you and your friend want to join us."

Oh my God! I nodded. "Sure, I'll keep that in mind. Take care of yourself, Chad." I shifted away from the table and rushed toward the front door.

How did I not know that he was a swinger? In all our conversations, he never even alluded to the fact that he and his wife used to switch couples. That was totally not my scene, and thinking about all the times we had been together now made me feel sick.

I headed to my father's house to see if Candy was still there and found her, Harley, and my father sitting at the kitchen table, finishing dinner. I paused beside my father long enough to brush a kiss over his cheek.

"What a nice surprise. What are you doing here?" he asked.

"I was looking for Candy."

"Oh, and here I thought you came to see me because you loved me."

"I do love you, Daddy, but I needed to talk to my sister."

"Then pull up a chair," he said.

"Um, this is a conversation better had in private."

Candy laughed. "Let me guess, you want to talk about Tim?"

"Tim, who?" my father asked immediately, looking curious.

Candy replied, "Tim Kohl, you remember him, don't you, Dad?"

He frowned. "Isn't he the one who broke your heart when you were a little girl?"

"I was seventeen, Dad. Not so little."

"He still broke your heart." He turned to Harley. "I sure hope you don't grow up to break girls' hearts."

Candy rolled her eyes. "Dad, I think we have some time before we have to worry about that. He's not even seven yet."

"You can never start too early. Why are you even talking about Tim Kohl?"

"Because he moved back to town," Candy stated energetically and grinned my way.

My father's frown deepened. "Why would he do that?"

Before Candy could say something else to upset my father, I stepped into the conversation. "He works for Alaina, Dad. He just moved here to run her new warehouse."

"Is he married?"

"Widowed."

His features softened. "That's too bad. Are you going to go out with him?"

"Dad, I don't know what I'm doing right now, but that's why I need to talk to Candy."

"All right, you two go do your girl talk. I'll make sure Harley understands the way of the world over ice cream sundaes."

Candy chuckled as she kissed Harley's head and came around the table, saying, "Don't go too deeply into the world, Dad, or give him too much ice cream. I don't want you to give him nightmares and a stomachache."

Candy and I went through the living room and climbed the steps to my old bedroom. I closed the door and dropped my coat over a chair in the corner.

"Man, this must be good if we had to sequester to your bedroom!"

I turned and stared at her, and then I wasn't sure what to say.

"Out with it!" she said with a laugh as she flopped to her side on the bed.

"Damn, Candy, I don't know where to start."

"What are the options?"

"Should I start with Chad being a swinger or the fact that Tim kissed me twice?"

CHAPTER TWELVE

TIM

S aturday afternoon, I worked around the house, cleaning up and doing a bit more unpacking. On and off during the day, thoughts of Carmen slipped into my mind, and I thought about the kisses we shared and the question I had posed to her before I left her the last time.

Was I ready to get involved with someone else? Since Emily died, I hadn't even considered it, but now I was suddenly thinking about how I could spend more time with Carmen. Did that mean I was finally ready? I wasn't sure.

It was during dinner that Savannah brought up Carmen, and I wished she hadn't. I didn't want the kids to know I was talking to another woman, not that anything was wrong with it. Emily had been gone for two years now.

"Did Carmen like my picture?"

Dean frowned. "Who's Carmen?"

"Dad's old girlfriend," Savannah supplied before I could finish chewing the food in my mouth.

Tripp froze, his eyes snapped to mine, and I saw anger starting to grow there. "You're seeing your old girlfriend?"

"No, I am not seeing anyone. I ran into Carmen on Friday

night, but we didn't get a chance to talk much, so we decided to have coffee this morning."

He dropped his fork to the plate. "Is that where you were last night? On a date? I thought you were at your boss' house for dinner. That's what you told me."

"I was at Alaina's house. That's where I bumped into Carmen. Alaina is married to Carmen's brother."

"Jesus, Dad! Is that why we moved here? So you could be closer to your old girlfriend?"

"Tripp, I came here for a job and no other reason. It was just ironic that this is where I used to live."

"Ironic? It's more like bullshit!" Tripp sneered as he pushed back his chair and got up.

"Where the hell do you think you're going?" I barked out the question, irritated that I was being questioned on this.

"I have plans. I told you that the other day. You said I could borrow your car."

I had completely forgotten about that. "Where are you going and with whom?"

He dropped his plate on the counter. "The movies with a friend."

"Who is the friend?"

"Just a friend," he muttered. "Why do you even care? You should be happy I am making friends."

I wiped my mouth and set my napkin beside my plate before I got up and blocked his path from the kitchen. "I am glad that you are making friends, Tripp. I'm not asking anything I didn't ask when we lived in California. If you took my car, you needed to tell me where you were going and who you were going with."

"Jesus, Dad, I'm going on a date, alright? Just like you did. I'm not going to go out partying. It's just a movie and then maybe some ice cream or something. It's no big deal."

I crossed my arms over my chest. "I did *not* go on a date."

"Yeah, whatever. Are we finished now? I have to get ready, or I'm going to be late."

I sighed. "Fine, but I want you home by eleven."

"Eleven? My curfew is at midnight."

"Yeah, well, nothing is open around here after eleven, so you be home then."

"Whatever. This place sucks," he muttered as he walked toward the steps, taking them two at a time.

I took a long breath, released it, and returned to the table. As I got seated, Savannah said, "Don't worry, Dad. It's just hormones."

I barked out a laugh. "Yeah, I know, Savannah, but thanks for that."

A few minutes later, Dean asked softly, "Did you really go on a date?"

"No, Dean. I ran into Carmen at Alaina's house, and we didn't get a chance to talk. We were good friends when I lived here, so we arranged coffee today. That's it. It wasn't a date."

"She's nice," Savannah told Dean. "She looks a lot like Mom too."

"Why does she look like Mom?"

"She has crazy blond hair and blue eyes just like Mom did."

Dean pushed food around on his plate. "I kind of forget what she looks like."

A rush of pain filled my chest. "It's okay, Dean. Sometimes when someone is gone for a long time, pictures in our mind start to fade."

"I don't want to forget her," he stated emphatically.

"You won't forget her. There is no way you will ever forget her."

Savannah chimed in, "Sometimes I wish I could hear her voice again. I don't remember what she sounded like."

I thought for a moment, and then I collected my phone.

"What are you doing?" Dean asked as I started to dial into my messages.

"I want to play something for you. I saved it."

A moment later, I put the phone on speaker and hit the play button. The night Emily died, she had left me a voice message, and I had listened to it a thousand times. I had almost deleted it, but now I am glad I saved it.

"Hi, I'm running a bit late as usual. My meeting lasted longer than I anticipated. I'm going to stop at the market and pick up something quick for dinner. Make sure Tripp is finishing his homework and Dean and Savannah have cleaned their rooms. I love you all, and I'll be home soon."

Dean and Savannah were both smiling as they listened to the message. "Thanks, Dad," Dean said after he heard it.

"Can we listen to it again?" Savannah asked.

"Sure." I played it again, then again, and the third time, Tripp stepped into the room. His features turned to rage as he heard Emily's voice.

"Why are you doing that to them? Why the hell do you still have that? You should have deleted that a long time ago. They need to forget her, just like you are doing."

"Tripp!" I burst from the table. "I am not forgetting your mother. Savannah said she forgot what her voice sounded like, so I played the message for her."

"You should delete that. She's dead, she's never coming back, and obviously, you are already moving on, so why should we remember her if you're just going to bring another woman into our lives?"

"Tripp, you need to calm down. That is not what I am doing."

"Yeah, right." He snapped and grabbed the keys off the hook where I hung them.

"Hey! You are not getting into the car when you are angry." I snatched the keys away from him.

"Give them back to me!"

"No! You calm down, and we can discuss it."

"Screw you, Dad! Give me the damn keys. I want to leave."

I pushed the keys into the front pocket of my pants. "Tripp, I think you need to cancel your date."

"No! This is the first good thing that has happened to me since we got here. I want to go out."

"Well, you can't drive when you are in this state, so either calm down or go to your room and cancel your plans."

"Screw you!" he hissed, his eyes filling with tears. "I hate you! I hate this place, and I hate that you fucking moved us here!"

"Go to your room," I said in a low, husky voice. His words had struck very close to home, and I needed him to leave before I lost my shit and started yelling. I never wanted to yell at the kids if I could help it.

"No! I'll walk!"

I grabbed his arm as he began to turn away and pushed him against the wall. "You will go to your room, Tripp Donovan Kohl! Do you understand me? This behavior will not be tolerated!"

Tears welled in his eyes, but they did not drop. Finally, he shrugged out of my hold and growled, "I hate you."

"And I love you," I replied as he stomped away and thundered up the stairs. A moment later, his door slammed, and I sighed.

I returned to the table and sat, and Savannah got up and hugged me. "He doesn't mean it."

"I know he doesn't, Savannah Bee." I forced myself to finish what was on my plate as I dwelled over what Tripp had said. I knew he didn't hate me, and as I sat there and chewed, I remember having an almost identical argument with my parents after we had moved. Eventually, he would get over it and adjust, just like I did.

AFTER I PUT the kids to bed that night, I paused outside his door. There was no sound from inside, so he was either listening to music with his headphones on or he was asleep. I would give him tonight to calm down and speak with him tomorrow.

I climbed into bed and turned on the television for a few minutes, but nothing captured my interest, so I turned it back off and rolled to my side. A few moments later, I began to drift and slipped right into the memory of kissing Carmen in her vehicle today.

Only it wasn't just the memory of today, but a mixture of then and now. I was kissing Carmen, but we were in the back seat of her SUV. We were making out like we had as teens, but in our adult bodies. Each of us made small, shy advances to tease one another. I wanted her to touch me, taste me, and let me deep inside her. I knew by looking into her eyes that she wanted the same thing.

I grasped her breast over her blouse. She gasped and dropped her head back so I could kiss her neck. The more I kissed her, the hungrier I got and the faster I moved. We got undressed, and she was suddenly her younger self again as she timidly sat over my lap and seated herself on me. I ravished her breasts as she rode me for the first time, more excited than I had ever anticipated. I could barely contain myself, and it didn't take long for me to hit my orgasm.

Only when I did, I woke myself up with my hand around my cock as sticky jets of come shot all over my sheets.

EARLY SUNDAY MORNING, I found myself in the shower, getting off to the memory of my dream for the third time. It had been months since I had gotten myself off. After Emily died, it was probably six or seven months before I even attempted it. It made me sad; after that, I had only done it a few times. Eventually, I didn't think much about it.

Now, I couldn't stop. I dropped my sheets into the laundry, and Dean, Savannah, and I made breakfast together. Since our fight the night before, Tripp still hadn't left his room, and I was giving him space to cool off.

"Dad, can we paint my room today?"

"What color did you want to paint it?"

"I don't know, maybe pink or purple? Mom always said that I could have a purple room."

"You aren't talking about a dark purple, are you? Because we aren't painting any dark colors."

"Why not?" She looked disappointed.

"Dark colors will make your room look smaller."

"But how can it make it look smaller than it is?"

"It just does. Lighter colors make a room look bigger."

She frowned. "But I want a dark color."

"How about we look at colors today and find something that might work? We can talk about a darker color when we buy a new house."

"Okay," she replied with a bit more excitement. "When are we going to buy a house?"

"Well, the lease for here is only six months, so hopefully around then."

"We aren't going to change schools again, are we?"

"No, we are going to stay in Millerstown."

"Good," Dean piped in. "I like it here. The school is pretty cool, and I can't wait for the pool to open."

"I bet you miss swimming, don't you?"

He nodded quickly. "Yes! I was just getting my butterfly down. Now I'm going to have to start over."

"I am sure it will all come back to you once you get in the water."

"Probably not," he said with a bit of a whine.

"Just wait and see."

"Do you think they have a pool around here?"

"Actually, they do." I thought momentarily. "There is a YMCA on the edge of town, and I am pretty sure they have a pool."

"Can I join it?"

"How about we look into it next weekend?"

The thought of the kids joining the YMCA was a good idea. Tripp used to go work out at the gym. It would be good for his frustration to get back there and do it again, and Savannah had taken gymnastics courses at our local one back in California. She would probably enjoy getting back to those too.

"Let's look on Saturday morning and see what they have."

"Can I take soccer?"

I frowned. "Soccer? Don't you want to take gymnastics?"

She shook her head. "No, everyone plays soccer here."

"You know you don't have to do what everyone else does, right?"

"Yeah, I know, but I want to play soccer."

I grinned at her. "Okay, we will look into swimming, soccer, and gymnastics."

CHAPTER THIRTEEN

CARMEN

Candy stared at me for three seconds, then she popped off the bed. "What? And what?"

I began to pace. "Which one do you need more explanation on?"

"Are you kidding? Both! How could you lead with that, Carmen?" She shook her head at me. "How about you start from when you left Evan's last night? I noticed shortly after that Tim was gone too."

"Yes, I left. I was overwhelmed and couldn't think straight. I just needed to go home and get in bed."

"Did bed include Tim?"

"No! Although I admit he did come over to talk, but that's all it was. We just talked." I paused. "Until he left, and then he kissed me."

"Like on the cheek, or did your tongues do the mambo?"

I gave her a droll look. "The mambo? Seriously, Candy? How old are you?"

"Younger than you, but that's beside the point! Did you kiss him back or act like a dead fish?"

"Of course, I kissed him back!"

"And was it good? Did it bring back memories?"

"Trust me; the memories have been there for a while."

She cocked her head like she was confused, and I sat on the edge of the bed. "I didn't tell anyone, but I knew Tim was coming back to town."

"You did? How long did you know?"

"For over a month."

"Then why the hell were you so surprised and upset to see him?"

"I wasn't upset to see him—surprised, yes—but not upset. I was overwhelmed from work, stressed, and anxious about running into him."

"Did you know he was going to be there last night?"

"No, not at all. Maybe it wouldn't have been such a shock if I had known."

"But things were better after you talked last night?"

"Yes, things were a little better, and then he kissed me when he said goodbye. Neither of us expected that to happen, and then when he said goodbye, he told me that he was sorry and that he had really loved me."

"That's good!"

"That's past tense and from a very long time ago," I stressed.

"So, how do you feel for him?"

"I don't know."

"Do you still love him? Several years ago, I know you told me that if you ever had the chance to see him again, you'd jump at it because he was the one who got away."

I winced. "Did I say that?"

"You might have been three sheets to the wind, but you said it."

I chuckled. "I probably did. I'm not sure that I ever entirely got over him. I think a little piece of me has loved him since I met him."

"I think when you love someone, that doesn't go away. It

might go dormant, but I don't think you can just fall out of love with someone like that."

"I don't know that I agree with that. I think you can fall out of love with someone. In fact, I know you can, but I agree that if you really love someone, that feeling doesn't ever go away—not entirely."

"Did you tell him that?"

"No! Are you crazy?"

"What happened after you kissed him?"

"He left. That's it. I went to bed—alone, I might add. Then I saw him this morning at Coral's."

"Did you two just bump into each other?"

"No, we arranged to meet there last night. We were going to talk, but he brought his daughter with him, and we didn't get to have much of a conversation."

"You met his daughter? How many kids does he have?"

"Three, two boys and a girl."

"Wow, and he's raising them alone. That's so sad." She grinned at me. "But you could be their stepmomma, maybe even adopt them like I am with Harley."

"I am not even going to dignify that with a comment."

"Fine," she huffed. "But what does this have to do with Chad being a swinger?"

"Last night, I thought I needed to tell Chad I had kissed another man."

"Oh, boy, you were feeling guilty."

"Yes, wouldn't you have?"

"It was a kiss, not a proposal or a night in bed."

"A kiss is still cheating, but it doesn't matter. After Tim kissed me again today, I had to tell Chad."

She smacked her hand on the bed. "You didn't tell me he kissed you today! You only told me about last night!"

"When I left the café, he ran to my car and got in. He wanted to know when he could see me again, and I told him I was seeing someone. He kissed me then and asked me if Chad made me feel the same way when he kissed me. Then he got out of my car and walked away."

"Well, does he?"

"Does he what?"

"Does Chad's kiss make you feel the same way that Tim's does?"

"Not even close," I said and then grinned. "Candy, when Tim kissed me, it was like something inside me broke open. I was flooded with all these endorphins, and I wanted to throw him into the back seat of my car and have my way with him."

She chuckled. "I bet he would have liked that."

"I'm not so sure his daughter would have enjoyed it, though."

Candy snickered. "Probably too early for that education."

"Definitely!"

"So you went to talk to Chad?"

"I did. I met Chad at the tavern and told him I had to confess to kissing someone else. He wasn't upset at all. Then he admitted that he was with someone else last night."

"Are you kidding me? You admit to kissing a guy, and he tells you he slept with someone else? What a douchebag!"

"He also said that if Tim and I ever wanted to join him and this new partner, he'd welcome it because he liked to swing. He said that's what he and his wife used to do."

"That's just wrong."

"Yes, it is."

"So, how did you two leave things?"

"I wished him well and left there as quickly as possible."

"So now, you can see where things go with Tim."

"I guess, but what if things don't work?"

"And what if they do?"

"We haven't seen each other in twenty years. Both of us are different. What if we don't get along? What if we end up hating one another?"

"First of all, I can't see you and Tim ever hating one another. You two were crazy about each other, and if the chemistry is already beginning to bubble after just two kisses, can you imagine what it will do when you two have a few hours together alone? Holy hell! You'll melt the paint off your house."

"You're funny," I said with a giggle. "I can't imagine having sex with him again, but then again, I kind of can."

"I wonder if he's thought about it," Candy said.

"Who knows, but probably. He is a man, after all."

"I wonder if he's had sex since his wife died."

I recoiled back. "That's a horrible thing to wonder."

"What? That's a legit question. Maybe he's not ready to take that step. He was married for a long time. I bet it's not easy to jump back in the saddle after all that time."

I sighed. "I guess you're right."

"You might have to give him time to make sure he's ready."

I chuckled. "You sure you're not the psychologist?"

"Absolutely not! I just listen to you carefully."

"I'm glad."

"What are you going to do now?"

"I think we need to talk and take some time to get to know one another."

"You're not going to jump into bed with him and make sure all the equipment works? He's not that far from forty, you know."

"Stop!" I chided her with a laugh. "I am sure all the equipment works just fine, and if it doesn't, there is medicine for that."

"I know, I'm just joking with you. I'm glad he's back, and I hope it works for you two."

"Yeah, me too. I think."

"How do you feel about him having three children?"

I thought about that for a moment. "I haven't given it much

thought. I mean, I met his daughter, and she's really sweet. She reminds me of me when I was younger."

"Oh, so she's a smart-ass, huh?"

"No, I mean, she looks like me at that age. Our hair is the same color, and our eyes are too."

"What color hair did her mother have?"

"I have no clue. I haven't seen a picture of her." I paused. "Would it be weird if he married a girl who looked like me?"

"Maybe, but maybe that's just his type."

"Yeah, perhaps." But I wasn't sure how I felt about that.

We talked for a bit longer, and then I talked with my father. I told him I'd be over early the next day to help with dinner and finally made my way home.

Once I got there, I contemplated texting Tim but decided to put my phone on the charger, turn on my music, and climb in the tub.

While there, I thought about those kisses, which led me to think about when Tim and I had shared a bath. Of course, that led to how we'd had sex in the tub, and before I knew it, my hand was slipping under the water to ease the desire building inside of me.

SUNDAY WAS FOR FAMILY, but that didn't mean I wasn't thinking about Tim. Back when we were dating, Tim used to come to our Sunday dinners. He didn't have any siblings, and he loved being around all my brothers and sisters. He had told me that he wanted to have a large family after we got married, and I had no trouble picturing the two of us with six kids.

But now he already had three, and I was of the age that having a child wasn't as safe. Would we have time to have three kids of our own?

I thought about texting him several times that day but

refrained and kept checking my phone on and off instead, wishing he would send me a message. It wasn't until I was home that I finally heard from him, but it wasn't by phone.

My doorbell rang at seven-thirty, and I opened it to find him standing on the porch. "Tim? What are you doing here?"

"I was in the neighborhood and thought I'd stop by to say hello."

I chuckled. "In the neighborhood, huh?"

He gave me a lopsided grin. "I made an excuse to run out to the store so I could see you for five minutes."

I let him into the house. "I remember you doing that from time to time when you were younger."

"Yeah, that was the only reason I would run errands for my mom. I think she knew that too." The two of us stared at one another before he finally spoke again. "How was dinner with your family? I assume you still do that."

"Yes, we do, and it was very nice. How was your day?"

"We were looking at paint colors. Savannah wants to paint her room purple or at least one wall."

"I hope you told her to go with a light purple," I said with a grin.

"Yes, I did." He studied me again. "Did you think about my question?"

I lifted my chin as if daring him to do something, but I didn't answer right away. He stepped forward, and I asked, "What question was that?"

His nose flared slightly, and he took another step forward as if he were prowling toward me. Instinct made me shift myself back as if I could run from him. Unfortunately, the door was behind me, and he would have me caged in another two steps. A shiver tore down my spine when I realized I wanted him to confine me.

"The question about whether your boyfriend's kiss can affect you as much as mine."

"How do you know that your kiss affects me?"

He stood only inches from me, and I felt my breath picking up excitedly. "Because I know you, Carmen. We might not have seen each other for twenty years, but I know what your face looks like when you enjoy something."

He ran two fingers over my cheek. "I know how you react when you want more." He lifted my chin with his thumb and leaned forward until his lips almost touched mine. "I know the look you get in your eye when you are turned on. It's not a look I could ever forget."

I whimpered slightly, begging him to kiss me without words, and unable to move as I waited for what would come.

"Answer the question, Carmen. Does his kiss excite you as mine does?"

"No," I breathed between us, and that was all it took. Tim's lips collided with mine, and for the first time since I was sixteen, I wrapped my arms around his shoulders and clung to him with everything I had in me.

CHAPTER FOURTEEN

TIM

I couldn't wait another minute to see Carmen and find out the answer to the question. I told the kids I needed to run to the store for a few lunch items, which wasn't a lie.

Dean and Savannah had already taken showers and were watching television, and Tripp was doing homework at the kitchen table.

Once I stepped into Carmen's house, I only had one intention: to get her to admit that my kisses turned her on more than her boyfriend's. Should I hate myself for causing her to cheat on him? Maybe, but I didn't care.

I ravished her lips, pressing her body tightly between me and the door. Carmen rose on tiptoe, and I lifted her off the floor, pressing into her as she wrapped her legs around my waist and whimpered again. I couldn't get enough of her, and my cock ached to be released and get lost in her, but that wouldn't happen tonight.

The kiss lasted over a minute before I pulled back and found that I wasn't the only person breathing hard. Our ragged breath mingled between us. "I'm sorry, Carmen, I couldn't help myself.

I haven't been able to stop thinking about you or kissing you again since I left you yesterday morning."

"I haven't either," she admitted.

I brushed my lips tenderly against hers again, and then I slowly let her body slip down mine. "I need to go. If I don't, I will have you naked and under me."

She shivered, and I saw the raw desire in her eyes. I closed mine and inhaled slowly to calm myself. "I understand," she finally said as she touched my cheek.

I smiled tenderly at her. "I'm not sure you do. It has been a long time since I have been with someone. I haven't even thought about doing so until recently, and now I can't get it out of my mind. Especially when it's you I want to be with."

She grinned up at me. "You do, huh?"

I nodded, brushed my lips over her cheek, and repeated it until I was near her ear. "Oh, yeah, I do. You have no idea how badly I want you, Carmen."

She shivered again, pressing her breasts against my chest. "I want you too, Tim. I can't believe how much I want you."

I nibbled on her earlobe, and she gasped as she ran her hand down my back, then pulled it around between us and rubbed her palm over my erection. I groaned at the touch and quickly retook her lips. She rubbed against me harder, and I adjusted my arms to pick her up.

She giggled as I did, and I carried her into the living room, where I put her back on her feet and let my hands move to the hem of her shirt. She was right there with me as she began to tug my t-shirt up too.

The two of us undressed in a rush, and it didn't take long before I was seated on the couch, and she was climbing over my lap, replaying the fantasy I've had of her for the last day.

I suckled on her breasts and palmed her ass as she moved faster, her head thrown back, moaning with plea-sure. It didn't last nearly long enough, and within a few minutes, I couldn't stop myself from hitting that high. Luckily, Carmen appeared to have been as into it as me because I felt her insides pulsing around me as we came together.

She collapsed against me, breathing heavily into my neck, and I held her tightly, placing soft kisses on her shoulder. It wasn't until then that I realized what I had just done, and a guilty weight descended over me.

"I hate to say this, but I need to go. I've been longer than I intended, and the kids will start wondering where I am."

She sighed but pulled back. "I get it." For a moment, we stared at one another, and I tried to hide the feelings that I was having, but I wasn't sure I was able to.

I had been with only two women in my life. Carmen was my first, and then Emily was my second. I had been faithful to Emily for over twenty years, and a part of me felt as if I had just cheated on her. Which wasn't possible since she was dead, but that's how I felt.

Carmen smiled slightly, then quickly climbed off my lap and gathered her clothing. "I'll be right back."

I watched her leave the room, collected my clothing, and began dressing. I was done, and she hadn't returned, so I went to find her bathroom and knocked. "Carmen, I need to get going."

"Okay, I'll see you later!"

I frowned. She wasn't going to come out and say goodbye? "Are you okay?"

"Yeah! I'll talk to you later. You better get going before the kids ask too many questions."

"Okay, I'll call you later?"

"Sounds good," Carmen said in a cheery voice from behind the door, and I furrowed my brow further. I left the house, feeling off-kilter about the whole situation.

"Jesus, what the hell did I just do?" I said as I sat behind the wheel. That was the last thing I had planned to do when I came to see her.

I started my car and began to drive away. I had only wanted to know if she was interested in seeing me and maybe getting another kiss. I never expected it to get out of control or to have sex with her on her couch.

What was worse was that I bolted as soon as it was over! I got dressed as quickly as possible and ran from the house without seeing her again. But maybe that was what she wanted. Perhaps she was embarrassed and didn't want to face me. Could that be possible?

I stopped at the store, grabbed the few things I needed in record time, and was back in the car and heading home as I continued to dwell over it.

This time I was pondering my reaction to having sex with Carmen and trying to come to terms with the guilt I felt immediately after. I knew that I didn't need to feel guilty, but I did. Was that natural?

I could have asked Carmen, but I didn't want her to know how I felt. If she knew, she would probably feel guilty, too; that was the last thing I wanted her to feel.

I slipped into the house to find all three kids watching television, and no one asked me any questions. A few minutes after I put the groceries away, Tripp turned the television off and told his siblings it was time for bed. Dean and Savannah hugged me and then headed up, but Tripp lagged until they were gone.

"Dad?" He stood at the counter's edge as I prepared some items for the next day for Dean and Savannah's lunches.

"Yes?"

"I'm sorry."

I studied him, not saying anything else because I wanted him to elaborate and tell me exactly what he was sorry for.

"I'm sorry for being a jerk last night. I shouldn't have gotten so mad but I freaked out hearing Mom's voice."

"I'm sorry it upset you so much."

"I didn't realize how much I missed her until I heard her voice, and then I just lashed out."

"You know that I miss her too, right?"

"If you miss her, why are you talking to your ex-girlfriend?"

He didn't ask the question in an angry tone but one of interest. I came around the counter and pulled out a chair. "Have a seat, Tripp." He joined me, and then I replied, "I loved your mother wholeheartedly, Tripp. I will never stop loving your mother, but I'm also tired of being alone. I'm tired of not having anyone to share my life with."

"But you have us," he replied.

"I do, but in a few years, you will be off to college, and then your brother and sister will be gone, and what will I have? Humans are meant to be mated. They need to have someone to share their lives with."

"And you plan on sharing yours with her?" His voice was taking on an angry tone.

"I didn't say that. I'm saying that, eventually, you will have to accept that I am getting involved with someone. I'm allowed to have someone in my life."

"That's not fair to Mom."

"Tripp, your mother is dead. That's what is not fair. She was ripped from our lives, but she wouldn't want us to wallow in our misery forever. Your mother and I talked about this, and we both said that should something happen to the other, we should move on with our lives and find someone to love and share our remaining years with."

He stared at me. "Did you really talk about that?"

"Yes, we did."

"Why would she want you to be with someone else?"

"It's not that she wanted me to be with someone else, but that she knew it wasn't fair to ask me never to be with someone else. I would never have asked your mother to remain faithful to me if I were dead. She had too much love to give and too much to enjoy to do it alone."

"But she's only been gone for two years."

"Yes, and that might not sound or feel like a long time to you, but to me, it does."

"But do you have to get back together with your ex-girlfriend?"

"You don't know her, Tripp. Don't judge her until you meet her."

"But it makes me feel like you had this whole thing planned before we arrived."

"Well, I didn't. I didn't even know for sure that Carmen was in the area. I haven't spoken to her in twenty years, Tripp. The first time I spoke with her was on Friday night at Alaina and Evan's house. I have been straight with you."

"You've been straight with me?"

"Yes."

"Then where did you go tonight? Because you went someplace else besides the grocery store, and before you deny it, I tracked your phone."

I should have been pissed off, but I laughed. "Watching me, huh?"

He shrugged. "Where were you?"

I sighed. "I went to see Carmen before I went to the store. I wanted to talk to her about something that had to be done face-to-face."

"What?"

"Tripp, some things are private."

"Fine, but next time don't lie to me. You tell me to give it to you straight. If you won't do it, why should I?"

"You're right, and I will from now on. I didn't tell you before I went because I didn't want to argue with you."

"I don't want to argue with you either, Dad, but I was really pissed at you for making me cancel my date."

"How about I make it up to you and pay for your next one?"

He grinned. "I'll take it, although I'm not sure when that might be. I'm thinking of getting a job."

"You are?"

"Yeah, I want to start making my own money, and I'm going to need to buy a car."

"We can discuss it later. You should get your shower and get ready for bed."

"Dad, it's not even nine. I don't go to bed until at least eleven."

"You should go to bed before ten."

He laughed. "That's for old men like you."

"Hey, I resemble that." I laughed with him, and he stood, and before he could walk away, I pulled him in for a hug.

"Dad," he said as he pulled away, "can I listen to Mom's message?"

I grinned at him. "I can do one better. I can forward it to you so you have a copy."

"Really?"

"Yeah, son. I can do that."

A few minutes later, Tripp headed up the stairs, and I was glad that the tension in the house had been alleviated. As I turned off the lights and ensured the doors were locked, I thought about sending Carmen a message but wasn't sure what to say.

Did I apologize for taking off so quickly? Should I say I was sorry for doing a wham-bam-thank-you-ma'am on her? Maybe I should tell her that I freaked out a little.

I wasn't sure what to say in the end, so I didn't say anything. I would figure out what to say to her tomorrow.

CHAPTER FIFTEEN

CARMEN

I t had been almost a week, and I hadn't heard from Tim. After having sex with him last Sunday night, I had seen the conflicted emotions in his eyes and had excused myself to the bathroom to allow him the privacy to get dressed and leave without confronting me. He hadn't been ready to do that, and I saw it in his eyes.

I didn't want to hear it in his voice, and after six days of no word from him, I realized that our quick tryst was all I would ever get from him.

It hurt, I wasn't going to lie, but I was glad we had the chance to be together at least once more.

Okay, that was a lie. I realized after that night that if I never had him again, there would never be another man who could satisfy me the way he did. I still loved him, even after all this time.

Which sucked because it was evident that it wasn't reciprocated.

I hadn't even told Candy or Cara about what happened. Part of me was embarrassed that I had let it happen, while the other part wanted to treasure the secret close to my heart.

I had just finished my yoga class when I stepped out of the room, mopping my brow when I heard a young voice down the hall that stopped me.

"Hey, Dad! Look, it's Carmen!" Savannah's voice echoed down the tiled hallway of the YMCA. "What are you doing here?" she asked after skipping toward me.

"Hello, Savannah," I replied as I tried to remember the image of myself in the mirror I had just passed and wanted to run shrieking down the hallway. My face was flushed, and sweat had been beading over my brow. My sports bra was wet, and my workout pants probably were too, making me look like I just peed my pants. How wonderful! "I was just finishing my workout. What are you doing here?"

Tim spoke for the first time. "Hello, Carmen. I didn't know you came to the Y."

I finally met his gaze. "How could you have? It's not like we have discussed it." I gave him a smile meant to take the sting out of my words and turned to the young boy beside him, leaning toward his sister, whispering.

"And you must be Dean, correct?"

He looked surprised I knew his name. "Yeah, I am."

"It's nice to meet you. Do you like your new school?"

"Yeah, it's pretty cool. It will be even cooler once the pool is in."

"You like to swim?"

"I was on the swim team back home. I was hoping they would have one here."

I grinned at him. "They do here at the Y, and it's pretty great. In fact..." I glanced at my watch. "They should be practicing now. Do you want to see the pool? I can introduce you to the coach."

"Really? You know the coach?" he asked excitedly.

My eyes shot to Tim's and then back to Dean. "Yes, I do.

Savannah, do you swim?" I asked her as I wrapped my towel around my neck and tried to pretend that Tim wasn't there.

"No, I don't swim like Dean. I was doing gymnastics, but I want to play soccer instead."

"Maybe you can do both," I suggested, glancing at Tim. "Do you mind if I introduce Dean to one of the swim coaches?"

"Not at all. I would appreciate it."

"Okay, then follow me. What stroke do you like to swim, Dean?"

"I'm really good at breaststroke, but I was learning butterfly. I really want to do that."

"Wow, that's a tough stroke to do. My sister was pretty good at it, but I couldn't do it very well."

"You have a sister?" Savannah asked.

"I have three sisters and two brothers," I told her as we turned down a hallway. "Do you remember the woman who gave you your hot chocolate last week?"

"Yes, and the chocolate croissant too!"

"Yes, that too. Well, that was Coral, one of my sisters."

"It must be really fun having that many brothers and sisters," Savannah giggled.

"Oh, it has its moments." As we got closer to the pool area, you could smell the chlorine in the air, and I knew that the moment we stepped into the pool area, the humidity would overtake us.

"It's right in here," I said as I pulled open the door.

Dean and Savannah stepped in, and Tim reached around me to put his hand on the door behind me and whispered, "You look cute in your workout gear."

My face snapped to his, and I knew my eyes were wide. I didn't need or want him to check me out. Okay, maybe I did want him to—a little bit—but I didn't need him doing it while I was a sweaty mess.

I ignored the comment and fled a few feet away onto the

pool deck. Dean was wide-eyed as he looked around and took everything in. I searched for the coach and winced a bit. This was going to be interesting, I thought.

The kids and Tim followed me, and we headed toward the coach, who had his back to us. As we got closer, he blew his whistle. "All right, guys, give me another one hundred freestyle."

"Carmen!" Chad said as he noticed us. He smiled at me and then glanced behind me, and his smile wavered when he saw Tim. "What are you doing here?"

"Hi, Chad. Sorry to interrupt practice, but I wanted to introduce someone to you."

Chad stepped closer to me and brushed his lips over my cheek. It was uncalled for, but I didn't make a big deal of it.

"This is Tim Kohl and his son and daughter, Dean and Savannah. They just moved to town, and Dean is interested in the swim team."

Chad grinned. "Is this the old friend you were referring to?" he asked me as he glanced over at Tim.

"That has nothing to do with this, Chad," I said softly, imploring him with a look to let it go.

He chuckled and reached around me. "Nice to meet you, Tim. Welcome back to town. Carmen mentioned you the other day."

"She did, huh?" Tim eyed him critically and then glanced at me with a brow raised. Damn, I was pretty sure he had just figured out who Chad was.

"She did, but that's not why you guys are here." He turned his attention to Dean. "Do you have experience with swimming?"

Dean grinned and nodded. "Yeah, I even have a bunch of ribbons from winning races!"

"What stroke do you do?"

"I'm really good at breaststroke and freestyle, and I was getting better at butterfly before we moved, but I'm not very good with backstroke."

He directed his next question to Tim. "Have you guys joined the Y yet?"

"Yeah, we just did."

"Good!" He looked at Dean again. "We can work on your butterfly and backstroke. Did you bring a suit by chance?"

He shook his head. "No."

"Well, I bet I have an extra team one you can use if you want to jump in and get some laps."

Excitement burst forth on his face, and he turned to his father. "Can I, Dad?"

"Um, I'm not sure today's a good day."

"But Dad! Come on!"

"Dean, I need to get you guys back home and head to work for a while. You know that."

Dean's face crumbled, and it broke my heart. "I can bring him home after if you need to go."

Both Tim and Chad looked surprised at my suggestion, and they looked at me and then at each other.

"Can I stay and watch?" Savannah asked quickly, just as Tim responded.

"I can't ask you to do that, Carmen."

"You didn't ask, I offered. I don't have any appointments today because I have plans for this afternoon, but I could bring them home."

"Please, Dad!" Dean begged.

"Are you sure?" Tim asked me, and I nodded.

"Okay, then I will leave them in your hands. Tripp will be home when you drop them off, so he can watch them."

"Sounds good. I just need your address," I told him, and Chad pulled Dean off to the side to get a suit to jump in the pool.

"Savannah, you need to stay out of the way and sit on the bleachers. Can you do that?" Tim asked her.

She nodded happily and quickly walked off to get a seat amongst a few other parents.

"I'll need to go shower quick. Do you want me to bring her to the locker room?"

"No, she should be good. She's the responsible one in the family. It's the other two you have to watch out for."

I laughed, and we stared at one another for a few seconds. "Are you sure this is okay?"

"Absolutely. If it weren't, I wouldn't have offered. I mean, that's what friends do, right?"

He stared at me momentarily. "Is that what we are? Friends?"

"I don't know, Tim. You tell me."

He started to step forward, but then his gaze shifted behind me, and he stepped back. "I'll text you the address."

"Alright," I replied, frustrated that he hadn't responded to my comment.

"Okay, well, then I'm going to go to get back sooner. How long is practice?"

"I think it is two hours, and they are an hour into it."

"Okay, that sounds good."

Dean waved at his father with a dark-blue bathing suit in his hand and then disappeared into the locker room to change.

"I appreciate this, Carmen. I really do. I haven't seen him this excited since he discovered they had a rock-climbing wall at school."

I laughed. "It's my pleasure."

The two of us walked over to the bleachers where Savannah was sitting, and Tim told her to behave. She rolled her eyes and said goodbye to him as he brushed a kiss on the top of her head. Then he smiled at me again and thanked me before rushing out the door.

"Savannah, I have to take a shower and change. Are you going to be all right here?"

"Yep." She hesitated as if she wanted to say something. "You don't know the soccer coach, do you?"

I chuckled. "I'm not sure, but I can find out who it is. I'll let you know if I do."

"Yay!" she said with a giggle.

I rushed away to shower and change and was back ten minutes later. While I'd done that, I kept wondering why I had offered to do this. It wasn't until I returned and saw Dean swimming his little heart out and Savannah cheering him on that I realized I'd done it to make the children happy. I always did things to make children happy. Or at least tried to.

Savannah and I went to the front desk and asked about the soccer coach. I didn't know the woman, but they gave me an email address I could forward to Tim so he could contact her.

Savannah and I wandered more around the Y, checking things out while she told me about her teacher and school.

When Dean finished swimming, he talked a mile a minute, and I laughed at him. We were walking to the car when his stomach growled so loudly that I could hear it, and we all started laughing. "I guess we should get you something to eat."

"Dad said we'd eat when we got home. Tripp can fix us something," Savannah said as we got in my car.

"What a nice brother," I said.

"No, he's not. At least not right now. He's a jerk." Dean groaned.

"Why is he a jerk?" I asked.

"Because he won't talk to anyone and keeps himself locked in his room talking to his girlfriend."

Missy. He must be talking to Missy. I had heard that the date hadn't happened because Tripp and his father had gotten into a fight, and he got grounded for a week.

"I am sure that things will get better soon," I replied, not wanting to give unsolicited advice.

I changed the subject and asked Dean what else he liked to

do and more about his school as we drove to their house. When we got there, I walked the kids up to the door, and they tried to get in, but the door was locked. We rang the doorbell, but there was no answer.

"Wait! I can climb in the back window. The lock is broken, and Dad needs to fix it. Tripp probably has his headphones on and his music too loud."

We walked around to the back of the house, and I wasn't thrilled about Dean climbing in a window, but it was a low one, and he easily fit. He opened the back door, and Savannah and I entered.

I couldn't help but look around and was surprised to find the kitchen so tidy. Dean had run up the stairs to find Tripp while Savannah opened the fridge to find something to eat.

A few moments later, Dean ran into the kitchen. "Tripp isn't here."

"What?" I asked.

"He's not in his room or the bathroom."

Well, hell. I couldn't leave the kids alone. I had promised I would deliver them home to Tripp. Dean might be old enough to stay alone, but Savannah wasn't. No matter how mature she was, she was under twelve and needed supervision.

I glanced at my watch. "Well, I guess you guys are coming with me then."

"Where are we going?" Savannah asked.

"To a birthday party at my friend's house."

"Will there be stuff for kids to do there?"

I chuckled. "Yes, and there will be other kids there too." I glanced at Savannah. "A couple of them are about your age."

"Who?"

"Do you know Tyler Young?"

"Tyler is in my class!" Dean said happily.

"Well, then you are in luck because he will be there. It's their stepmom's birthday party."

"Cool!" Dean said.

As we locked the house back up, I pulled out my phone and sent Tim a message, hoping he wasn't upset that I was taking them there. *Change of plans. I am taking the kids to the Youngs' house for a party. You are welcome to come over once you finish. No hurry!*

I didn't bother to mention that Tripp hadn't been home. He would need to deal with that later, and adding stress while he was at work probably wasn't a good idea. I just hoped that I was right.

CHAPTER SIXTEEN

TIM

My one day lasted a lot longer than that. The next morning, I still had no idea what to say to Carmen, and then I was back to work, and everything was an issue. Occasionally, I would scold myself for not contacting her, but the longer it went, the easier it was to ignore.

If she had wanted to contact me, she could have. She did have my cellphone number too. The fact that she didn't reach out bothered me each night as I lay down to sleep.

Unfortunately, nothing was going as it should at work, and I left early and arrived home late every night. A belt malfunction on our priority shipping line was the latest thing to go wrong.

That's why I had to come to work on a Saturday. It was the earliest we could get a technician in from the manufacturer. The issue was taking longer than expected, and while this usually wouldn't be my issue, the foreman had twisted his knee and was on bed rest for a couple of weeks. There was no one else I knew well enough to trust to oversee the problem with the machinery.

While I assisted the man, I dwelled over my run-in with

Carmen today. Seeing her made me want to slam my head against the wall for being an asshole and not reaching out to her. She must think I was a grade-A asshole for coming over and screwing her and disappearing. She was right. I was.

However, she had been incredible with the kids, and the fact that she offered to watch them and bring them home meant more to me than she knew.

While waiting for the technician to test something, I also thought about the swim coach, Chad. Neither of them had said anything, but I had a feeling that was the guy she had been dating. What had she told him? Did he know that we'd had sex? Was she still seeing him? The only way I would get my answer was if I finished this up, got out of there, and went to talk to her in person. I owed her at least that after disappearing on her.

I felt my phone vibrate, but my hands were occupied, and I couldn't reach it. Hopefully, it wasn't a problem with the kids. More likely, it was Carmen letting me know they were home safely. Man, I had to repay her for this favor, not only for taking the kids home but for introducing Dean to the coach.

Almost thirty minutes after I received the message, I could finally look at it. I stared at the message, wondering why the hell she would decide to take my kids to a picnic. They had chores to do. They should not be gallivanting around at someone else's party. Carmen didn't have any right to do that, and I hit the call button to ask her to bring them home.

It rang three times, and I wondered if it would go to voice-mail when she picked up. "Hey, are you on your way?"

"Why the hell did you take my kids to a party? You should have asked me before you did that, Carmen."

"Whoa! Hold your horses, mister. We went to your house, and it was all locked up. Dean climbed through the back window and let us in, and we found that Tripp wasn't home."

"What do you mean he wasn't home?" I stared at the wall, unsure if I should be pissed off or worried.

"Just what I said. Dean checked around the house, but he was gone. He even looked in the garage to make sure he wasn't hiding in there and found his bike missing."

"That little shit!" I growled. "He knew he had to watch the kids this afternoon."

"Well, he might be home now, but I didn't feel right leaving the kids without knowing how long you would be gone. I brought them over to the Youngs' house. It is Nolan's birthday, so we are doing our traditional party, and there are quite a few kids here, so Dean and Savannah are happy and fine."

"I'm sorry you had to do that."

"Tim, it's okay. I don't mind. You have good kids. I have enjoyed hanging out with them. They are eating and making new friends. Although, you might have to look into horse riding lessons for Savannah."

"No!" I snapped more forcefully than intended and then softened my voice. "Soccer is dangerous enough. Savannah is active, but she's accident-prone."

Carmen chuckled, and I found myself smiling as I listened to it. "It's the age. She'll get over it soon. Are you coming over?"

"I'll be here for about another twenty minutes, and then I can head out. I will try calling Tripp now and see where he is. If he doesn't answer, I'll stop by the house to see if he is home yet."

"Okay, just let me know when you'll be here. There is plenty of food, and I am sure everyone will enjoy seeing you."

"Is everyone there?"

"Everyone and their spouses and kids, well, except Cara, of course."

"I hope one day you can tell me where she is."

"Maybe," she replied noncommittally.

"I'll let you know when I am on my way."

"Sounds good, and take your time." She hung up before I could say anything else. After we hung up, I finished what I needed to take care of, but my attention was divided by her friendly demeanor and where the hell my son was. I had tried to call him and sent him two text messages but hadn't heard from him yet. That boy would be grounded for a month if he wasn't home by the time I arrived.

I tried calling him a couple more times but never got an answer. Furious, I drove home and burst into the house like a bull going after the red cape. I searched every inch of the house for him and signs of a note but found nothing.

I called him again, and this time I left a voicemail. "Tripp Kohl, you better have a damn good reason for why you are not home, and you better get your ass here soon. Call me when you get this!"

I hung up and wondered if I should pick up the kids and then come back here and wait for him, but then I figured it would be better if I had a chance to calm down. I would go to the picnic, visit with everyone, and then come home once I knew he was there. That would give me time to think over what I needed to say to him and hopefully have that conversation with Carmen that I needed to have.

I didn't need directions to the Youngs' house. I had spent enough time there when I was growing up. Wes and I had been good friends, and I had spent several nights camped out in his basement on the couch.

When I pulled down the long driveway, I noted all the cars. There had to be over a dozen, and kids were running everywhere around the side yard. I parked off to the side and got out, looking around. It looked the same as I remembered.

They were lucky that it was a mild day in March, and the temperatures were in the high fifties. It was perfect weather for the kids to be out running around.

I climbed the front steps and walked around the porch to the back side. As I rounded the back corner, Kayley turned toward me; it took her a second, and then she laughed. "Well, I'll be damned. I heard you were back in town."

She got up and came to hug me. "Yeah, I tried to hook up with you when I came house hunting, but you were out of town."

She wiggled her ring finger. "Cam and I finally got a chance to take our honeymoon. I hope that Brianna was good to you."

"She was great, but when I'm ready to buy a house, I hope you will be willing to help me."

"Absolutely." She peered into the yard. "And with those kids, you need some room."

"Yes, I do. Where is Carmen?"

"I think she is inside getting more salad. I saw her walk in with a bowl a minute ago."

"Thanks," I told her and started to walk away. Luckily, I could slip into the house without seeing anyone else and I paused inside the kitchen. Carmen was rinsing something in the sink, and I walked up behind her. The urge to slip my arms around her was so damn strong that I almost did but refrained and instead leaned over her shoulder and spoke softly. "Hi."

She jumped and dropped the spoon into the sink as she spun around. "Damn you, Tim! Don't sneak up on me like that!" She smacked my chest playfully, and I grabbed her hand before she could let it drop.

I chuckled as I approached her. "I'm sorry."

She lifted her chin, her wild blond hair falling away from her face as she did. She had a spot of something on her cheek, and I reached out, wiped it off, and then put my finger to my lips. She watched my every move. "Yum, barbecue sauce."

Her hand remained on my chest where I had captured it, and I wondered if she could feel how hard my heart was beating. She was so damn beautiful. Did she have any idea how gorgeous she was? Time seemed to stand still for a few moments, and I irrationally wanted to lean forward and kiss her, but just as I began to move, the back door closed as a man laughed, and I quickly stepped back from Carmen and let go of her hand.

She immediately spun back to the sink, dropping her head so her hair covered her face.

"I heard you were here," Wes said as he approached the corner. He looked between us. "Did I interrupt something?"

"No, I was just letting Carmen know I was here."

"Oh, good, come on out. We need to catch up, and since Carmen isn't freaking out at your presence, you can stay for a while."

"Screw you, Wesley!" she called out as Wes laughed and led me from the room.

"You look like you could use a beer," he said.

"And then some," I muttered.

He led me over to a group of people sitting around a large fire pit, and while he grabbed me a beer, I said hello to Mr. and Mrs. Young, along with Mr. Winston. The Youngs were happy to see me, but Carmen's father was more reserved in his greeting. I could understand that. What father wanted to greet someone who broke their daughter's heart with open arms?

I said hello again to everyone I had met at Evan and Alaina's that night and quickly fell into conversation as I watched my kids play with the others. At one point, I sat there and looked around, marveling at how far we had all come. Almost everyone was married off and had kids.

Emily and I had a good life when we lived in California, but her family wasn't around very often. I only had my parents, and there were no weekly dinners or birthday parties. I envied the hell out of these two families—and I always had.

My gaze drifted around the clusters of people and landed on Carmen. She watched me, and as our eyes locked, she didn't look away. She just smiled, and I wished like hell I knew what that smile meant.

I was about to go over and ask when she looked at her phone and then stood, putting it to her ear as she walked away. It was probably her boyfriend, Chad. Why wasn't he here? Had he been invited?

Carmen stopped as she approached the house and turned slightly, a concerned look on her face. She spoke for a moment and then turned toward me, waving her hand as if to call me over to her.

I set my beer down and approached her as she listened to the person on the other end.

"Okay, I'll be right there." She paused. "And I'll bring his father. He is actually standing right in front of me."

"What?" I asked, suddenly concerned that she was talking about Tripp.

She hung up and looked at me. "Don't freak out, but I know where Tripp is."

"Where?"

"The hospital."

"What?"

"Come on, we need to get down there, and I will explain on the way." She started to walk away from me, and I grabbed her arm.

"Carmen, is my son all right?"

"Yes, he's fine. He is a little shaken up, but he's fine. Come on."

"Wait! What about my kids?"

She looked around, then ran over to Nolan. "Tim and I have to go. There is a little emergency. Can you keep an eye on his kids until we get back?"

"Sure, is everything okay?"

"Yes, it will be fine, but we need to go. I'll explain later." With that, the two of us rushed toward the front of the house. "I'll drive."

"I am capable of driving."

"Have you not had like three beers? I'm not drinking, and you are in no state of mind to drive."

"Fine." Once inside her car, I asked, "What the hell is going on? What happened to Tripp? You said he was okay."

"He is okay," she stated as she backed up and did a U-turn in the driveway.

"Then why is he at the hospital, Carmen? And why the hell did they call you?"

She paused at the end of the driveway to look back and forth. Once she had pulled onto the roadway, she said, "My client's mother called me. Do you remember the bridge over Old Man's Creek?"

"Yeah, what about it?"

"Well, it seems my client and your son were hanging out with other kids. Missy jumped off the bridge and didn't come up, and Tripp jumped in to rescue her."

"What?"

She glanced at me. "From what Maureen said, Tripp saved Missy's life."

CHAPTER SEVENTEEN

CARMEN

He looks like he fits right in—like he is part of the family. That's what I was thinking as I observed him.

"I don't know how, but he got even cuter than he was," Kayley said as she sat beside me.

"You think so? I haven't noticed."

She laughed and slapped a hand onto my leg. "Come on, girl, you can't tear your eyes away from him. Don't tell me you haven't noticed."

"Is it that obvious?" I asked as I peered at her.

"To anyone with eyes." She paused for a second and then continued. "How is it having him back?"

"Weird. I don't know what to think about it."

"How did you come to bring him today?"

"Ironic coincidences," I replied dryly and then explained what had happened today.

"Or maybe it was fate. Everyone always said you two were destined to be together."

"Oh, bullshit! That was twenty years ago. Our destiny changed when he broke up with me and married another woman."

"It's not like he broke up with you *to* marry another woman. You guys were young and had too much to learn about life. Perhaps fate took you apart so that you could come together now."

"That's not going to happen, Kayley."

"Why not? You're single, he's single, and it is obvious that you're still into the man."

"Into the man? What the hell does that even mean?"

"You like him."

"I don't know him, Kay. Whatever feelings I have for him have been dredged up after years of being dormant."

"Then get to know the man. He looks like someone worth knowing."

The baby monitor on her side squeaked, and her son's voice babbled over the speaker. She sighed. "I guess my resting time is over. The little monster is awake."

I laughed. "He's not a monster."

"No, you're right, he's not. If you hooked up with Tim, you could have three instant monsters."

I laughed harder. "Let's not jump the gun, okay?"

Kayley squeezed my shoulder as she stood up. "You never know, Carmen." She paused and looked over her shoulder at him. "And damn, girl, if you don't go after that, I might have to file for divorce."

"Get out of here!" I burst out laughing.

After she left, I watched him more, and he turned to look at me. Our eyes locked, and everyone else around us faded. It was just the two of us like it had always been when we were together. Was this fate? Should I tempt it?

The memory of his coming to my house last Sunday night and us having sex on the couch in a whirlwind moment filled my mind, and I was tempted to lure him into the house and find someplace to reenact the event.

I was about to approach him when my cellphone rang. Well,

crap, it was Maureen, Missy's mother. "Hey, Maureen, how are you?"

"Dr. Winston, it's Missy. She's at the hospital."

"What? What happened?"

"She jumped off the bridge at Old Man's Creek. She was there with friends, and she jumped off the damn bridge! She didn't come up, and another kid, I think his name is Tripp, jumped in to pull her out. She was unconscious when they pulled her out, and he got her breathing again, but I don't know if she did this intentionally to hurt herself or if she was doing it for fun."

"Is Tripp okay?"

"Yeah, he's fine. He looked a bit spooked, but he's fine."

"Okay, I'm on my way."

"Do you know this other kid? Has she said anything about him?"

"Kind of. I'll bring his father. He is actually standing right in front of me."

Tim instantly looked confused and panicked as I explained what was happening. It wasn't until we were in the car together that I filled him in on what I knew.

"Does Tripp know CPR?" I asked him as he sat there staring at me.

"Yeah, he learned it last year at school. He was thinking of becoming a paramedic."

"He should speak to Henley. He's a paramedic."

"Why did you ask about the CPR?"

"Because he might have done it to her. Maureen said that she wasn't breathing when she came out of the water."

"Holy shit!"

He stared out the window for a few minutes, saying nothing, and then my cellphone rang over the car speakers. "Hello?"

"Where did you two go?" Wes asked.

"I have a little emergency and am heading to the hospital. Tim is with me; his son is at the hospital too."

"Oh crap, he's not the one who almost drowned, is he?"

Tim looked at me as I answered, "No, that was my patient. I think Tripp, Tim's son, pulled her out and gave her CPR."

"Okay, they were going to transfer her to Summersville, but I told them to keep her there since I was out here. I'll see you over there."

"Great, thanks, Wes." He disconnected as I heard his car door close.

"Why would they want to fly her to another hospital?"

"Because Millersville doesn't have a great pediatric unit, but Wes has privileges there. He is trying to get them to open a pediatric unit here. I think Alaina will donate money to the hospital to make it happen so Wes can be closer to family."

"Must be nice to have someone in the family who has money," he muttered.

"Yes, I guess it is, but she uses it wisely. She is very shrewd with her money, but she loves helping an underdog and children. She will do anything for children."

"She is a good person."

"Yes, she is. Evan is lucky to have her."

The two of us were quiet as I drove. When he spoke again, I was surprised by his question. "What's the deal with the swim coach?"

I frowned. "You want to talk about that now?"

"I need to talk about something so I don't freak myself out."

"Makes sense," I replied softly. "Chad is the guy I was seeing."

"Was?"

"Yes, I broke it off with him after I told him we'd kissed."

"Did you tell him it was me?"

"I just told him it was an old friend who was back in town."

He snorted. "So he knew it was me. I'm surprised he didn't take a swing at me."

"Oh, I doubt that would have happened," I muttered.

"How come you have never been married?"

"Who said I wasn't?"

"Wes told me you weren't. I asked him."

"I am married to my career. After almost nine years of college, starting my career, then building my practice, I haven't had time."

"But you do now?"

I shrugged. "I don't know."

"You don't know?"

"Yes, I don't know. What about you? Are you ready for a new relationship?"

He paused. "I don't know how to answer that right now, Carmen."

"Okay, then how about we table this conversation for now, Tim? I think we both have more important things to think about."

He sighed. "You're right. I was just trying to make conversation to keep myself calm."

"Tripp is all right, Tim. You don't have anything to worry about."

"Except he lied and left the house when he wasn't supposed to, and God only knows what he was doing with that girl."

"He was being a kid, Tim. That's what they do. How many times did we hang out at Old Man's Creek?"

He grinned. "Quite a few, and I remember having the police knock on the truck door a time or two."

I shook my head. "Don't remind me, Tim. My point in bringing that up was that we were teens. He is a teen. He is doing the same kinds of things that we did."

"God, I hope not, or at least I hope he is being safe and smart."

I frowned, suddenly thinking that we hadn't been safe last week. I didn't mention that, but I did comment about our past.

"I can remember a few times that we were neither of those things."

"Yeah, I do too. Could you imagine if you had gotten pregnant?"

Or what if I were pregnant now?

I parked the car and turned it off before I looked at him. "No, I can't, and I'm glad I never did. I would have had to raise a child alone while you went off to California and started a new life."

I didn't wait for a response and climbed out of the car. Tim rushed out the other side and met me at the back. "I would have helped you."

"Oh, I'm sure you would have," I said somewhat sarcastically. "Can we please not talk about this? It has nothing to do with what is going on."

"Doesn't it?"

I stared at him. "Tim, I have a patient and her mother in there who need me right now. The last thing I want to do is debate a nonexistent issue between us. We have enough real ones to discuss at another time."

"Like what?"

I scoffed. "Forget it. I need to get in there."

"Carmen, what do we have to talk about?"

Maybe it was the fear of what had almost happened to my patient and knowing that she wasn't out of the woods yet, or it might have been because I had been in close quarters with Tim, and he had brought up things that should have stayed buried, but a switch had flipped, and the words began to pour from my mouth.

"Jesus, Tim, are you that ignorant? You gave me a damn promise ring! You promised you would come back for me, or we would meet again in college. You promised me that we would have a future! I waited for you, even after you broke it off with me. I waited because I hoped that one day you would realize you made a mistake and return for me.

"Then I moved on. I finally moved on, and I am finally at a point in my life where I have time to get into a relationship, and you show back up in my life; only, you clearly don't want a relationship. Or you aren't ready for one, but there you are, and I can't get you out of my head, and then we have incredible sex together, and you ghost me! You fucking ghosted me just like you did when we were teens.

"And do you want to know why I never really got into a serious relationship? Because of you! Because I always felt like I was cheating on you! You left me behind twenty years ago, and I still thought I should be faithful to you. How messed up is that? I'm a freaking psychologist, and I know how wrong it is, but I still couldn't get over you!

"I spent years hoping that one day you would return. Well, here you are, and you know what? Now I don't know why the hell I was waiting for you because I was obviously the last thing on your mind. There is no doubt that you probably never thought of me in all the years we have been apart. Of course, you didn't. You had the perfect family, the perfect wife, the perfect life! You probably would have dumped me in college anyway, and I should be thankful that you did it when you did, but I'm not.

"Instead, I stand here staring at you and wishing like hell you hadn't returned and opened all these old wounds. And at the same time, I wish I could fall into your arms and pretend like we were sixteen again, but that will never happen, Tim. And do you know why? Because we aren't sixteen and seventeen! We are in our thirties, you have three kids, and I have a patient who needs my attention."

I stopped talking and tried to calm my breathing. I was shaking from head to toe and absolutely stunned at all the things I had said. I might have been mortified at my behavior if the adrenaline wasn't flowing so quickly.

Tim opened his mouth and then closed it, and then suddenly someone took my arm and pulled me toward the hospital. "Come on, Carmen. You can pick that up later. This is not the time or place for your breakdown or makeup kiss."

I stared up at Wes, surprised by his arrival and thankful for his interruption. I didn't even bother to glance back but assumed that Tim was right behind us.

Once inside, Wes went to the window to talk to the nurse behind the glass. I glanced around and saw a boy sitting off to the side. His hair was a mess, and his clothes still looked damp as he stared at the floor. I glanced back at Tim and pointed toward the boy.

The door opened to the back, and Wes escorted me through to the patient area. I would check on Missy and figure out what to do about Tim later. Jesus, had I just flipped out in the hospital's parking lot? Freaking great!

As it turned out, Missy had a skull fracture and would be under close supervision. They would put her into a drug-induced coma to keep her calm while they watched her brain to make sure it didn't swell anymore.

I consoled Maureen the best I could, then walked out to the waiting room. Tim and his son were sitting in the corner, neither speaking and both staring out the window. Tripp looked exactly like his father did when he was a teenager. It made my heart constrict, but I pushed on.

Tim glanced my way as I approached and burst to his feet. "How is she?" Tripp was by his side, and I glanced at him and gave him a reassuring smile.

"Not great, but not horrible. Wes said they were putting her into a coma to protect her. She has a skull fracture, and they have to wait until the swelling goes down in her brain before they will know if there are any deficiencies."

"Deficiencies?" Tripp echoed the word in a confused manner.

I nodded. "Yes, Tripp. You did a great job pulling her out of the water and giving her CPR. That was very brave of you, but Missy has a major concussion, and there could be complications from the trauma to her brain."

Tears welled in his eyes, and I wanted to pull him into my arms, but he wasn't mine to help. I stepped back as he crumpled into his father's strong embrace and wept. Tim glanced at me once, then closed his eyes, and I stepped away to leave father and son in peace.

I knew that with this trauma, both were probably thinking of the day Emily was killed. Trauma traveled that way, and it only took a similar life-threatening incident to bring all the feelings and emotions back to life.

I stopped at the front desk and spoke to the nurse. She handed me a piece of paper with a pen, and I wrote a short note for Tim.

Tim, take my car back to the Youngs' house so you can get your kids and go home. It would probably be better to wait there. I will send word of any news when I have it. I will ride back with Wes later. Carmen

I didn't add anything else, and who knew if we would ever see one another after the tirade I had given him outside. As I stepped back through the doors to the patient area, I thought, it's for the best anyway. It was time to move on without him.

CHAPTER EIGHTEEN

TIM

I was dumbfounded at the explosive words that tumbled from her mouth and couldn't even attempt a response for the life of me. Thank God Wes interrupted us and saved me from having to reply.

I followed behind Wes and Carmen, trying to digest what she had said. Inside the waiting room, she pointed off to the side, and all thoughts of Carmen fled as I rushed to my son's side.

"Tripp!" I called as I got closer, and his head snapped up. He burst from his seat and launched himself into my arms.

"Dad, I'm sorry. I'm so sorry." He sobbed into my chest, and I held him, saying a prayer that he was okay. We would deal with his disobedience later. Right now, I was just glad that he was safe.

"What happened, Tripp?"

"I was hanging out with Missy and some of her friends. We were sitting on the stone above the creek, and she decided to jump off the top. I told her not to because it didn't seem deep enough, but she did it anyway. She went under, and she didn't come back up. I thought she was messing with us, but then she still didn't come up. I ran down to the water and went after her. I found her just floating to the top, her face down, and she wasn't breathing. I dragged her to the side and got her out, and I did CPR on her, and after a few minutes, I don't even know how long it was, she finally coughed up the water and began to breathe on her own, but her head was bleeding, and her eyes looked weird."

"Weird?"

"Yea, like one pupil was really big, and the other was small."

I winced, knowing enough about head injuries from television to know that wasn't good. "Are you okay?"

"Yeah, I'm okay."

Just after I asked that, two cops stepped into the waiting area and came in our direction.

"Tripp, how are you holding up?" one of them asked.

"I'm okay."

The officer looked at me. "Mr. Kohl, I'm Officer Robinson, and this is Officer Tuckerton. We need to get Tripp's statement. Do you mind if we talk to him?"

"Not at all."

We sat down in the corner, away from other people in the waiting room, and Tripp went through what he had told me in more detail for the police. They asked a bunch of questions, like if they had been drinking or doing any drugs. Tripp admitted that they had each had two beers but hadn't used any drugs. The conversation took about fifteen minutes, and they said they might have to come back for more questions later, but that was all they needed for now. They disappeared into the patient area a few minutes later.

Tripp and I sat there for a long time, both lost in thought. Finally, Carmen let us know what was going on. It didn't look good, and Tripp again fell apart in my arms. I could remember four times that Tripp had cried since he was a teenager. The day we learned his mother died, the day of her funeral, and the other two times today.

After Tripp had calmed down, the nurse waved me to the window and handed me a note with a set of keys. I read the message from Carmen and frowned that she didn't want us to wait, but then I realized she was right. I needed to get my children and go home. This was not the place for Tripp right now.

"Come on, Tripp, we are going to go."

"Go where?"

"We need to pick up your brother and sister, and then we are going home."

"But I don't want to leave until I hear how Missy is doing."

I took him by the shoulders. "Carmen will let me know how she is. As soon as I hear something, I will let you know."

"Okay." We started toward the door. "That was Carmen? Your old girlfriend?"

I led him out of the hospital. "Yeah, that was Carmen."

"What were you doing with her?"

"It's a long story and something we will discuss later."

I led him to her car and opened the door. "Whose car is this?"

"It's Carmen's. I came with her."

Tripp's face turned into a mask of rage. "Were you on a date with her? You said you had to work."

I glared at him over the roof of the car. "And you were told to stay the hell home and watch your sister and brother while I went to work. Carmen helped me out today and took them to a family event so I could finish work. I was at her friend's house picking them up when this shit happened."

He looked less angry and, in fact, a bit contrite as he pulled the door open and got inside. I adjusted the seat for my larger frame and then started the car.

His voice was soft as he spoke again. "I'm sorry, Dad. I

shouldn't have gone, but Missy would be dead now if I hadn't, because none of them knew how to do CPR."

"Tripp, we will discuss this later. I don't think now is an appropriate time."

"Okay," he said softly, and then a few seconds later, he spoke again. "She does look a lot like Mom."

I sighed. "And I'm not talking about Carmen either. Just sit there quietly and think about everything that happened today."

"I was just saying."

"Yeah, when I want your input, I will ask you for it."

"Fine," he grumbled.

At the Youngs', I told Tripp to get in our vehicle and went around back to collect the kids and thank Nolan for keeping an eye on them.

"Is everything okay?" she asked.

"Yeah, a friend of Tripp's got hurt."

"That's why Wes tore out of here, I guess."

"Yes, he went to the hospital to see her."

"Well, the kids have been great, and they can come to our house anytime. God knows something is always going on with four kids in our house."

"I didn't realize you and Brad had more kids."

"Brad has two, and I have two from previous marriages. Two girls, one older and one younger than Savannah, and his daughter and son."

"Oh, great. We will have to get them together."

"Have Carmen give you our number."

"I will." If she ever spoke to me again, I thought. I said goodbye to a few other people and then corralled the kids to the car. They were a bundle of chatter, and I heard about everything they had done all day. Tripp remained quiet in the passenger seat, and the kids were so excited by their day that they didn't even notice the tension in the car. If they did, they probably assumed it was because Tripp had left the house that day.

That was fine. They didn't need to know what was going on. The last thing they needed was to be reminded of the day Emily died.

When we got home, I sent them up to shower and to get ready for bed. Tripp had gone straight to his room and told me to tell him if I heard anything. I grabbed a beer and went out on the back deck to decompress.

As I leaned back on the chair, my mind drifted back to the night Emily had been killed.

The kids had been watching television, waiting for their mother to get home, and I had been in the garage, straightening up a few things and taking the trash out. I had just come in when I saw I had missed a call from Emily. I listened to the message. No sooner had I listened to it than a news report came on the screen about a shooting at the local market down the street. My blood ran cold because I knew Emily would go to that market. Maybe she wouldn't be there yet. Or maybe she had already left.

The younger kids were staring at the television, but it was just another story to them. Tripp looked tense, but that could be because he understood more than his siblings.

The news reporter talked about how a man with a gun had gone into the store and started randomly shooting people. As the reporter spoke, I stared at the screen, trying to see anyone in the background. A couple of cops walked by, then a paramedic rushed through the front door, and the camera panned the parking lot a little bit to a witness they were interviewing.

My heart thudded in my chest as the person began to talk. Right behind the man was Emily's car. I knew it was hers because she had a Lake Tahoe sticker in the back right-hand corner of the window, and there it was.

My stomach rolled, and I collected my phone and returned to the garage. I called her phone, but it just rang. I called again, and it went to voicemail. I called it a third time and was about to leave a message when I heard a car door, and I hit the garage door button, ready to pull her into my arms.

Only it wasn't Emily. It was two police officers coming to give me the news. "Excuse me, sir, are you Timothy Kohl?"

"Yes."

"And you are married to Emily Kohl?"

"Yes, I am." My knees almost buckled. "Please tell me she's only hurt. Tell me she's at the hospital. Please."

"I'm sorry, Mr. Kohl, but your wife was shot multiple times at Ames Market on Quandary Street. She didn't make it. I'm afraid she's dead."

I covered my mouth, but I wasn't sure if it was to keep me from throwing up or screaming. I felt like doing both then, but it only got worse when I returned to the living room and the officers followed me.

The kids took in the somber faces of the police officers and my stricken expression and knew something was wrong. Tripp had been the first to speak. "What's going on?"

I took the remote control off the couch and turned the television off. "Kids, I have to tell you something."

I sat between Tripp and Dean on the couch and pulled Savannah onto my lap. "Something happened tonight. Something bad."

"What?" Dean asked and then glanced at the officers. "Why are the police here?"

Tripp looked at the television and then at the police. "She was there, wasn't she? Did she get hurt?"

"Yeah, she was there, Tripp. She didn't just get hurt, though. She's —" I swallowed, unable to say the word.

I didn't have to because he jumped off the couch and said, "She's dead? Is that what you are going to say? She's dead?"

"Yes," I replied as I looked up at him, and the tears began to leak from my lids. My wife was gone. Just like that, minutes after she left me a message, she was gone, and now my children were without a mother.

"What?" Dean asked. He was only ten at the time, and Savannah was nine. They didn't have a huge understanding of death, not yet.

"Your mom is gone, Dean. She's dead. She was shot and killed tonight."

Savannah immediately crumpled into my arms and sobbed. "I want Mommy!"

I held her close to me and put my other arm around Dean. Tripp sat back on the couch with us, and the four of us cried for a few minutes before the police said a few more words and left. That night, Dean and Savannah slept with me on the couch. Tripp dozed in the recliner. None of us wanted to go upstairs.

I blinked and was back on the porch in Millerstown. It had been a brutal night, and I shivered as I thought about how Tripp could be in the hospital and not his friend. I wasn't sure I would be able to live if I lost someone else whom I loved.

CHAPTER NINETEEN

CARMEN

I
t had been a long day, and at eight o'clock that night, Wes
and I finally left the hospital. Missy's condition hadn't
gotten any worse, but tonight was critical.

As her psychologist, it wasn't my place to stay there. If it had
been anyone other than Missy, I wouldn't have. I would have
checked in and then made my goodbyes.

But it was Missy, and I had so many reasons to stay. First,
because I liked this kid; second, her mother had no one else to
support her. Third, I was concerned about what her mental
capacity was going to be and how that might affect her depression and suicidal ideation. If she had lasting issues, those could
compound her mental health.

I also had concerns that weren't even really related to Missy.
I was worried about Tripp. I didn't even know the kid, but I
knew his father, and if there was anything I could do to help
Tripp get through this, I would.

So I stayed and chatted with Maureen and the nurse occasionally, and when I wasn't talking to them, I was stewing over
the incident in the parking lot. God, how could I have said all

those things? What did Tim think of me after that? Did he think I had lost my mind? Was he sorry he had even hooked up with me again?

After five hours, I still had no answer, and now I was too tired to think about it. When we returned to Wes' parents' house, I climbed in my car and headed home.

Inside, I didn't bother turning on the lights. I walked through the dark to the kitchen, grabbed a half-full wine bottle from the fridge and a wineglass from the cabinet, and dragged myself up the stairs to my room.

I poured a glass of wine, had a nice long guzzle, and then turned on the tub, adding extra bubbles. In between my sips—okay, gulps—I undressed, put music on my phone, turned down the lights, and slid into the hot water, easing as deeply under as I could as the water finally reached its limit.

I closed my eyes, inhaling the sweet scent of honey and lemon from my bubbles, and sighed in relief.

A moment later, my phone buzzed, interrupting the music, and my eyes popped open. With that notification, I remembered that I hadn't texted Tim to let him know what was going on and promised that I would.

I dried my hands and then reached for my phone. Ironically, the notification was from Tim asking if there was any news. I was about to start typing when I stared at the tiny phone symbol on the screen. I was too tired to type. I punched the call button and waited for it to go through.

"Hey, you didn't have to call. A text would have been fine."

"Sorry, you probably don't want to talk to me, but I am too damn tired to text."

There was a long pause, and then he asked, "What's going on with the girl?"

"The girl has a name, and that name is Missy."

"I know her name, but she is your patient, so I wasn't sure you wanted to use her name."

"You have a personal connection to her, and this incident has nothing to do with why she comes to see me."

"Okay." He paused. "What is that noise? Are you washing dishes?"

"No, I'm soaking in the tub." The line grew silent for a long moment, and I wondered what he was thinking. Did the memory of us using his mother's claw-foot tub so many years ago spring up?

"I'm sorry for interrupting your quiet time. I'll let you go."

"No, you wanted to know how Missy was doing. I will tell you. There hasn't been much change, which is good, but things will be rough for her. A lot is going to depend on how she does tonight."

"I can't even imagine what her parents are going through."

"It's just her mom. Her dad has been out of the picture for a while, and her mother is an absolute mess. That's one of the reasons I stayed as long as I did."

"What time did you get home?"

"About ten minutes ago. I literally grabbed a bottle of wine and a glass, then filled the tub. I had just gotten in when I got your message."

"I'm sorry for bothering you," he said in a husky voice.

That voice was disturbing me, but not for a bad reason. "You're not. How is Tripp?"

"Upset, but he has reason to be."

"How long did you ground him?"

"I didn't, at least not yet. He is punishing himself enough right now. He admitted to drinking two beers today; it was probably more, but at least he admitted that to the cops."

"Did the cops do anything?"

"No, they just wanted his statement. I think they felt sorry for him."

"Good, I'm glad they didn't try to hit him with underage drinking."

"Yeah, me too."

There was a momentary lull in the conversation. "How are Dean and Savannah? Did they have fun today?"

He laughed, and the sound caused me to shiver. "They had a blast. They couldn't stop talking about everything on the way home. You might regret taking them there."

I smiled. "Why is that?"

"Because they will beg to attend more of your family's parties."

"Well, it's easy to get invited. You just need to be partnered up with one of the kids." I froze after the words left my mouth. Whoops! "You know Coral is single." I would die if he started dating Coral. Why had I even suggested such a thing?

"Coral? Really? You don't want me, so you pawn me off on Coral?"

I never said I didn't want him. Or did I say that earlier today? Shit, I might have said that. I heaved a heavy sigh that I had no doubt he could hear. "I'm sorry about earlier."

"Which part? There was a lot that happened."

"The part where I lost my mind on you in the parking lot."

He didn't reply immediately, and I gave him time to process what I said. "Did you mean it?"

I frowned. "Did I mean that I was sorry? Yes, I mean that."

"No, the part about how you felt you were cheating on me?"

I winced. Of all the things I said, that was the one Tim latched on to? Crap! Crap! Crap! "A lot was going on this afternoon."

"So you lied to me? That's not like you, Carmen."

"No, I didn't lie. Okay, maybe a little." I groaned. "Why do you have to know me so well? No, it was not a lie. I don't think I ever really moved on or took any relationship seriously because I always hoped you would come back for me. Trust me, I tried, but I always seemed to measure every guy to you."

"Jesus, Carmen. Why would you deny yourself a relationship? I sure as hell was not worth ruining your life for."

"Hey! Wait a second! I never said I ruined my life. I just said that I never moved on. I am quite happy in my life." Except for the fact that I have no one to love, no one to share my life with, no one to have kids with, and no one to have sex with. Gah!

"I didn't mean that."

"I think you did." I felt a bit angry and used that to give me the confidence to speak my mind. "I think you are so confident in yourself that you think because I didn't find someone else to take your place, you're the best there is out there. Well, I am quite aware that other great men are out there. I just haven't had the time or willpower to search for them."

"Is that so?"

"Yes. There are at least a dozen men I could call to go out with."

"Oh, yeah? If that's the case, then why don't you?"

"Maybe I will."

"Or maybe you won't."

"It doesn't matter what I do since it's none of your damn business."

"You sort of made it my business, Carmen."

"Yeah, and how is that?"

"You made it my business when we had sex the other day."

"Oh, you remember that happening, do you? When I didn't hear from you after that, I assumed you had forgotten all about it, or I had dreamed it all up on my own."

"Come on, Carmen. I didn't forget about it. I was busy."

"Too busy to send me a damn text to say hello?"

"The phone works both ways, you know."

I bit my tongue to keep from lashing out and closed my eyes. He was right. The phone did work both ways, but why should I have been the one to reach out? "I was worried that you regretted it."

"Me? No, Carmen, I didn't regret it." He sighed heavily. "I think I just needed time to process it. You're the first person I have been with since Emily died."

"I kind of figured that."

"I felt guilty right after."

"I know. That's why I let you leave without having to make excuses."

He scoffed. "You hid in the bathroom so I could deal with my guilt?"

"Yes, and perhaps I was feeling a little overwhelmed myself."

"Why would you feel overwhelmed?" he asked.

I hesitated but continued. "Because of what you made me feel, Tim. It had been so long since I felt that, and it was overwhelming."

"I will admit it was a little overwhelming for me too. Not just because you were the first since Emily, but because it was with you, and it brought back many buried memories."

I nibbled on my bottom lip. "Is that a bad thing?"

"No, that's not a bad thing, Carmen. I'm sorry for not contacting you this last week. I should have, and I guess I was hiding from how I felt."

"What do you mean?"

"You made me feel things I haven't felt in a long time. I wasn't sure if I was ready, and I needed time to consider all of it."

"Do you know the answer to that question now?"

"I think so."

"What is the answer?"

"I'd like to see where this goes, Carmen. Maybe we are caught up in the excitement of being back together, or maybe it is meant to be, but I want to find out. Would you be interested in that?"

I almost squealed but held it back with a palm over my lips. I nodded, knowing he couldn't see me. "Yeah, I could be interested in that."

He chuckled huskily. "Could be?"

"Okay, I am."

"All right, then, how about we start over, and I take you out on a date?"

"A date, huh?"

"Yeah, dinner, drinks, getting to know you, chitchat, that kind of thing."

"I could probably do dinner later this week. I'll have to check my schedule and get back to you."

"You do that, and if you hear anything else about Missy, can you let me know so I can pass it on to Tripp?"

"I can do that."

"Okay, thank you." He paused and then lowered his voice. "And while you are in the tub, maybe you can think about that time we took one together."

I grinned. "I have no idea what you are referring to."

He chuckled. "Yes, you do, and don't deny it. That was the best bath of my life."

I laughed out loud. "Oh yeah, I'm sure! I don't doubt that you have since had better baths."

"Actually, no, I haven't." He was quiet for a few heartbeats. "That memory is reserved for you and you alone, Carmen. I'll let you go so you can think about that. Night, Carmen. Sweet dreams."

"Night, Tim," I said right before the line clicked, and my music started to play again. Maybe there was a chance after all.

A moment later, I got a text and looked at it. *You could send me a picture of the bath.*

I snickered and put my foot up on the side. Bubbles ran down and dripped off my heel and ankle, and I snapped a picture. Before I could overthink it, I attached and sent it.

A moment later, I got a reply. *Holy crap. Now I need a cold shower.*

Or you could join me for a hot bath.

Girl, don't you tempt me, or I will be banging down your door in about ten minutes.

I laughed. *Fine, another time, then.*

I will hold you to it, Carmen. Enjoy your bath.

I grinned at the phone and said softly, "Oh, trust me, I will."

CHAPTER TWENTY

TIM

The kids were in bed, tuckered out after their long day of adventure. I stopped by Tripp's room after I checked in on them.

"How are you doing?" I asked from just inside the door.

"I'm okay. Have you heard anything?"

I shook my head. "No, I'll text her in a few minutes and see if she has an update."

"Okay." He paused. "Dad, do you think Missy's going to be okay?"

"You have to believe that she will be."

"What if she isn't?"

I sat on the side of his bed. "You did all you could, Tripp. I'm proud of you for how you jumped in and rescued her. You'll make a damn good paramedic one day."

"But what if it wasn't fast enough? What if I did something wrong, and it made her worse?"

"You did the best that you could, Tripp."

"Maybe I'm not fit to be a paramedic."

"Hey, I bet if you ask any of them, they will say they second-guessed themselves. That's normal, but you did the best that you could. In fact, you did more than you had to. You stepped up when no one else did."

"But if I did something wrong, are the cops going to blame me?"

"No one is going to blame you for what happened to her. No one made her jump off the bridge; she made that choice herself." I stopped as he winced slightly. "Unless someone did make her? Did someone push her off?"

He quickly shook his head. "No, she decided to jump."

"Are you sure? You can tell me if someone did."

"No, she jumped by herself." His words sounded confident, but he looked away from me while he spoke.

"Then no one is responsible for her action but her. You went above and beyond what was expected of a young man. You said you were the only one who knew how to do CPR. That's impressive on its own."

"Yeah, I guess."

"You're a hero, Tripp."

"I don't feel like a hero."

"Maybe not now, but I bet her mother thinks that. I know I do."

He smiled faintly. "Thanks, Dad."

"You're welcome."

"I'm sorry that I left today."

"I guess now is as good a time as any to discuss that. Why did you?" I asked him.

He shrugged his shoulder. "Because I wanted to go hang out. Missy was having a hard day and begged me to come."

"What do you mean she was having a hard day?"

He glanced at me and then looked away. Finally, he sighed and shifted on the bed to sit up more. "Missy has depression. She was feeling down today. She said if I came, it would make her feel better."

"Did it make her feel better?"

"Yeah, I guess for a little while."

"What do you mean, for a little while?"

He huffed, "I don't want to talk about this anymore. Can we just let it go? I'm tired."

"Okay, you get some rest."

"Will you let me know if Carmen updates you?"

"I will. You try and get some sleep."

"Thanks, Dad." He slipped down on the bed, and I stood. "And Dad, I know I'm grounded for like a month. I get it."

I almost laughed. "I'm glad you understand how important discipline is."

"Yeah, I do, but I couldn't very well not go when she was begging me."

"You could have invited her over here. Then you would have been able to watch your brother and sister."

"I'll do that next time."

"Okay, get some sleep, Tripp. I love you."

"I love you too, Dad."

I slipped out of his room and went downstairs to get another beer. It was after nine, and there had been no word from Carmen. Would she be upset if I texted her? I hoped not.

A few moments after I sent her a message, she called me, and that conversation went in a different direction than I had planned.

I had expected an update on Missy, not a hard-on and fantasy about Carmen in the bathtub. After we hung up, she sent the picture, and the blood in my veins warmed about ten degrees.

Thinking about that made me start seriously considering something else we had discussed. What if Carmen and I did start dating again? Would we still get along as well as we had? God knows that we'd had chemistry when we were younger, and it still appeared to be there.

She was my first love, my first everything. We experimented

and learned with one another, and after our quick tryst the other day, it was apparent that both of us had expounded on our knowledge. How many partners had she had over the years? I'd had two my entire life, but I wasn't stupid to think she hadn't been with more.

A little twist of jealousy hit my gut, but I didn't have the right to be jealous of the men she had been with. I had broken up with her. I had ended it, and she had every right to be with others.

For a few minutes, I thought over some of the things she had said earlier today. It bothered me that she had not moved on, even though she appeared to have gone through the motions. If I had handled things differently when I was younger and told her it was over for good, would that have changed things? I thought it was over, but I guess she was right. I never made it clear to her.

Should I feel guilty for it? I honestly couldn't. Not after I had such a wonderful marriage to Emily that gave me three incredible kids. Our marriage wasn't without strife. We argued and fought. We had money issues and differences of opinion over how the kids would be raised, but we'd gotten over all of it.

After she passed, my heart had been split in two, and I never imagined having a life with anyone else again. Returning here and seeing Carmen again made me wonder if it was possible.

ON SUNDAY MORNING, I received a text from Carmen. It said there had been no change in Missy, and they kept her heavily sedated. She would update me when there was a change.

When Tripp came down for breakfast, the first thing he asked was, "Is there any news?"

"News about what?" Savannah asked.

"None of your business," Tripp snapped at her.

"Hey! Don't talk to your sister that way." I shifted my focus to my daughter. "One of his friends got hurt yesterday and is in the hospital."

"Oh," Savannah replied and resumed eating her cereal.

"Carmen texted me that there has been no change, and she is still sedated. She will let us know when there is news."

"Okay, thanks." He turned to his sister. "Sorry about snapping at you. I didn't sleep well."

"That's okay," she replied. "I slept great!"

I chuckled. "That's because you were worn out from the picnic."

"Where were you guys again?" Tripp asked, and Savannah told him about how Dean had joined the swim team, and I went to work, so Carmen brought us home. Then she told him how Dean climbed through the back window. She turned to me. "Carmen said you need to get that window fixed."

I chuckled. "Yes, I already talked to the landlord."

"Sorry about that, Savannah, but I guess it turned out all right."

"It did! They have horses, and Tonya and Tyler both play soccer, so they taught me things, and now I want to play on Tyler's team. He's going to talk to the coach because he said I'm pretty good for a girl."

Tripp and I chuckled, and Savannah continued her story, telling her big brother everything they had done.

We hung out as a family for the rest of the day and did things around the house. Tripp even helped without complaining, and by dinnertime, we were all too tired to cook, so I took them down to the tavern.

We had just gotten seated when Candy came over to say hello. "Tim, it's great to see you." She glanced around the table. "Hey, Dean and Savannah. Did you two have a good time yesterday?"

"We did!" Dean replied. "How's Harley?"

She chuckled. "He is good. He's upstairs watching television right now."

"You have an upstairs?" Savannah asked.

"Yep, we do, and I will show it to you another time." She looked at Tripp. "And there is no doubt you are Tim's son. You look exactly like him when he was your age."

"You knew my dad then?"

"Oh, yeah." Candy laughed. "We all knew your dad. He was a pretty popular guy around here."

"I was not," I said with a laugh.

"Come on. You were a baseball star! Everyone talked about you during baseball season. In fact, after you left, we lost several games, and they blamed it on you not being there."

The kids were all grinning at me, and I chuckled again. "Don't believe everything you hear about me, and this is Tripp. Tripp, this is Candy Winston. She owns the tavern with her fiancé, Mike. She's also Carmen's sister."

Tripp's features darkened at the mention of Carmen, but he smiled politely at Candy. "It's nice to meet you."

"You too, Tripp. How do you like it around here?"

He shrugged. "It's okay, I guess."

She grinned. "I bet it was hard moving here in high school. I remember Carmen telling us how much your dad first hated California."

"You hated California?" Dean asked.

"At first, I did."

"When did it change?" Savannah chimed in.

"Probably after I met your mother." I peered at Candy to see if she would be upset, but she didn't appear to be.

"Your mom was a lucky woman. Your dad has always been a great guy. I wish I could have met her."

"I wish you could have, too," I replied.

"Well, I just wanted to say hello. Have dessert tonight. It's on me." She grinned at the kids and wandered away to speak to another table.

"She's so nice, and I love her name," Savannah said as she watched her leave.

"Her name is weird," Dean commented.

"A lot of people used to give her a hard time about her name growing up. Her father still calls her by different candy names."

"How do you know that?" Tripp asked.

"Because he was there yesterday. I heard him call her Twix."

The kids giggled, and as the server approached our table, I looked past her and saw Carmen enter the restaurant. She was smiling and looked back over her shoulder. Behind her was a man I hadn't met before, and I couldn't help but frown.

I pried my eyes off them as the server took our orders and forced myself not to seek her out in the crowded dining area. Unfortunately, I didn't have to look to know she was about four tables away because I could hear her tinkling laughter over the din of the diners.

It didn't take Savannah long to hear it either. "Hey, Carmen is here."

"That's Ms. Winston to you, young lady."

"She told me to call her Carmen, and it's actually Doctor Winston, Dad." Savannah put me in my place.

"I guess it is, but you should still respect that she is an elder," I told her.

"But she did tell us to call her Carmen," Dean added.

"What's the big deal about her?" Tripp growled.

"She's Dad's friend and used to be his girlfriend," Savannah replied to her brother.

"So?" Tripp sneered. "Who cares. She's not his girlfriend now."

"Tripp, watch your tone and lower your voice. Carmen is a good friend of mine."

"Are you going to start dating her now?"

I paused. I hadn't planned on bringing this up anytime soon. "I don't know what the future might hold, Tripp, but if and when I decide to start dating again, it will be my choice. Not yours."

"How can you just forget about Mom and start dating another woman?" he asked rudely.

"We already discussed this, Tripp. Your mother wouldn't want me to be alone forever. She would want me to be happy."

"You don't know that."

"I do know that, Tripp." I inhaled deeply and released it to keep myself calm. "Let's table this discussion for another time."

"Whatever," he replied, leaning back in his seat with his arms crossed, looking sullen as hell. I sighed.

Carmen approached the table a few moments later. "Hey, guys. How are you?"

"We were fine until you came over," Tripp mumbled.

"Tripp Kohl," I growled at him, and Carmen's brows rose, but she forced a smile over her lips as Dean and Savannah said hello.

"I'm sorry you feel that way, Tripp. I only came over to give you news about Missy. I just got word about five minutes ago that she is awake."

His entire demeanor changed. "She is? Is she okay?"

"They don't know the extent of her brain injuries yet, but she is awake and communicating. It will take a little more time before they can start running tests and know for certain."

"Can I go see her?"

Carmen shook her head, giving him a gentle smile. "No, not yet. She is in intensive care, and only her family can see her now. Would you like me to tell you when you can see her?"

"Yeah, please!" he said quickly. "I can give you my cellphone number so you can text me as soon as you know something."

Carmen glanced at me with surprise. "Is that okay that I speak with him directly?"

"Sure," I stated, as shocked as she was by his request.

"Here, let me have your phone. Mine is in my purse. I'll put my number in and text myself so I can save your number."

He handed over his phone. "Thanks, Dr. Winston."

"You are most welcome, Tripp," she replied and typed into his phone before handing it back to him. "You guys enjoy your dinner. Sorry to interrupt."

"No problem, Carmen. Thanks for the update."

She nodded. "Have a good night."

"You too," I stated, but then finished up in my head, but not too good of a night. I watched her take a seat and again wondered who the man was seated across from her. Was he one of the men she had mentioned she could call at any time to go out with? I fucking hated that thought.

21

CHAPTER TWENTY-ONE

CARMEN

The last person I expected to see at the tavern was Tim. I was walking to my table when Candy approached us and gave me a hug, whispering in my ear, "You're with the wrong man."

I gave her an odd look and glanced over her shoulder to see Tim and his family. Well, crap. "That's not funny, Candy."

She chuckled. "But it's true." She said hello to Matt, one of the psychologists I considered adding to my practice, and then walked away so we could get seated.

Matt and I discussed a few things about the practice, and I was considering bringing him on as a partner. That's what dinner tonight was about. I tried to be a good companion, but while facing Matt, my mind was otherwise occupied on the other side of the room. Maybe we should have asked for a table in the bar area.

A few minutes later, I got a text from Wesley with an update and figured that now was probably a safer time to pass the information along. I wasn't ready for another private conversation with Tim. The one last night was enough and had left me tossing and turning until I had pulled out my battery-powered best friend and relieved the tension.

I wasn't surprised by Tripp's curtness at my approach, but I made sure to let him know I was there for him. I was, however, surprised by his request that I contact him directly.

I was fine with that as long as Tim didn't mind me communicating with his son.

When I returned to the table, Matt was frowning. "How do you know them? Are they clients?"

"No, Tripp was the one who saved Missy," I replied as I laid my napkin over my lap.

"Wow, good for him. Who is the man?"

"Um, that's Tim Kohl. He moved away many years ago but recently came back."

Matt chuckled. "He can't seem to keep his eyes off you—or me, for that matter."

"Don't mind him. We went to high school together and just reconnected."

"Did you date in high school?"

I studied Matt, wondering how much I should say. "We did date. We dated for four years, then he left and broke up with me to start a new life."

His gaze traveled across the room, and I knew he was looking at him.

"He might have broken up with you, but it looks like he wants to mend fences." He grinned.

"You have no idea what you are talking about. We are just friends."

"Yeah, okay, you keep telling yourself that, Carmen."

"Seriously, Matt. Can we drop it? I think we have more important things to discuss." The last thing I wanted was to have Matt dissect my relationship with Tim. I had done that enough for both of us.

"Yeah, okay. I'll drop it, but I feel this conversation will come back around," he said with a chuckle as the waitress appeared beside the table.

We had a pleasant dinner and discussed the possibility of him becoming a partner. I wanted to bring one on so I could expand the practice. It was growing by the day, and we needed more good pediatric and teen therapists with the growing population of Millerstown.

Occasionally, I drifted off and thought about Tim and his kids. I had already picked up on the fact that Tripp wouldn't be all that on board with the idea of his father in a relationship, but was that because it was with me, or would it be the same with anyone?

Not that there was a relationship between us. What we had between us was still clearly undefined.

Two hours after getting home, I sat on the couch, trying to lose myself in a television program.

My phone beeped, and I looked at the message that had just come through. It was from Tripp. *Hi, it's Tripp. Have there been any changes with Missy?*

I typed back: *I have not heard anything, but let me call Wes Young and see if he knows anything.*

Thanks, was his reply.

I pulled up Wes' number and hit call. He answered on the second ring. "Hey, Carmen, what's going on?"

"Any word on Missy? I have an anxious teenage boy wondering how his friend is doing."

He chuckled. "Tim's son?"

"Yep."

"I called the hospital about an hour ago. She was talking, but she was still heavily medicated. There hasn't been any more swelling. Tomorrow we will start running more tests to see if there are any deficits."

"Do you think there will be?"

"I would be surprised if there isn't."

"Hmm, okay."

"I'd let the kid know she's doing a bit better, but she's not out of the woods."

"All right, I will let him know that."

He was quiet for a few seconds. "So, what is going on with Tim?"

"What do you mean?"

He laughed. "Come on, Carmen, I know how bad you had it for him when you were younger. You two going to get together?"

I scoffed. "That was a long time ago, Wes. I'm not sure what will happen."

"Are you open to the idea? You two were good together."

"I might be open to it, but since his wife recently passed, I don't want to put that kind of pressure on him along with everything he has going on with his kids."

"His wife died two years ago, Carmen. It's time for him to move on."

"Who knows when he will be ready to move on or if he would even be interested in doing so with me?"

"You're kidding, right? The man couldn't keep his eyes off you at the picnic. I think he is ready."

"We had sex." I blurted the words out and closed my eyes. I had been dying to tell someone, and Wes just happened to be the person it was shared with. I winced as the quiet on the line grew almost deafening.

"That was the last thing I expected you to say." He chuckled.

"It wasn't a big deal. He came over to talk to me, and it was a spur-of-the-moment thing, and then I knew he would feel guilty about it, and I was right, he did."

"Wow, what are you going to do now?"

"Well, please don't tell everyone else, Wes, but we already talked about going out on a date and seeing what might be between us."

"That's great, Carmen."

"Is it?" I sighed. "I almost feel like this might be a bad idea."

"Why? You guys were fantastic together. You're single, he's single, so why not try it out."

"I guess."

"Don't look too deeply into it. Just get to know one another again. It might not work, but then it might. You aren't going to know until you try it."

"You're right."

"In the meantime, you should probably stop dating other guys."

I frowned. "What are you talking about?"

"Who is the man you had dinner with tonight?"

"How do you even know about that?"

He snickered. "Carmen, there are no secrets between our families. One person makes a call, and before you know it, everyone knows what is going on."

I sighed. "Well, everyone can just butt out of my life. That was Matt; he might start working with me, and we were discussing business."

"You know we all just want you to be happy."

"I am happy."

"Happy with someone in your life," he quickly added.

"All right, enough of this. Have a good night. Tell Charlotte I said hello, and tell everyone else to stop talking about my love life."

"Or lack of one," he tacked on. "Night, Carmen." He disconnected while my mouth hung open.

I quickly typed back to Tripp the update, and he said thanks. After that, I stared at the television for a moment and decided to video chat with my big sister.

"Well, hello!" she said, and I heard Luke yelling in the background.

"Good Lord, what are you doing to that kid?"

"Oh, don't mind him. He's upset because his father went to the barn and wouldn't take him to feed the horses."

"Why didn't he? I thought that was what they did at night."

"Because it's storming, and Luke is getting a cold. Hence the reason he is throwing a mini temper tantrum."

"Aww, poor guy. Tell him Aunt Carmen is on the phone. Maybe that will cheer him up."

"Hey, Luke, Aunt Carmen is on the phone. Do you want to come to say hello?"

"No!" he shouted from off in the distance.

Cara shrugged. "Don't mind him. I told you he's not feeling well."

"I will try not to let it bother me," I said with a grin. "How are you doing?"

"I am doing well."

"Hey, why didn't you tell me you and Brian were trying to have another baby? I had to hear that from Candy."

"Because it just came up. You know you will be the first person I call when I have a positive test. Besides, don't you have other things to be worried about now?"

"What are you talking about?"

"I'm talking about the fact that you were out on a date with another guy tonight while your hottie boyfriend was sitting on the other side of the restaurant."

My jaw dropped again. "You guys are killing me here! Tim is not my hottie boyfriend, Cara, and I wasn't on a date. It was business."

"Since when do you have business dinners with attractive older men?"

"Since Matt Concordia might become a partner in my practice. How do you even know about this?"

"Candy told me tonight."

I rolled my eyes. "Sometimes I hate siblings and other people's siblings. Wes was questioning me on this too."

"We know you."

"Yeah, well, you all don't know everything. Everyone just needs to butt out of my life."

"So, you weren't on a date tonight? He was cute, by the way."

"No, and of course, she sent you a picture." I sighed.

"If Tim asked you out, would you say yes?"

"I already have."

She paused and then squealed. "Wait! He asked you out?"

"Yes, and I said yes."

"When?"

"I don't know. I still have to look at my schedule."

She sighed. "Come on, woman! Look at your schedule already."

"I will. Relax, okay?"

"Fine, I'll relax, but you need to make sure he knows you are interested."

"He knows."

"Good, I hope things work out for you."

"What if it doesn't?"

"Then you move on."

I laughed. "Yeah, because I moved on so well the first time he ended things."

"You are a mature woman now who sees things for what they are. You aren't a lovestruck teenager in la-la land."

"True," I replied with a weary sigh. We talked for a few more minutes, but then Luke had another meltdown, and Cara said she had to put him to bed.

I went up to bed and climbed in, thinking over what we had discussed. What if things didn't work between us? Could I get over him this time?

We had already had sex, but was he ready to move on? He

still wore his wedding ring, which made me think that he wasn't.

Eventually, I drifted off to sleep and woke up to my phone ringing. I glanced at the clock to see it was almost two in the morning. Who the hell was calling me now? I grabbed my phone and saw Tim's name on the screen.

"Why are you calling in the middle of the night?"

"I'm sorry, Carmen, but I need your help."

I heard the panic in his voice, and I threw back the covers and sat on the edge of the bed. "What's wrong?"

"It's Tripp. He's freaking out, and I don't know what to do with him. I think he might be sleepwalking, but he is sobbing in the corner of his closet. I can't get through to him."

I jumped up and rushed to my closet. "Does he have a habit of doing that?"

"He did when he was younger but hasn't in a while. I have never seen him this way, Carmen. I don't know what to do with him."

"Okay, let me throw on clothes, and I'll be on my way. Just keep your distance and make sure he remains safe. Don't try to wake him if you don't have to."

"Okay, I will, and thank you."

"Don't thank me yet, Tim," I said and hung up the phone.

CHAPTER TWENTY-TWO

TIM

I was glad when dinner was over. As pleasant of a meal as it was, I hated being there and seeing Carmen with another man.

I didn't have a right to feel that way, but I did. The more I saw her, the more I wanted to get to know her again, and her comment from last night about having ten different men she could call for a date irked me more than I cared to admit.

I sat on the edge of my bed that night, staring at the ring on my finger. I hadn't lied when I told Tripp his mother and I had discussed it. Years ago, we had said that if anything happened to one of us, the other should go on and love again. Suddenly a memory drifted back to my mind.

I had been going through some old boxes of stuff from when I was a kid and was telling Emily about the items inside the box. I pulled out a picture of Carmen and me sitting on the deck of her house.

"Who is that?"

"Carmen Winston. We dated for about four years before I moved to California."

She took the picture from me. "Timothy Kohl, I never knew you had a type."

"What do you mean?"

"I mean, look at her. We could be sisters with our hair color and skin tone. How tall is she?"

I frowned and thought for a moment, then stood and put my hand just under my collarbone. "I guess she came up to here on me."

Emily stood, laughing, and put her head on my chest. "Yep, we could be sisters. That is exactly how tall I am."

"That's ironic."

She stepped back, looking thoughtful. "Tell me about her."

I scoffed. "Why would you want to know about her?"

She lifted her shoulders and smiled as she sank back to the sofa. "Because I'm curious about her. Don't you think it's ironic that you dated her for so long and then moved out here and we found one another? She and I could be long-lost siblings."

"I doubt that. She already has five siblings."

"Big family."

"Yeah, it is. It was a great family. I really enjoyed hanging out with them."

"What was she like?"

I inhaled and then released it in a huff as I stared at the picture, seeing now how right she was about the looks. "She was really smart, wanted to be a doctor or shrink or something like that. She was caring. She cared about everyone and always wanted people to be happy."

"Do you think she is now?"

I looked at Emily. "I have no clue, but I hope she is."

"I hope she is too. I hope that she found someone to love as you did."

I leaned forward and kissed her. "I do love you very much."

"And I love you." She kissed me again, then pulled back, looking thoughtful. "If something ever happens to me, you should look her up."

I laughed. "Why would I do that?"

"Because it is obvious that you cared a great deal for her. If the least you do is make sure she is happy, then great."

"Yeah, well, if something happens to you, I won't be in any mind to be looking up old girlfriends."

"Not right away, but I don't want you alone, Tim. I know you wouldn't want that for me either."

"No, I wouldn't. You're right. I would want you happy, even if that were with someone else."

"And I would want the same thing, so promise me that if something ever happens to me, you will look her up."

I laughed. "Sure. If that's what you want, I will promise."

I snapped back to the present, and my eyes locked on my ring. I had forgotten that promise to her. In fact, after that day, I never thought of it again. I had packed up the items and returned them to the attic.

The only thing I remembered of that conversation was that we had said we would eventually move on and find someone else to share our lives with if one of us died. Had Emily somehow known she would pass before me and that I would move back here?

That was honestly some twisted fate, and it unnerved me slightly.

I put the thoughts out of my head and forced myself to lie down and try to sleep. I must have dozed off because I woke with a start of a shout in the other room. I was on my feet and racing toward the sound when Dean came out of his room.

"What's going on, Dad?"

"I don't know. Go back to bed, kiddo."

"Okay," he replied as he rubbed at his eyes.

I rushed into Tripp's room, but he wasn't in bed. I was about to leave when I heard a noise coming from his closet. "Don't! Please don't!" he begged someone.

"Tripp?" I pulled open the closet door and found him on the floor on his knees, pleading with the wall. "Tripp! What are you doing?"

"Don't! You can't mean it! Please don't!" he plead toward the wall.

"Tripp, buddy, come on. You are dreaming. Let's go back to bed." I touched him, and he freaked out.

"No! Don't touch me! Don't you see what she's trying to do!" he shouted at me, but I didn't think he knew who I was.

"Tripp, it's okay. Calm down." I tried to touch him again, but he punched and hit me in the jaw, knocking me back on my ass.

"Stop! I'm not going to let her kill herself! Please don't jump!"

I stared at him, fear gripping my chest as I suddenly realized what was happening. He was sleepwalking, and he was dreaming about the incident with Missy.

I slipped out of the closet and found Dean and Savannah staring at me from the hall door. "Both of you go back to bed. Your brother is sleepwalking. Do not go near him."

They looked on wide-eyed and moved as I rushed from the room to get my phone. I had no clue what to do with Tripp in this state, but maybe Carmen might.

I didn't even think as I called her, and after we hung up, I went back to Tripp's bedroom and sat on his bed, watching him through the closet door. My hands shook as I sat there, and suddenly, I thought about the fact that the front door was locked. I quickly unlocked it, turning on the lights so she could find her way inside.

Front door is unlocked. We are upstairs, I typed to Carmen but didn't get a reply. I assumed that she was probably driving.

I had stopped shaking but was still tense as I waited for her to arrive. A few minutes before she did, Tripp finally stopped calling out and slipped to the closet floor.

I heard her car door close, and I winced. I should have just waited. He would have come out of this on his own. Now I had woken her up and gotten her out of bed for no reason. Shit.

I heard the front door open and close, and I stepped out into the hallway just as she reached the top. "Where is he?"

I put my hand up and looked behind me. "He just fell asleep.

Literally, while you were pulling in, he stopped crying and lay down."

"Can I see him?"

"Yeah." I stepped to the side so she could enter the room. I watched as she walked cautiously toward the closet and stood at the door, looking in.

She turned after a moment and pulled his comforter off his bed and disappeared into the closet.

When she emerged, she put her finger to her lips and joined me in the hallway, closing his door behind her. "Best not to wake him after that. Do you want to tell me what he was doing?"

"I feel like an ass for getting you out of bed and making you come over here."

She put her hand on my arm. "It's okay. I know that can be scary. How about we go downstairs and talk for a little while? What happened to your face?"

I touched my cheek and winced. "He punched me. Probably the only time he could get away with doing that."

"Let's put some ice on your jaw while you tell me what happened. I might have some ways to help if it happens again."

I checked in on the other two kids, found them both sound asleep again, and followed Carmen down the steps.

"I'm sorry for waking you," I told her as I pulled an ice pack from the stack in the freezer. With three active kids, we always needed them.

"It's okay. I assume this was not the first time he has done that."

I shook my head. "No. When he was younger, he would sleepwalk if he had difficulty with something. The doctor said he'd probably grow out of it."

"Did he have them after his mother died?"

I paused to think. "Maybe, but nothing this bad. I have never seen him like this. He was crying and begging someone he couldn't see."

"I'm sure he could see, but you couldn't. He was deep inside his mind, playing out a dream. What was he begging?"

"He was telling someone not to do something. I think he said don't jump."

"Aw, he was probably revisiting the incident with Missy."

"Yeah, I am sure that is what it was." I paused. "What do I do if he does it again? He's never gotten violent before."

"If he is going to endanger himself or someone else, you need to wake him up."

"But I was always told not to wake him."

"That is an old myth, although waking them during a dream can be very disorienting. It's better to try and reassure them and get them back to bed."

I sighed and took a seat on the stool beside her. "Thank you for coming over."

"You're welcome, Tim."

"I owe you," I said.

Carmen studied me. "You could repay me with that dinner you mentioned."

I peaked a brow. "You'd be willing to have dinner with me?"

"Yes."

"Can it be someplace different from the tavern?"

She chuckled. "I would appreciate a different location."

"What about the guy you were out with tonight? Won't he get jealous?"

"No."

"Why not? Did the date not go well?"

"It wasn't a date, Tim. It was a business dinner. Matt is a colleague who might become a partner."

"Oh," I commented, shifting closer to her. "So, he's not a romantic interest?"

"Not even in the slightest. His wife might have something to say about that if he were."

Before I could tell her I was glad to hear that, a shout came from the stairs, and Carmen was already getting to her feet. "Let me see if I can coax him back to bed."

"Just watch his left hook," I said from behind her as we raced up the stairs.

Carmen slipped into his room and approached the closet. I wasn't far behind her but did stay back to watch.

Before she did anything, she paused and listened to him. "Get down, please! You don't want to kill yourself. Please get down."

He paused, and Carmen stepped forward. "Tripp, honey, it's okay. She's not going to jump."

Tripp's face swung around so fast that I thought I was watching that exorcist movie, but my knees almost buckled when he spoke.

"Mom? Mom!" He burst to his feet and threw his arms around Carmen so fast that neither of us had time to move. "Mom, I couldn't stop her! I tried. She said she wanted to die, but I tried to stop her."

I thought I was going to be sick. The girl hadn't just jumped off the bridge for kicks. She had done it to commit suicide. Holy fuck!

CHAPTER TWENTY-THREE

CARMEN

I didn't think about going. I just did. When it came to children, I understood them more than anyone, and if Tripp was sleepwalking and in a bad place, I needed to help him. This had nothing to do with Tim.

I heard the message on my phone, but I was too close to his house to stop and read it. Perhaps he had said everything was okay, but when I pulled into his neighborhood, I checked my message and saw that the door was unlocked for me.

I rushed into the house, thankful that there were lights on, and made my way up the stairs. At the top, Tim stepped out of a room, and I forced myself not to take in his shirtless chest.

I checked on Tripp, glad that he was calm now, but not sure that would be the last of it tonight. Many times, there was more than one episode a night, especially after trauma.

I sat at the kitchen island as Tim got an ice pack from the fridge and let my gaze drift over his back. He looked pretty damn good for someone who was getting close to forty.

We were sitting side by side, talking softly, and I decided to take Cara's advice and put it out there. It didn't take long for him to come on board with the idea of going out together, but Tripp was back in a state before we could cement the time.

We returned to his room, and I stepped into the closet quietly, watching him and trying to decide the best way to approach him.

The words he said took me back. Had Missy been trying to kill herself? Or was he adding more to the conversation? The best way to ease him out of this was to reassure him and get him back in bed safely.

"Tripp, honey, it's okay. She's not going to jump."

Tripp spun so fast that I almost screamed. He threw his arms around me, calling me mom and sobbing into my neck about how Missy was trying to kill herself.

I held him tightly. If he thought I was his mother, it might comfort him enough to let me get him back to bed and into a more relaxed dream state.

"It's okay, honey, it's okay," I repeated as he squeezed me so hard I thought he might crush me. After a few minutes, I tried to pull back a little. "Come on, Tripp, let's get you back to bed."

"Okay," he whispered and wiped his nose, and then he let me lead him back to his bed. He lay down, and I covered him with his sheet and blanket. His comforter was still in the closet, but he wouldn't pick up on that.

"Mom, stay with me. Don't go."

"Okay, I'll stay for a little while. Close your eyes and go back to sleep. You are okay, and Missy is okay too. She's alive and healing. I'm proud of you, Tripp. You saved her life."

He smiled sleepily. "Thanks, Mom. I missed you."

"I know," I stated softly, not wanting to say too much.

"I love you, Mom," Tripp said groggily, and I ran my hand over his head, brushing the hair back from his face. I knew Tim was watching from the door, so I remained quiet, although I wanted to tell Tripp that I loved him too.

How could I not after how this boy had reacted at the

thought of his mother coming to save him from his dream? No wonder he was brash with me last night at the restaurant. He was protecting the memory of the only mother he knew.

"Sleep well, Tripp. You are safe now, and your job is done. Rest, sweetie."

He sighed contentedly in his sleep, and then I stood, brushed my hand over his forehead one more time, and before I knew what I was doing, I bent over and kissed his forehead tenderly. He smiled in his sleep.

I turned and found Tim watching me, although, with the light behind him, I couldn't see his face. I could only tell that he was staring in my direction.

I slipped past him and was heading toward the stairs when Tim snatched my hand and pulled me to a stop. I turned back to him. "What?"

The look on his face made my knees weak, and he stepped forward until he was close enough that I shifted back against the wall.

"What? Did I do something wrong?"

He touched my face. "No, you did everything right."

Before I could think, he leaned forward, and his lips landed on mine. Suddenly, the sun burst from behind a dark cloud, and I felt weightless. My mouth instantly opened for him, and our tongues brushed together in an almost urgent manner.

I would have clung to his shirt if he had been wearing one, so instead, I spread my hands wide over his firm chest. There was hair there that hadn't been when he was younger, and I wanted to thread my fingers through it, but I also wanted to get lost in his kiss and never return.

It didn't last nearly long enough, and as he pulled back, he stared at me and then looked down the hall. Oh, holy crap! I hoped that he didn't invite me to his bedroom. Kissing him was one thing, but I wasn't ready to have sex with him, surrounded by children.

Then I realized he was checking the other doors to make sure no one saw us. "Let's go downstairs."

I followed him down, feeling very unstable and light-headed. Thankfully I had a handrail to hold on to. At the bottom of the stairs, I turned toward the door. That was what I needed to do. I needed to get out of here and go home. Maybe this was all a dream.

"Where are you going?" Tim asked from behind me.

"I should go," I said with my hand on the door and my back to him.

He put his hands on my shoulders and then wrapped his arms around me, putting his cheek to the side of my face. "I'm sorry if that upset you. I had no idea he would respond like that."

Oh man, he thought I was concerned about how Tripp called me mom. He had no idea it was because I wanted to drag him into his room and have my way with him, only I couldn't. "It's okay. You aren't upset, are you?"

"No! It floored me how you just handled my son and how incredible you are." He turned me in his arms.

I blinked at him and then blinked again. "Well, I'm glad I could help."

He brushed a lock of hair away from my face. "Thank you for coming tonight."

"You're welcome."

He shuffled closer. "When can I see you again?"

"This weekend. I'm swamped for the rest of the week."

He spiked a brow. "Don't tell me you have more dates."

I shook my head. As far as I was concerned, I would never be going out with anyone ever again. "No, I have a busy week with work."

"Okay, then this is going to have to last me until the weekend," he said as he descended on me again, and I happily wrapped my arms around his neck.

I kissed him even more passionately than I did in the upstairs hallway, and he seemed all for it. He ran his hands down my back and over my butt, curling his hands around my cheeks and lifting me off the floor. It was almost exactly how it had been at my house, and my body ached for him. The kiss intensified, and I wished I had gotten him into his room. To hell with my earlier thought!

However, he slowed down and pulled back. Both of us were breathing hard, returning me to our teen years when we used to make out in the car.

"Damn, Carmen, I can't believe how good you feel." He pressed his hips forward, and I groaned. "You like that, huh?"

"Yes," I practically purred in his ear.

He kissed down my neck while he ran his hand over my breast. "I would do anything to have you naked right now." I wanted to ask him why he didn't, but he continued. "But not with the kids here."

Kids! Way to splash the cold water on. My eyes flashed open, and I looked at the stairs. Luckily, no one was there watching. I pushed him back. "We should probably stop."

He sighed but slowly put me down. "Yes, we should."

"I should go and try to get some sleep, and so should you."

"Gonna be hard now."

I laughed slightly and knew he was talking about more than just sleeping. "I am sure you know how to deal with that."

He winked at me. "As I am well aware that you are too."

He stepped back, running his hands up and down my arms again. "Thanks again for coming over tonight."

"You are welcome. I am glad that you called."

"Is he going to remember any of that?"

"Maybe some of it." I gnawed on my bottom lip for a second. "I'm going to want to speak with him again. He mentioned that Missy was trying to kill herself. I need to know if that was true or just his perception."

"Of course, whenever you have time."

"Okay, thank you."

"No, thank you, Carmen." He brushed one last kiss over my lips and reached around me to open the door.

The night air was refreshingly cool after the steamy kiss, and I gulped it down as I made my way to the car after saying a quick good night.

He stood in the doorway watching until I had started the car and backed out. Then he waved and shut the door.

I grinned to myself all the way home. Holy smokes, I had just made out with Tim Kohl—again! If only there had been no kids in the house.

When I got home, I found a message on my phone that I hadn't heard on the drive, probably because I was lost in my mind.

Let me know when you get home.

Hi, I'm home. Thank you for checking on me.

You're welcome and thank you for coming over to help. I'll talk to you tomorrow. Get some sleep.

I will try. Night, Tim XOXO

XOXOXO, he replied, and I sighed dreamily as I climbed my stairs to head back to bed.

Unfortunately, I didn't get much sleep. Once I was back in bed, my mind flipped back and forth between what Tripp had said and what happened between Tim and me.

24

CHAPTER TWENTY-FOUR

TIM

The following day, I was thinking back on the night before—not only about what happened with Tripp but what occurred with Carmen when she was here. I was pouring my coffee, and music was playing quietly from my phone when I heard footsteps behind me and turned to see Tripp enter the room. "Hey, kiddo. How are you today?"

He shrugged slightly. "I'm fine, although I don't think I slept very well last night."

Should I tell him he was sleepwalking again? Maybe I'd wait to see what he said. "Sorry to hear that. Were you dreaming?"

"Yeah, I guess." He frowned as he set his backpack down. Then he looked up, and his eyes looked clearer than they had in a long time. "I had a dream about Mom last night."

I froze, the mug two inches from my mouth. "You did?"

"Yeah, she was there and hugging me, and she told me she was proud of me and missed me."

I smiled at him. "That was a nice dream."

"Yeah, it was, except it almost felt real too. It was like I could feel her arms around me, and she was there when I fell asleep, brushing my hair off my brow like she used to do."

"Powerful dream," I told him, then sipped my coffee before saying more. "Hopefully, it made you feel good."

"It did. I needed that last night."

"Then I am glad you got it." The toaster popped my bagel up, and I turned to it. "Are your brother and sister awake?"

"Yeah, I checked on them before I came down. They are getting dressed."

"Thanks, I appreciate it."

"Dad, was I talking in my sleep last night?"

"Why do you ask?" I queried over my shoulder as I put cream cheese on my bagel.

"Dean said I was talking loud and woke him up."

"You might have said a few things."

"Like what?"

I set the knife down and turned to him. "You were telling someone not to jump. I assume you were pleading with your friend."

His face instantly shuttered. "I don't remember."

"Don't you?"

He shook his head and grabbed his backpack as his phone buzzed. "I gotta go. Kyle is picking me up for school."

Before I could say anything else, he rushed out of the room, and I heard him say goodbye to his brother.

"Hey, Dad," Dean said as he entered. I finished chewing the mouthful I had.

"Morning, Dean, how are you today?"

"Tired. Why was Carmen here last night?"

"You remember Carmen being here?"

"Yeah, I saw you kissing her in the hallway. I thought she wasn't your girlfriend."

I stopped in mid-chew. "You saw that, huh?"

"Yeah, it was gross."

I chuckled. "Sorry about that. Did it bother you to see me kissing her?"

"Who did you kiss?" Savannah asked as she hustled into the room.

"Dad kissed Carmen last night."

"When?" Savannah asked, looking confused.

"When she came over after we were in bed. Tripp was yelling."

"Aww, Daddy and Carmen sitting in a tree—"

I put my hand up. "None of that, please." I set my plate down and studied them. "Would it bother either of you if I took Carmen out on a date?"

"Are you going to marry her?" Savannah asked immediately.

"No, I said date, not marriage."

"I don't care. I like her, and she has a cool family and knows a lot of people around here," Dean supplied.

"What about you, Savannah? Do you mind?"

"No, I like her too. She's really nice and pretty too."

"She is pretty, and I appreciate you two telling me your feelings."

"Tripp won't like it, though," Dean commented.

"Yeah, I don't think Tripp will like it, but he will get over it." I paused. "Dean, I know you said something to your brother this morning about his talking in his sleep, but I think you better leave out the part about Carmen coming over to help him."

His eyes grew wide. "You want me to lie? You told me never to lie."

"No, I'm not telling you to lie. I'm telling you not to talk about it."

"But why?" Savannah asked.

"Because I think it might embarrass your brother if he knew someone else saw him like that. He doesn't remember it."

"Oh," Savannah commented.

"All right, I won't talk about it, but if he asks, I won't lie. You told me never to lie."

"Yes, I did, and I appreciate your willingness to be honest. Now what do you want for breakfast?"

LATER THAT DAY, I got a text from Carmen. *Can you talk?*

I closed the door to my office and called her. "I can. How are you?"

"A little tired. I had a hard time sleeping when I got home. I wonder why?"

I chuckled as I sank back in my seat. "Yeah, me too, but it was worth it."

She laughed softly. "I wanted to see how Tripp was this morning. Did he remember anything?"

"Not about what happened in the closet, although he did say that he dreamed that his mom was there."

She sighed. "Yeah, I wondered if he would remember seeing me. What did you tell him?"

"I told him it was a good dream to have."

"Wait, you didn't tell him the truth?"

"No, why would I do that? The kid doesn't remember you being there, not for real. He thinks that his mother came to visit him in a dream. I didn't want to burst his bubble. It was the brightest I had seen my son in months."

She sighed heavily over the phone. "Because it's lying, Tim. You should have told him the truth."

"Jesus, you sound like Dean."

"Why do you say that?"

"Because I told Dean not to mention that you were here last night, and by the way, he saw us kissing in the hallway."

"He did?"

"Yes."

"What did he say about it?"

"He said it was gross."

She chuckled, and I smiled at the sound. "I'm sorry that he saw it. Did he tell Tripp?"

"No, and I asked him not to say anything to him. Neither Dean nor Savannah has an issue with me going on a date with you, but I don't think the idea will as easily win over Tripp."

"No, I don't think he will be happy about it. Teens can be tricky. They feel a loyalty to their deceased parent that is hard to battle against."

"What do I do to get him over it?"

"Nothing. He needs time to adjust to the fact that you might be with someone new."

"Might be?"

She grew quiet momentarily. "I know we said we would go out next week, but we have no idea if it would work between us."

"You doubt that it would?"

"I'm a realistic person, Tim. We have both changed quite a bit over the years. Just because we might be attracted to one another, that doesn't mean we will actually get along."

I sighed. "I guess you are right."

"And the last thing you want to do is jump into a relationship with someone new. That's not a smart thing to do, and you might find yourself regretting it."

Somehow, I couldn't imagine ever regretting anything with Carmen, but whatever. I wasn't going to argue with her. "Fine. We can debate this later. Did you figure out when you wanted to go out?"

"I can do Saturday."

"What time on Saturday?"

"Would five-thirty be too early?"

"No, that will work for me."

"All right, then I will talk to you on Saturday."

"I'm not going to hear from you before then?"

"Maybe or maybe not. I don't want to give too many secrets away before seeing you. You might stand me up."

I laughed. "I don't think I can do that."

"You have done it before."

"When?"

"Prom? Remember you promised to come back for prom?" She chuckled. "I have to go. I will talk to you on Saturday."

"Bye, Carmen."

After I hung up, I fretted for a moment over her comment. Was she still upset that I didn't come back for prom? I also wondered if she was right about the other part. We did have an attraction to one another, but did we have more?

The memory of talking to Emily about her came back to mind. Maybe I was only interested in dating her because of that. That thought didn't feel right, and I decided not to look too deeply into it. If we went out and things worked, then it was good. If we didn't, then we would know that it never would have worked in the first place.

For now, I would wait to see what happened, but that didn't mean I wasn't looking forward to taking her out.

Tripp had been quiet since Thursday morning after the sleepwalking incident, and there hadn't been another. Perhaps his dream of seeing his mother had calmed him enough that he had gotten past the incident.

"What time are you leaving?" Tripp asked as he came into the kitchen on Saturday afternoon.

"In about an hour."

He grunted.

"Do you have a problem with me going out?"

He pulled the container of milk from the fridge. "No. I have a problem with you going on a date."

"Tripp, we talked about this."

"No, you talked about it. Just because you think you're ready to move on doesn't mean I have to like it."

I sighed. "Your mom has been gone for two years, Tripp. Would you rather I spend the rest of my life alone? What happens when you go to college in a few years, and then your brother and sister leave the house a few years later? What am I supposed to do then? Sit on my ass and be lonely?"

"You could at least wait a few more years."

"Yeah, well, that's not happening. I'm ready to start living again."

He laughed. "You've been living. You're lucky! Mom didn't get that choice."

"No, she didn't, and if I could have traded places with her, I would have."

He stared at me. "Do you mean that?"

"Yes, Tripp. I understand how difficult it has been not having a mother to help you. We have all had to make a lot of concessions for her loss."

His face looked suddenly sad. "Do you miss her? I mean, do you even think about her anymore?"

"Yes, I do—all the time. She might not be here in person, but she's with us in our hearts. She would want us all to be happy." I sighed. "Sometimes, on my way home from work, I have silent conversations with her about my day. It's like I'm pretending she's at home waiting for me."

He poured the milk into a glass but said nothing for a few seconds. "Yeah, I do that too."

I remained where I was, leaning back against the counter, and waited to see if he would say more.

Finally, after he drank about half his glass, he looked at me and then at my hand. "If you're so ready to go on a date, why are you still wearing your wedding ring?"

Good question. Was it wrong to wear it while I was dating

another woman? Probably, but I wasn't quite ready to part with it.

"I'll take it off when I'm ready. It's not like Carmen doesn't know I was married."

"Why her?"

"What do you mean?"

"I mean, there have to be other women here. Can't you date someone else?"

"What do you have against Carmen?"

He shrugged. "Nothing, but it's weird that she looks so much like Mom. It's like you are picking her because of that."

I laughed. "You could say I picked your mother because of Carmen's appearance. I did meet your mom right after I broke up with Carmen."

"That's stupid," he growled.

"Well, it's good that your opinion does not matter in whom I date."

"That's even stupider. You should care what we think."

"I do care what you think, but if you brought a girl home that I didn't like, would you care what I thought or said?"

He gave me a lopsided grin. "Probably not."

"Then you get where I am coming from."

He sighed, then drank the rest of his milk, putting the glass beside the sink and the milk in the fridge. "I'm going to give you the same advice you give me when I go out on a date."

"Yeah, what's that?"

"Make sure you wear protection; I wouldn't want you to screw up your life." He smirked as he turned and walked out of the room. I shook my head at him and chuckled once he was gone.

25

CHAPTER TWENTY-FIVE

CARMEN

Thursday night, I got a text from Tripp asking how Missy was. I asked him if he could talk, and after a few seconds, he replied yes, so I called him.

"Hello?"

"Hi, Tripp. Missy is doing pretty well. She will probably move out of intensive care on Friday, so you might be able to visit with her this weekend."

"Is she okay?"

"Well, she has a serious concussion, but she is healing quickly. Dr. Young is impressed by her recovery so far."

He was quiet for a moment. "Is she different?"

"Do you mean, does she have any deficiencies?"

"Yeah, that."

"Well, most people with concussions have issues, and she's not up and moving around yet. When she sits up, she gets dizzy, so she is not allowed to stand or move around on her own yet. She has a long road ahead of her."

"Oh."

"I bet she would be happy to see you."

"I don't know about that," he muttered.

"No, I think she would." I gave him a second, and then I broached a different subject. "Tripp, how are you doing?"

"I'm fine."

"I'm glad to hear that, but if that incident bothers you, it's okay. That was a stressful thing to do, and I know it can have a lingering effect."

"I said I was fine," he replied, but he didn't sound convincing.

I decided to take the focus off him. "Tripp, can I ask you a question about Missy?"

"Yeah."

"Was Missy messing around on the bridge and just jumped, or did she jump because she was unhappy about her life and wanted it to end?"

He didn't respond, and I gave him a few seconds to think about his answer.

When he didn't respond, I continued. "I think maybe she might have done it because she was unhappy. That's why she comes to see me every week. She's talked about killing herself before, and I am concerned that she did this hoping she might die."

He replied softly, "That's why I don't think she will want to see me."

"Do you think she will be mad that you saved her?"

"Yeah, I do."

I sighed softly. "I figured as much."

"I tried to talk her out of it. I did. I begged her not to jump, Dr. Winston."

"I am sure that you did, Tripp. No one could have stopped her if that's what she wanted to do."

"I should have said something to you before."

"No, that's okay that you didn't. You were trying to protect her."

"What is going to happen now? Is she in trouble?"

"She's not in trouble, Tripp, and neither are you. I appreciate you telling me. I'm not sure what will happen to Missy, but I know that she has a lot of healing to do, both physically and mentally. I also know she is going to need a friend."

"I'll do anything that I can."

"That's sweet of you, Tripp. If you can visit her, make sure you tell her that."

"Are you going to tell her that I told you?"

"No, I'm going to get her to admit it." I was already working on that part. After hearing Tripp in his dream state, I had a strong feeling that was what she had been doing.

"Oh, okay."

"Is there anything else you want to talk about?"

He was silent for a few seconds. "I had a dream about my mom the other night."

"You did? I bet that was a good dream." I didn't want to play into this dream bullshit and almost told him it had been me and not his mother. However, I kept those words out of my mouth.

"It was. She made me feel safe again."

"I'm sorry you didn't feel safe, but I am glad you do now."

"Thanks, and thanks for letting me know about Missy."

"You're welcome, and if you ever want to talk about what happened, you have my number."

"No, I'm fine."

"Okay, I'll leave the offer open."

"All right." I was about to speak again when he continued. "Dr. Winston, do you know any paramedics?"

"I do. Henley Young is a very good friend of mine. Why?"

"Do you think maybe I could talk to him sometime? I'm thinking about being one, but I don't know anymore."

"Tripp, I think that would be a great idea. I am sure that Henley would love to talk to you. I'll reach out to him tomorrow, and if it's okay with you, I'll pass along your number."

"Yeah, that would be cool."

"Great, well, you have a good night, Tripp."

"Yeah, you too, Dr. Winston."

After we hung up, I spent a lot of time thinking about Tripp. Out of the three kids, he had probably taken the loss of his mother the hardest. Being fourteen at the time of her death was a difficult period for a boy in general, and not having the loving hand of a woman around might have made it harder for him.

If things worked out with Tim, I hoped Tripp learned to accept me. Not that I had any crazy thoughts that it would work out. I was still undecided on that.

Yes, I was open to it, but would it be what I wanted it to be? Would we be able to build a relationship with who we are now? Only time would tell.

Friday morning, I texted Henley. He said he was away for tactical response training over the weekend but would be happy to reach out to Tripp early next week to set up a time to talk.

I was almost ready Saturday afternoon when Tim knocked on my door at five-thirty. With butterflies flying madly in my stomach, I wiped my hands over the skirt I wore and shook back my hair before I opened the door.

Tim stood on the other side looking mouthwatering in a navy sports coat and a white button-down shirt with dark jeans. "Hi," he said with a smile that made the butterflies go crazy.

"Hi, come in. I am almost ready."

He stepped into the house, and I stared at him, unsure how to greet him. Did I hug him? Kiss him?

He seemed as confused about it as I did and leaned forward after a moment and brushed his lips over my cheek. "You look beautiful."

"You look pretty good yourself." I grinned at him and got lost in his eyes for a moment. "Um, let me grab my purse and check the back door."

He stepped into the living room, and his eyes went to the wall of pictures again while I gathered my purse and ensured the back door was locked.

"Okay, I'm ready. Where are we going?"

"It's a surprise."

I laughed. "I don't love surprises."

"I know you don't. But you are going to have to trust me on this."

I chuckled as we headed toward the front door again. Tim reached around me and grabbed the doorknob, and I glanced at him. Our faces were mere inches apart, and he glanced at my lips.

"Before we go, I need you to do one thing," I said breathlessly.

"What's that?"

"Kiss me so I don't drive myself crazy thinking about it."

He chuckled as his hand curled around my neck and pulled me closer. "Thank god you said that."

It wasn't a crazy intense kiss, but it helped to calm my nerves and possibly his, and after he pulled back, he said, "That's all you get right now. Otherwise, we will never leave your house."

"That's not a bad thing." I giggled.

"You are trouble." He stepped away and opened the door for me. He then held the door of his SUV open so I could get in.

Once on the road, the butterflies began to calm, and I enjoyed the company and the ride. We talked about his work while we drove, and Tim told me about a few other people he had run into from childhood.

We drove about thirty minutes outside of town, and he turned down a long drive into a winery. "A winery?"

"Yes. They just opened a small restaurant here. The wife of one of the men I work with runs it."

"Wonderful! I love trying new places."

"He said it is pretty special, so I hope it is good too."

"I am sure it will be." I had been to the winery once many years ago for a girls' afternoon of wine tasting and frivolous girl talk, but I had not heard about the restaurant.

He parked, and there were only about ten cars. "I guess they aren't that busy right now."

"It is by reservation, and they only have a few tables. Nate had to pull some strings to get me one." He held his arm out to me, and I curled my arm around his.

"Nice to know people, isn't it?"

"Yes, it is." He covered my hand with his other one and escorted me up the stairs. Little fairy lights burned along the wood beams, and soft music played from hidden speakers.

Inside, we stepped into the winery storefront, and I glanced around at all the bottles in the racks. A man in a suit stood behind the tasting area and smiled brightly. "Evening."

"Good evening. I have a reservation for Tim Kohl."

"We have been expecting you. Right this way, sir."

Tim let me proceed in front of him, and I followed the man through an arch and into a hallway. Back here, you could hear a little chatter and a few utensils clicking against china, but it was muted.

He walked us through another arch and down a set of terracotta steps. At the bottom, he glanced back and smiled, then turned to the right and proceeded down another hallway. A waitstaff member came through an arch and politely stood to the side so we could pass.

We went under that arch, and I quickly peered in to see three tables, all occupied by couples. We turned into the next arch, and in that room, there was a single table in the middle. On the opposite side was a wall of windows that looked out over the field of vines.

"Wow, this is breathtaking," I said as I glanced around.

"This is our best room," the man said. "I'm Jerome, and your server will be Annabelle. If there is anything that we can get for you, please let us know."

Tim held my chair out for me, and I sat down and set my purse at my feet as Tim took the other seat. Jerome poured us water and then collected two menus from a small table off to the side. He held them out to us. "The special tonight is a lobster ravioli with fresh squash puree and linguini, and a filet with roasted peppers and cauliflower mash, with a red wine gravy."

"Oh, yum," I said. "I'm not sure I need to see the menu after that."

Tim laughed. "Look at the menu. You will change your mind five times before you finally decide."

Jerome excused himself and left us alone in the room. I took a moment to glance around, loving the atmosphere and that we were alone.

Tim glanced over the menu, and I took a moment to study him unnoticed. Small lines were around his eyes, and his skin was tanned from the California sun. His jaw was clean-shaven, and my fingers ached to run over his face. There was a small scar on his right cheek, and I wondered how and when he got that. I had missed so much of life with this man and my heart ached at that thought.

He glanced up. "What did you decide on?"

"I haven't even looked yet," I replied.

"Don't you think you should? I am sure the waitress will be here soon."

I nodded and opened the menu, but all I could see were the years that passed us by and the things I wanted to know about his life—starting with why he broke things off.

I forced myself to concentrate for a few moments and decided it was easier to just get the filet that Jerome had mentioned. I set the menu aside as Annabelle entered the room.

Tim asked what I was having and then decided to get the same, along with whatever bottle of wine they thought would pair the best.

He looked at me after she left the room. "You're staring."

"I am."

"What's on your mind, Carmen?"

I swallowed; it was time to talk this out. If there was any chance that we would work things out and build a relationship, I needed to understand why it ended in the first place. After that, we could move forward because I couldn't do that with unanswered questions. "Why exactly did you break up with me?"

CHAPTER TWENTY-SIX

TIM

I blinked and returned the intense stare. "You want to start the night with that one?"

"I think we need to start with that. If we don't, I will spend the entire night wondering."

I sighed and opened my mouth to speak when Annabelle returned and showed me the wine she had chosen. We went through the rigamarole of opening the bottle, pouring some, and then she told me to let it breathe for a few moments before I tasted it. She set the bottle aside and said she would return shortly.

During that time, it gave me the moments I needed to come up with a reply.

"For months, I was devoted to you and our relationship. I wanted nothing more than to come back and be with you, but I was ending my junior year, and there was so much to do."

"You mean other girls to sleep with?"

"No, that's not what I meant. Yeah, I met a lot of girls, but none of them compared to you, Carmen. I didn't date anyone until after I had decided to call it off."

"But you never actually did. You just told me you needed some time. Then you disappeared."

"I thought I had made it clear."

"You didn't." She lifted her chin defiantly. "Maybe if you had, I wouldn't have sat around waiting for your needed time to be over."

"I'm sorry, Carmen. That's all I can tell you. I was young and stupid, and as much as I loved you, I needed to see what else was out there."

"Well, you found something," she said as she leaned back in her seat and messed with her napkin.

"I did, and I'm not going to apologize for that. Emily and I had a good life, and I loved her very much."

She was quiet for a few seconds as she stared out the window, then smiled brighter than I expected. "I'm glad you did. I am not angry that you found love, Tim. I am happy for you and sorry that she died. I can only imagine how difficult that was for you and the children."

"Thank you for saying that." I contemplated if I wanted to bring this up but decided now was the time to clear the air. I had thought over this several times, and it bothered me more than I cared to admit. "Were you serious when you said you never moved on because of me?"

She lifted her shoulder slightly. "Maybe, I don't know. I blurted all of that out because I was worried, confused, and being dramatic at the time."

"You? Dramatic?" I replied with a grin.

"Yes, I know, it's crazy." She smiled back at me, and Annabelle returned to check on us and see if I had tasted the wine. I did and told her it was good. She poured our glasses, left us some warm bread, and disappeared again.

If we were going to be asking difficult questions, then it was my turn. "How many men have you been with?"

Her brows rose. "Wow, talk about a personal question."

"You started it, and since you probably know the answer to how many women I have been with, I figured it was only fair to know about your past." I paused. "Especially since we have already been intimate."

She sipped her wine, then fiddled with the stem momentarily as she contemplated her answer. "Not counting you, I have been with five. Two in college and three since."

Five over twenty years wasn't as bad as I expected. I could deal with five. "And none of them worked out?"

"No, none of them did."

"I'm sorry you never found someone. When I returned here, I was sure I'd find you married with several kids."

"No husband, no kids," she stated before she sipped her wine again.

"Well..." I lifted my glass and held it out to her. "To us getting to know one another again."

She clinked her glass to mine and sipped. "Do you miss California?" she asked after putting her glass down.

"Some parts of it. I don't miss the traffic." I laughed. "You can't go anywhere out there without traffic. Unless you are up in the mountains."

"Did you go there often?"

"Emily loved to ski, so we went to Lake Tahoe once or twice a year."

"I hear it is beautiful there."

"It is. Words can't describe it. You should go sometime. I could take you."

"I'm not a skier. However, Coral is. Perhaps you should take her."

I gave her an irritated look. "I am not interested in taking your sister."

"But you would be interested in taking me?"

"Maybe, if you'd like to go."

"I guess we will see what happens."

"You could always go during the summer. The lake is incredible. No matter what time of year you go, there are always things to do. The kids always like to go zip-lining while we are there."

"I did that once. That was fun."

"It is fun."

"Maybe I will visit sometime," she replied casually, and suddenly, I wanted nothing more than to take her.

Emily and I loved going there, and our rented house had a great view of the lake from the Nevada side. It was only a short walk down the hill to get to an area where the kids enjoyed climbing over the rocks.

Our conversation progressed over dinner, and we talked about different things, from places in California to people we had known in school. There was never a lull or any awkwardness, and as we finished our dessert of homemade chocolate cheesecake, I realized how quickly we had slipped back into our easy banter.

After dinner, Annabelle suggested we slip out the back door and walk through the vineyard. There was a fire pit back there, and we could watch the sunset.

We took her up on her suggestion, and as we strolled down the path, Carmen's shoulder kept brushing against my arm. It was driving me nuts, but not in a bad way. The sensation was traveling from my arm straight down my spine into my groin, and I ached to pull her into my arms and kiss her again.

We paused down the path and stared at the stars that filled the sky above. It was a beautiful way to end our date here, and I put my arm around her back and pulled her to me. It felt right, and she cozied up to my chest, wrapping her arm around me and resting her head on my chest.

I looked down at her and lifted her chin so she looked at me. I stared into her beautiful blue eyes, leaned down, and kissed her full lips. The kiss was tender and loving and full of unspoken promises.

Eventually, we made our way back to the building and around to the front parking lot. There were a few more cars than before, but not many, and I would have to thank Nate for his suggestion to come here. It was perfect.

We were both a little quieter on the ride home, and I wondered what she was thinking. I also wondered if she would invite me in when we returned to her house. I glanced at the clock on the dashboard and saw it was still early, so hopefully she would, and we could drink another glass of wine and talk more. Or snuggle up on the couch and kiss a little bit.

After I pulled into her driveway, I glanced at her. She was watching me. "Yes?"

"Do you want to come in?"

"I'd like that."

She nodded and climbed out of the car before I could get out. She walked straight toward the door, not looking back, and I wondered if she was nervous to have me here.

She unlocked it, stepped inside, flipped on the lights, and then closed the door as soon as I entered.

She turned to me, her lips parted, and I saw something I had not expected to see—desire. I inhaled sharply as I took a step forward, and like magnets, the two of us collided in the space between.

My lips crushed against hers, and her arms banded around my neck, pulling me down more. I walked her back a few steps to the door and let my mouth travel down her neck. Jesus, she felt so good, tasted so good, and the perfume she wore had been driving me nuts all night.

She whimpered as I kissed down her neck, and then I stopped and pulled back. "Carmen, if you don't want to take this any further tonight, tell me now because I'm not sure I'll be able to stop if we continue like this."

She didn't speak words, but her actions said it all. She cupped the back of my head and brought my mouth to hers as she ran her other hand down my back to my waistband.

I moaned as I deepened our kiss, and after a few minutes of heavy petting in the foyer, we pulled back, breathing hard, and she took hold of my hand and pulled me toward the steps.

I didn't even hesitate to follow. She led me up the steps to her room, and once inside, I spun her around and began kissing her again. She pushed my jacket off and started to unbutton my shirt immediately. It reminded me of when we were younger.

She wasn't the shy girl she had once been, and within a few moments, we were both naked and falling onto the bed.

I propped myself on my elbows and stared at her. "You're beautiful, Carmen." The words were said with a reverence I felt deep inside of me.

"Thank you," she replied shyly.

"I'm sorry that I hurt you and wasn't there for you." I meant those words too.

"You're here now."

"Yes, I am."

I leaned forward, taking her lips again. As we kissed, she laced her hand with mine, and I felt my wedding ring pushing against her skin. For a moment, I almost stopped as a pang of guilt filled me. Yes, we had already had sex before, but that wasn't like this. This was methodically making love, not just bringing our bodies together for satisfaction. Was I ready to let go of what I had shared with Emily and move on—letting someone else in?

Carmen pulled back, gauging the change that had come over me. "Are you okay? We can stop."

The fact that she cared enough to ask meant the world to me. I brushed my hand along her face. "I'm okay."

She nodded. "It must be difficult."

"It's a little strange," I told her, being honest.

"We can stop."

Holding her chin between my fingers, I shook my head. "I don't want to stop, Carmen. I want to make love to you."

She ran her fingers through my hair. "Then make love to me, Tim."

And that's what I did. Carmen and I took it slowly and got to know each other's bodies in a way we never had before. When we were teens, it was about the act of sex, but now it was so much more. Feelings were involved, and the need to please and be pleased.

Afterward, I lay with her head on my shoulder, her arm over my chest, and I tried not to compare sex with her to what I had shared with Emily, but it was hard.

They were both such loving women, and I had known Emily so well that I only had to listen to the sounds she made or notice how her body moved to understand what she needed next. With Carmen, I had to pay a bit more attention. It was exciting and fun, and as I released a heavy breath, I felt content for the first time in a very long time.

"Are you all right?" Carmen asked softly.

"I am, are you?"

She lifted her head. "I am more than all right. I am pretty damn fabulous right now."

I chuckled. "I'm glad to hear that. It was a little different than when we were younger and last time."

"A little?" She laughed. "That was a lot different than when we were younger, and our last tryst was more about being horny and not connecting the way we just did."

I tweaked her nose. "Yes, I agree with you."

She gnawed on her bottom lip for a few seconds. "You aren't disappointed, are you?"

"What? No! How could I be disappointed?"

She shrugged lightly and rolled to her back, staring at the

ceiling. "I guess I assumed you were comparing me to your wife."

Ouch, I winced. "Maybe a part of me was, but not really. I thought more about how easy it was to read Emily, but I need to pay closer attention to you."

She turned and looked at me. "Is that a bad thing?"

I smiled and rolled to my side before stroking her cheek. "No, Carmen, that is a very good thing, and I look forward to listening a lot more."

27

CHAPTER TWENTY-SEVEN

CARMEN

Yes, we had previously had sex, but that episode had been frantic and exciting. It had been strictly about physical closeness, not a more profound mental connection. I knew it might be difficult for Tim to take that step, but I was ready. I needed to know if this attraction was because of the past or if it could be the start of a future.

So far, so good, I thought as he said that my being different from his wife was a good thing.

I was glad to hear that because Tim had rocked my world. I wasn't ready to admit that to him, but I did to myself. I had slept with other men, and none of them had ever turned my insides to jelly as he had. His strong hands had been firm but not abrasive, and his mouth—my god—his mouth had been masterful in all the right places.

So much so that I was practically ready to go again, but he lifted his arm and looked at his watch—a telltale sign that he was probably starting to overthink things a bit, and it was time to let him go so that he could ponder them alone. Although, this time, I wouldn't hide in the bathroom until he left. I'd make him feel comfortable enough to go without things being odd.

I pretended to yawn and stretch. "You should probably get going."

He chuckled. "Are you kicking me out already?"

"Oh, I'd invite you to stay, but I know that's not happening. You have kids waiting for you at home."

He sighed. "That is true. I should get going. I told Tripp I wouldn't be too late."

"Then you better get a hustle on because it's almost ten." I pushed his shoulder playfully. "I don't want you to get yourself grounded."

He chuckled. "Now, that would be funny."

I pasted on a grin, but it slipped away as he sat up and put his back toward me to gather his clothes. "Do you mind if I use your bathroom?"

"Be my guest. Clean towels are in the linen closet if you'd like one."

He winked back at me and then padded into the bathroom, glancing around the room a little as he went. He closed the door, and I stared at where he had been lying. It had been a few years since I'd had a man in my bed, and no man had ever slept there all night. Would the day ever come when I would have a man beside me all night? Could Tim be that man?

I continued to dwell on that as I collected my robe and then sat on the bed, staring at his shoes lying haphazardly on the floor where he had kicked them off. How badly I wished that he could stay, but I knew he couldn't. When we were growing up, we were always hiding and sneaking around to have sex, but now we were adults, and we could be more open about it.

The bathroom door opened, and the smile magically appeared back on my face. Tim grinned. "You look adorable sitting there in that robe."

I giggled playfully. "You want to take it back off me?"

"Oh, don't tempt me. I want to, but I need to get going." He collected his shoes and then sat beside me. "I have to ask you a question, Carmen."

"Then ask."

He turned and looked at me seriously. "Are you on anything?"

Well, talk about taking the fuel out of the fire as I realized what he was asking—and the associated answer. Whoops! "Um, no. I should have mentioned that earlier."

His brows jumped. "You think?"

"Hey, you didn't think about it either," I said, and then I mentally calculated where I was on my cycle. It wasn't good news.

"Because I just assumed," he stated. "Does that mean you aren't taking birth control?"

I stood and tightened the tie on my robe. "No, actually, I'm not. It's not like I have sex regularly, and in case you forgot, I am above the age that taking birth control is safe."

"But you've been dating Chad?"

I shrugged a shoulder. "Yes, and he always used a condom."

He frowned. "Carmen, is there any chance you could get pregnant?"

"Tim." I rolled my eyes and chuckled. "There is always a chance you can get pregnant if you don't use protection. I would think that you would understand that by now."

His brow furrowed deeper, and he focused on shoving his feet into his shoes and tying them.

"Don't tell me you are mad."

"Well, I'm not happy about it."

I laughed. "What's the worst that could happen?"

He finished tying his shoes and stood. "You could get pregnant, and then I'd have to worry about raising another child."

I stared at him, shocked by his harsh tone and his words. "Are you telling me you don't want any more kids?"

"No, I don't. I have three already. I don't need any more."

My heart dropped. Suddenly, the fairy-tale ending that had been building in my heart went up in flames. "So, if you decided to be with someone else, you wouldn't be open to having more children?"

"No," he stated flatly.

"Oh, I see," I replied and turned to leave the room.

"I'm sorry, Carmen, but I've been through the baby stage and am not keen on going through it again."

I kept walking and heard him follow me after he sighed heavily. I was trying not to cry and hustled down the steps to the foyer. Once there, I went straight to the door and prepared to open it.

"Carmen." He took hold of my arm. "I'm sorry that's not the answer you wanted to hear."

"No, that's fine. That's how you feel. I'm sorry that we didn't have this conversation sooner. It might have saved us both some anguish."

He tried to take me by the shoulders, but I sidestepped. "Come on, Carmen. I don't want you to be upset."

I snapped my face up to him. "Upset? I'm not upset."

"The hell you aren't."

I glared at him. "Okay, maybe I am upset, but that's not your problem." I stepped out of his grasp and grabbed the doorknob. "If by chance I get pregnant from tonight, I will make sure not to bother you with the baby stage."

"Carmen, if you get pregnant, you know I wouldn't let you do it alone."

"Do I? I don't know that Tim. You just told me that you didn't want to go through that again. Unlike you, I don't have a family and want one. So, if you are saying that you won't have more kids, this thing between you and me is over before it can begin again."

"You're going to end it because of that?"

"Yes," I stated forcefully, holding back the tears. "I want kids, Tim."

He looked suddenly angry. "Did you want to have sex with me tonight because you were hoping you'd get pregnant?"

"What?" I snapped back at him. "How dare you even say that!"

"I say that because you were in an awfully big rush to get me back here tonight and seduce me."

I scoffed. "Me? You were right there with me! It's not like I had to try hard!"

He huffed and shook his head. "I should get going before we say something we can't take back."

"Too late for that, but I agree—you should leave."

He shoved his hands to his hips and stared at the floor. "Carmen, can we just calm down for a moment and talk?"

I yanked open the door and stood back. "I believe you were just leaving."

"Carmen."

"Goodbye, Tim. Your *children* are waiting for you."

He glared at me but didn't say anything else as he stepped out of the house. I promptly closed the door and turned the deadbolt. Then I flipped off the lights and ran up the stairs to my room. I threw myself on the bed and let the tears explode.

That was the second time that he had broken my heart. No, I had not purposely brought him to my bed to get pregnant, but would that be a bad thing? Obviously, to him, it was.

I cried for what once was and for what would never be. On our date tonight, I saw how perfect our lives could be. I saw the man I had once fallen in love with and imagined how incredible a life with him would be. I had even pictured us with his children, which broke me the most.

Maybe subconsciously, that was what I had wanted all along. I saw his children and how beautiful and special they were, and I was jealous of that. I had lost him many years before, but he was back now, and I wanted a piece of him. A part that I thought I deserved.

I put my hand to my stomach, willing myself to conceive from the seed he had planted. I could do it alone. I wouldn't need him. I had my family to help me. Hell, if it got too hard to be around him here, I could move to Texas and live near Cara. I could quickly get hired by a practice there.

I wept on and off as I pictured myself going through a pregnancy alone and how I had lost the man I loved twice in my lifetime. Eventually, I drifted off to a fitful sleep.

I HOPED that the light of the day would make me feel better when I woke. It didn't.

I went downstairs and saw my purse lying on the floor. I quickly gathered it and pulled out my phone to find the battery had died. I plugged it in to charge before I made coffee.

After brewing my coffee, I sat on a stool at the island and turned on my phone. I wanted to see if Tim had sent me any messages. It took a moment, but finally, the notifications came down. I skimmed through them, noting several texts from Candy, Cara, and Evan, but there was nothing from Tim.

Nothing! He didn't even try to send me a message to say he was home or he was sorry. What the hell?

I set my phone on the counter and massaged my temples. What did I expect? He did not leave on good footing last night. I knew Tim well enough to know that it lasted a few days when he was angry. We'd had many arguments when we were younger, and it would always take a few days for him to cool down. Then he would show up at my door, begging me to forgive him, and the world would right itself.

Would that happen again? Sadly, I had a feeling it wouldn't. This wasn't an argument over something simple we disagreed on. This was a fundamental life-changing decision, and he had told me his stance on it.

Cara's face popped up on my screen as if knowing I needed to talk, and I answered.

"How did it go?" she asked after I said hello.

"Horrible," I groaned.

"How could it have been horrible?" she asked in surprise.

"Oh, Cara, the date itself was perfect. It was romantic and sweet, and we had a great time." I proceeded to tell her about the winery and dinner.

"What's horrible about that? It sounds perfect, Carmen."

"It was after he brought me home that it took a downhill turn."

"Why?"

"He came in, and we ended up in bed together."

She chuckled. "Was the sex that bad?"

"No, it was perfect too."

"Then I don't understand. What aren't you telling me?"

"We didn't use protection."

"So, that's not the end of the world. God knows, Brian and I didn't use protection the first time we had sex either."

I laughed. "Yeah, but that's because he was claiming you." Brian had been Ryan back then, and he had infiltrated a biker gang. To protect Cara, he had claimed her. To do that, he had to have unprotected sex. It was just what biker gangs did.

"True, but I know you care about him, Carmen. What's the worst that can happen? You get pregnant, fall in love with him again, get married, and live happily ever after."

"That would all be well and good, except he doesn't want any more kids."

"Oh—" she said softly. "Why doesn't he want more kids? Did he say?"

"Yes, he told me he's been through that stage before and doesn't want to do that again."

"Well, that sucks."

"It does, and he insinuated that I brought him home to seduce him and get pregnant. Like I had the whole thing planned."

"Did you?"

"No! Of course I didn't have it planned."

"And what would you do if you found out you were pregnant?"

"Well, now if I find out I am pregnant, I will have to decide what to do."

"Would you get an abortion?"

"No! I could never do that." I sighed. "If I were pregnant, I would do what I needed to do. I even thought a few minutes ago I could move to Texas and start over."

"You could, or you could tell him to suck it up and be a father."

"I would never make him do something he doesn't want."

"Do you think he might have been overwhelmed?"

"I don't know, maybe."

"Maybe you should just give him some time. He will come around, just like he always did."

"Yeah, maybe. I don't know that he will, but we'll see."

"Not to rub it in, but I have some news for you."

"What's that?"

"I'm pregnant."

Despite feeling like crap, I grinned. "Are you really?"

"Yes, I am. I just found out a few minutes ago and wanted you to be the first to know."

"You mean second."

"No, first. Brian doesn't even know yet. He's not home."

I laughed. "Okay, now that's awesome."

"I hope it's a girl this time."

"Yeah, I do too. I'd love to buy Daisy Duke shorts for her."

"No, you won't!" she said with a laugh. "That will never

happen." She got quiet for a few seconds. "It would be pretty cool if you were pregnant. We could go through it together."

Now that was a nice thought, but then again, maybe not. "Yeah, that would be good," I said softly, knowing that if I were pregnant by chance, I would have many hurdles to overcome before I could enjoy it.

28

CHAPTER TWENTY-EIGHT

TIM

I sat in my car for a minute, trying to understand what the hell had just happened. One minute we lay cozily in bed, and the next she marched me out the door.

I stared at her dark house, half tempted to bang on her door and hash this out immediately, but I didn't. Instead, I started my SUV and drove home.

Emily and I had made a pact many years ago to never go to bed angry. There had been times in our relationship when we had stayed up for hours rehashing something that had caused an argument, but in the end, we had always climbed under the sheets and kissed each other goodnight.

The following morning, we would discuss it further over breakfast, and usually, by lunch, we were completely over the night before. We had learned to make concessions and to admit fault. We had learned to listen to one another and try to see things from the other's point of view.

I hated leaving Carmen when she was so upset, but I needed to give her space unless I wanted to stay there and argue with her over something that might or might not happen. I knew that, eventually, she would understand. If there was anyone who could understand my thoughts, it was Carmen. She had always been able to see my point of view, and while she might disagree with it, she would understand where I was coming from.

I pulled into my driveway and stared at the house I had rented. What would I do if Carmen were pregnant? I had no clue. Emily and I had decided shortly after we got married that we wanted three kids. After Savannah was born, Emily tied her tubes, and we never had to worry about it again.

I didn't even think about that tonight until I was in the bathroom cleaning up and reached into the closet to get a towel. On the middle shelf was a box of tampons, and it immediately got my mind spinning. Where was Carmen in her cycle? Was there a chance?

I pushed the door open, not wanting to think about it anymore, and went inside. The television played softly in the family room, and I found Tripp kicked back on the sofa, watching a movie.

"How was your night?" I asked him as I dropped my keys on the counter.

"Fine," he replied.

"I'm surprised you are down here."

He grinned. "I just wanted to make sure you got home safely."

I chuckled. "Yeah, well, I'm home. You can go to bed."

He paused his movie and entered the kitchen while I poured myself a glass of water. "How was your date?"

"Dinner was very nice. I know a place you can go if you want to impress a girl, although you better start saving your pennies."

"Or get a job," he suggested. "I was thinking about that."

"What? Getting a job?"

"Yeah, would that be okay?"

"I guess. Where are you thinking of working?"

"I noticed that they needed a busboy at the tavern. I could

apply there." I knew he wanted to say something else, so I waited. "I was also thinking that I need a car."

"We went from a job to a car pretty fast."

"Yeah, well, it's not like I could hop on a bus," he retorted. "It's hard to get around out here. Unless I borrow your car, and you need it."

"That is true," I said with a sigh. "Let me think about it, Tripp. It's been a long night."

He studied me as I sipped my water and set my glass near the sink.

"Did something happen?"

"No."

"You look upset about something."

I walked toward him. "Nothing that concerns you, but I appreciate you asking. I'm going to head up to bed."

"Okay, I'm going to finish my movie down here and head up."

"Enjoy," I said as I walked away.

It would probably be helpful for Tripp to have a car. He was right that it was hard to get around out here. The town had grown a lot in twenty years, but not enough that it had a major bus line. He could probably call a car service, but that added up.

I would start looking around to see what I could find for him. Maybe if he got a job, too, he could contribute toward it a little bit. That would be helpful.

I was in bed, staring at the ceiling, reflecting on my night. It had been the perfect evening—great company, delicious food, excellent location, and then sex. God, I had missed having sex.

At first, I felt a little guilty, but then I forced myself to let it go. Emily had wanted me to move on, and she had even suggested it be with Carmen.

I frowned. Was I only interested in Carmen because of Emily? Had I gravitated toward her the moment I was back because Emily had mentioned I should look her up years ago?

That didn't feel right. Perhaps Carmen and I were meant to be together. Maybe back then hadn't been right, but now was the right time. How could it be the right time if she wanted kids and I didn't?

It wasn't that I didn't like kids. I loved them. I had three great kids, but my kids were finding their independence. Tripp wanted a job and a car; Dean was getting into swimming again, and Savannah would be neck-deep in half a dozen activities in no time.

Plus, I had a new job. How would I ever have time to deal with a baby? The thought gave me a headache, and I shoved the thoughts aside to consider them later.

―――――

WHEN I WOKE UP, I had hoped to find a text from Carmen, but I didn't. Perhaps it was too early. She did like to sleep in on the weekends. She always had. I was sure that later in the day, she would reach out. Probably apologize for last night.

I spent the day working around the house, and Tripp helped me organize the garage. I didn't want to unpack everything because I knew we wouldn't be there long, but I wanted my tools and such organized. When we finished, I had enough room to put my SUV inside.

"Dad, what's for dinner?" Savannah asked.

"I hadn't thought much about that, Savannah Bee."

"Can we go to the tavern for dinner?" Tripp asked. "I could see if that busboy position is still open."

"What's a busboy?" Savannah asked.

"The person who clears off the tables and makes sure the dirty dishes are taken to the back to get washed," I replied.

She wrinkled up her nose. "You want to do that?"

"No," Tripp grumbled. "But I want a job."

I glanced at my phone for the fortieth time that day. Why hadn't Carmen sent me a message?

"Can we, Dad?" Tripp pulled me back to the conversation.

"Sure, but after, we need to stop by the store and get groceries. We need some quick meals for this week."

Dean groaned. "I hate grocery shopping."

"Grocery shopping is fun," Savannah said to him, and I chuckled.

"I have to agree with Dean. I'm not a fan of grocery shopping," I stated.

"Then I can't wait until I'm old enough to drive to go for you."

"Honey." I grinned at her. "You got yourself a deal!"

We were in the car heading to the tavern for dinner a few minutes later. Candy wasn't there this time, but the assistant manager told Tripp to fill out the application and she would give it to Mike when he returned. She mentioned that he was at dinner with the family, and I remembered being invited a few times to Sunday dinner at the Winston house.

Maybe that is why I hadn't heard from Carmen. Perhaps she had been busy with her family today. That made more sense than her ignoring me.

We were halfway through dinner when Candy entered the front door, and Carmen was with her. They were laughing about something, and they disappeared into the bar area. Well, she looked to be in a better mood than she had been in last night. That was good. I would talk to her after I finished eating.

I was almost done when I glanced up and saw Chad enter and glance around. He skimmed right past me and then headed toward the bar. No freaking way. Was he here to see Carmen?

"Excuse me, guys. I need to use the restroom." I set my napkin beside my plate and headed toward the entrance to the bar. The restrooms were just around the corner, so the kids wouldn't know I wasn't going to use them.

I paused as I entered the bar and scanned around, instantly finding Carmen at a table on the other side. She was smiling at Chad as he approached the table. He paused beside her and then leaned down and kissed her cheek. What. The. Actual. Fuck!

The two of them laughed over something, and he took a seat and glanced at the server approaching the table. On the tray in her hand was a dark brown-colored martini, and she set it down in front of Carmen. I started marching toward her, not even thinking about what I was doing.

Carmen picked up her drink as she laughed at what the server had said, and I reached around the woman and took the glass from Carmen's hand. "What are you doing?"

Three pairs of eyes snapped toward me, but Carmen was the only one who kept her attention locked. I heard Chad order a beer, and the server rushed off as I set the drink on the opposite side of the table.

"I'm having a drink. What is your problem, Tim?"

"You're drinking? What if you're pregnant?"

Her eyes went as wide as possible and then narrowed into dangerous slits. Then I realized what I had just said in a public place.

Before we could say anything, a female voice rang out behind us, "Well, Tim, that's a great way to break the ice. Why don't you and I take a little walk before Carmen tosses her drink in your face."

Candy snaked her arm around my elbow and pulled. I shifted back to look at Carmen's face and saw fury written over it. I glanced at Chad, and he looked both confused and humored simultaneously.

"Come on, you look like you could use another beer," Candy said as she pulled harder on my arm. Carmen reached over the table and collected her glass, then took a very precise sip while keeping her gaze locked on mine as if taunting me.

I let Candy lead me away, and I shook my head and winced

at myself. Shit! I never should have done that. Candy pulled me from the bar and down the hallway toward the bathroom.

"What the hell was that?" she said when she finally stopped and let me go.

"I don't know. I wasn't thinking."

She crossed her arms over her chest and leaned her head to the side. "That was obvious."

"I just—" I stopped and shook my head, unsure what to say. I had no clue if Carmen had told Candy anything about what had happened.

"You just thought that because you had sex with her, and there is a slim chance that she might be pregnant, you had any say in what she does?" She hiked a brow and continued before I could reply. "What makes you think you have the right to say anything after telling her you didn't want any more kids?"

"Jesus, she told you all of it, didn't she?"

She nodded dramatically. "You were a big topic of conversation tonight at the dinner table."

"What? She talked about that at the dinner table?" Just freaking great!

"Yes. Most of us found it amusing; unfortunately, not everyone."

I heaved out a sharp breath. "Let me guess? Your father had something to say about that?"

"Only that you have never been worth the heartbreak, and she was better off avoiding you at all costs. I think he said something else about wishing you had never returned to town."

"I am sure he did."

"Hey, no daddy likes their daughter to be brokenhearted."

"Candy, I'm not trying to break her heart."

"Oh, no? Then why tell her you don't want kids—after you have sex—and then come in here and demand to know why she might be drinking if she is pregnant?"

I leaned against the wall and closed my eyes. "Because I'm an asshole."

"You said it. I didn't." She touched my arm. "You better give her time to calm down after that."

"What is she doing with that guy?"

"Why? Are you jealous?"

"No, I'm wondering if she played me. She told me it was over with him, yet here she is, and I saw him kiss her when he got to the table."

"Tim, I'm pretty sure nothing is going on with Chad."

"Then why is she with him?"

"I guess you will have to ask her—later. Don't do it tonight unless you want to cause more of a scene than you already have."

"Fine," I growled.

"I see your son wants a job here. Do you want him to work here?"

"I don't have a problem with it. He's the one who suggested it."

"Okay, well, do you mind if I have a word with him? Mike just got back, and we'd love to fill the position as quickly as possible."

"Sure," I told her. "And Candy, thank you for pulling me away."

"You're welcome." She paused. "You might want to think about your response last night and how you acted tonight. They don't quite match up."

"Yeah, I realize that now. Thanks," I replied dourly.

CHAPTER TWENTY-NINE

CARMEN

My date with Tim had come up at our Sunday family dinner, and while I didn't want to talk about it, everyone else seemed happy to—except my father—especially when I admitted that things had taken a wrong turn when the topic of kids had come up. I hadn't told everyone at the table that we had already had sex, but I suggested it was a topic of conversation at dinner. I also didn't tell them that I had kicked him out of my house after that either.

Only Candy and Cara knew because I had told Cara, and she had called Candy to check on me. Was it wrong to leave Coral out of the girl chat? Maybe, but she always seemed so preoccupied that no one ever wanted to bother her with our nonsense.

Candy, Coral, Alaina, and I did the dishes. Evan and Mike sat at the table with my father. Ethan and Riley were at Riley's parents' house for dinner this week. The Young family had the same tradition.

My father got up from the table and came to the sink where I stood. He set his glass down and leaned close to me. "Can I have a word with you?"

"Sure, Dad," I responded. Dad turned and walked away, and

everyone gave me different facial expressions, like I was heading to the principal's office. I rolled my eyes at them and followed my father out the back door to the porch, where it was a mild night.

"Did you need to tell me something?" With Cara in Texas, I was the oldest of the group, and sometimes the serious matters landed on my ears first.

"I wanted to talk to you about Tim."

I sank into the chair beside him. I should have known. "Dad, you don't have to worry."

"Don't I? That boy moved away many years ago and took a piece of you. It took a long time before you smiled again and did things with friends. I don't want to see that happen again."

"Dad, I was sixteen at the time. Yes, I was crushed that he moved away, but I'm fine now. If he were going to up and leave tomorrow, I would be sad to see him go, but it wouldn't break my heart."

"I'm not worried about him leaving. From what Alaina says, he's doing a good job and she wants to keep him. I'm more worried about things not working out between you two and you having to lose him again while he's still right there in front of you."

I considered what he was saying. Yes, it would suck if things didn't work, and already I was getting the feeling that they wouldn't, but I was mature enough—and I hoped he was too— to remain friends and put the past away where we should have put it before.

"Dad, I appreciate what you are saying, but I will be okay."

"Are you going to continue seeing him?"

"I don't know. I might."

"Didn't you recently go out with another man?"

"Chad, but that's over."

"So you aren't dating two men at once?"

I glanced at my watch. "Actually, I'm not, but I need to meet

Chad in a few minutes. He said he wanted to speak to me about something."

He frowned slightly. "Are you going to keep seeing Tim?"

"I don't know what I'm going to do, Dad. I need a little time to figure things out."

My father studied me, and I was a little shocked at the words out of his mouth. "Have you been intimate with Tim?"

"Um, do you really want to talk about that?"

"Yes, because I know for him to be intimate with someone else after being married for so long is a big deal. I wanted to make sure you were aware of that."

"Dad, I am very aware of that."

"I would think long and hard about what kind of a relationship you want, Carmen. You have always wanted children, and it would be a shame if you never got to experience that for yourself. Tim was married and had a life for himself. He's more set in his ways, with different concerns than yours. His priorities are to his children before anyone else, including you."

"I get what you are saying, Dad. I do."

He hesitated. "Before we go back in, I need to ask you a question."

Oh, man, now what? "Sure, do you need help with something?"

"Not really, but I wanted to ask if you might be upset if I started dating someone." My father's face pinkened slightly as he waited for my response.

That honestly had been the last thing on my mind. I reached over and took his hand. "Dad, if you think you are ready to do that, and you met someone, then go ahead and date them. You don't need my permission to do that."

"No, I know I don't, but I wanted to make sure that it wouldn't bother you or your siblings."

"We all want you happy, Dad. Mom has been gone for a while now, and we all know you are lonely."

He nodded. "There are moments."

"Then have fun, Dad. Go out and have fun."

"Do you think I should tell everyone else?"

I chuckled. "I think you should, or you risk the chance of it reaching them through the grapevine. Do you have someone special in mind?"

He nodded. "Silvia. Her name is Silvia. I met her at the doctor's office a few months ago." He glanced away, and I knew from the look on his face that he was thinking about my mother. "Do you think your mother would be disappointed in me?"

"No, Dad, I do not. I hope we get to meet Silvia sometime soon."

"Well, as long as no one has a problem with it, I'd like to invite her next week. She's also a widow but lost her only son recently. We have had coffee a couple of times and talked about it."

I grinned. "So you have already been on a date with her."

He scoffed. "Coffee isn't a date, Carmen."

I laughed. "I agree with you, and I am sorry to hear of her loss. How is she doing with it?"

"Handling it the best that she can. She had three children, and all have passed. She is the last in the family, and it weighs heavily on her."

"Aw, that's so sad, Dad. You need to invite her to dinner."

"Okay, I should ask the rest of the family."

I squeezed his hand. "No, I think you should invite her and introduce her next weekend. There is not one person in this house who doesn't want you happy."

"You think I should surprise them?"

And get them off my back, hell yes! "Of course! Let's keep it a secret, and next week bring her. I can't wait to meet her."

And now it made sense why he talked about intimacy after losing a wife. I did not doubt that subject had been on his mind.

I WAS at the tavern waiting in the bar for Chad to arrive. Candy had gone off to do something else and told me she would order a drink for me. Chad strolled into the room a few minutes later, and a few nervous twitters shifted through my belly.

"Thank you so much for meeting me," Chad said as he reached the table and brushed a kiss over my cheek.

"You're welcome. I have to admit, you have my curiosity."

He chuckled, and Tammy, the server, set a chocolate martini down in front of me and asked Chad what he wanted. Before he could reply, a hand reached between the server and me and took hold of my drink.

"What are you doing?" a deep voice asked, and I turned to see Tim.

"I'm having a drink. What is your problem, Tim?"

"You're drinking? What if you're pregnant?"

Oh, you did not just say that! How dare he say that in front of all these people? I glared at Tim, and before I could lose my mind on him, Candy dragged Tim away as I reached for the glass and took a sip.

I almost immediately spit it all over the table as I had expected a chocolate martini, but instead, it was chocolate milk. Gag! I hated chocolate milk.

I didn't have time to be angry with Candy because I was furious with Tim. How dare he do that to me! After not even communicating with me today, and then after what he said last night! Damn him. Damn him to hell! What did he even care if I was drinking and pregnant? He already told me he didn't want anything to do with a kid!

"Um," Chad stated on the other side of me, and I winced and prepared myself to face him. I tried to plaster on a smile, but I knew it was more of a grimace. "Is there something you want to share with me?"

I shook my head. "No, I'm sorry. Tim was way out of line for approaching this table, much less saying what he said."

"Is there a chance you could be pregnant?"

"No, I don't know, maybe," I quickly said and hesitated, but I told myself that I had no clue if I were or not, and until I did know something, I would treat it as if it were a no. "We were together, and we didn't use protection. It's no big deal."

"It seems like it is a big deal to him."

"Yeah, well, he's an ass." I rested my forearms on the table. "Anyway, I'd prefer not to talk about Tim. Why did you want to meet with me?"

"I needed to ask you a favor," he said as Tammy set his beer down and smiled at me.

"How is your martini?"

"Tell my sister that she is hilarious. Can you bring me a Coke, please?"

She laughed. "Sure."

I turned to Chad. "What can I do for you?"

"Well, I have a friend with a kid acting out. I was wondering if you might be able to help them."

And just like that, the stress of Tim vanished as I listened to Chad talk about his friend's kid. Of course I would help him, and we spent a few minutes discussing what he knew and the best way for them to contact me for an appointment.

Before we left, Chad leaned forward and put his hand over mine. "I hope things work out with you and Tim."

"I don't know if they will, Chad, but thank you."

"I am sure there is a very long story there."

"There is, but not one I feel like discussing."

"I appreciate you meeting with me."

"Of course," I replied, and then he dropped money on the table to cover the drinks and tip, brushed my cheek again with a kiss, and left me staring at the vacant seat.

Tim and I needed to chat, but I didn't think tonight would be a good night to have that. I quickly gathered my things and hustled out of the restaurant, hoping I wouldn't run into Tim again.

Halfway to my car, I noticed Tim's SUV and Chad walking away. Tim was staring after him, and he turned to see me.

I clenched my jaw and spun to return to the tavern. I did not want another scene.

"Carmen!"

I ignored him, and a few moments later, I heard his feet hitting the pavement as if he were running toward me. I had never run from a fight before, so I spun around, and he nearly plowed over me. "How dare you!"

"I'm sorry." He held his hands up to his sides. "I am very sorry. I had no right, but when I saw you with him after being with me last night and saw you drinking, I didn't stop to think."

"So, you had to announce to everyone in the bar that we slept together and didn't use protection?" I snapped, and he winced as he looked over my shoulder.

"Fuck," he muttered.

I heard a gruff laugh and turned to see Tripp approaching us. I just couldn't catch a break.

CHAPTER THIRTY

TIM

I returned to the table with Candy, and she spoke with Tripp for a few moments and then took him away for an interview. I paid, and the kids and I went outside. It was better that I wasn't in the building to avoid being tempted to go back to her table.

The kids were in their seats, and I stood beside the vehicle, talking to them through the door.

"Give me a moment, guys," I said as I saw the man who had been with Carmen heading my way. I closed the door to prevent them from hearing what was said.

"Do you have any idea how incredible that woman is?"

"I do," I stated.

"I don't think you do. You might have known her years ago, but you don't know who she is now. She's an incredibly caring woman who would do anything for anyone and tries everything she can to keep from hurting people."

"I already know that. She's been that way since she was twelve."

He blinked, unaware that I had known her quite that long. His gaze drifted down my chest to my feet and back up. "I don't know how you got her into bed, and that's not my business, but if you hurt that woman, I swear, I will come after you. You got that?"

"I'm not going to hurt her," I replied and fought not to wince because hadn't I already done that?

He scoffed. "Well, you already broke that promise." He sneered and leaned forward. "I'm watching you, Kohl. I might not be with Carmen anymore, but I will pick up the pieces after you break her heart. She deserves better than the stunt you pulled in there."

I wasn't sure if I should wish him good luck, tell him to take a hike, or hit him in the face. I decided to do nothing and instead watched as he walked away.

He paused a few steps away and turned back. "And your son is a damn good swimmer. Make sure he comes back to practice."

I shook my head as he turned to leave again, having not expected that, and glanced toward the tavern's entrance where I saw Carmen standing, but the moment I saw her, she turned back to the building. I guess she had hoped that I would be gone by now.

"Carmen!"

She kept walking, but as I reached her, she surprised me and turned around, getting into my face as she growled at me, "How dare you!"

"I am very sorry. I had no right, but when I saw you with him after being with me last night and saw you drinking, I didn't stop to think."

That was as much truth as I could give her.

"So, you had to announce to everyone in the bar that we slept together and didn't use protection?"

No sooner had she spoken the words, than I noticed someone approaching us and realized it was my son. "Fuck."

"You should have taken your own advice, Dad," he said as he skirted around us.

"Get in the truck, Tripp."

He didn't respond, and when I focused on Carmen again, she was massaging her temples. I touched her arm. "Carmen, I'm sorry."

"It was such a mistake."

"No," I told her as I stepped closer and ran my hands down her arms. "It wasn't a mistake."

"How can you say that? You got mad at me last night because you thought it was my responsibility to be on birth control. You never asked! Then you got rude about not wanting any more kids. Plus, we have tonight. It was a mistake to even go out with you. I should have known that things would never have worked."

She stepped back and put her hand up as I spoke. "Carmen, please—"

"No, Tim, there is nothing else to say. I need to go." She quickly stepped around me and hustled to her car.

I made my way back to my vehicle and climbed in. "Not a word," I growled toward my son, who sat in the passenger seat smirking.

"What? You don't want a lecture on what happens when you have unprotected sex?"

I slammed my eyes at him. "I know damn well what happens. I have three times the proof."

"Why?" he barked. "Why did you have to sleep with her?"

"Tripp, I am not having this conversation with you right now." I glanced at the other two kids in the back.

He shook his head and stared out the side window as I started the car. I was on the main road when I glanced his way. "How did the interview go?"

"Fine. I have a job. I start on Thursday."

"What time?"

"They want me to start right after school. Candy even

offered to pick me up and bring me to work until I could get a car. I told her I could walk."

"Okay, how often will you be working?"

"They asked if I could work Thursday through Sunday this week to get trained."

"How much are they paying you?"

"Twelve an hour, plus Candy said that the waitresses sometimes pass along some of their tips to the busboys."

"Twelve? That's pretty generous for a busboy position."

"That's what I thought. I heard a few kids at school talking about making nine or ten, and they thought that was good."

"I will have to speak with Megan and make sure she doesn't mind watching your brother and sister after school."

"I don't need a babysitter, Dad," Dean whined from the back seat.

"No, you don't, but your sister is not quite ready to be on her own, and it would be nice if you knew that there was someone who could help you if you needed it."

"I guess," Dean muttered.

We made it home, and I told the younger kids to head up, take their showers, and get ready for bed. I felt Tripp and I needed to discuss what happened.

No sooner had they disappeared up the stairs than Tripp turned on me, "Why did you sleep with her? How could you do that to Mom?"

"Did you forget that your mother is dead?"

"Of course I didn't forget that."

I sighed as I leaned back against the counter with my arms crossed. "I know that you think I should be faithful to your mother forever, but that's unrealistic, Tripp."

"I don't care! It's only been two years."

"Yes, two years without any affection. Without me having someone to confide in and share things with."

"You have us!"

"That's different, Tripp." I sighed again. "One day, you will understand. It's hard to explain it to you, but you must understand. I loved your mother very much. I still do. Just because I am dating—"

"Screwing someone else."

"Hey, watch it. Don't be rude. Just because I am being intimate with someone doesn't mean that I love your mother any less. Your mother would understand. We talked about this. We both promised one another that we would mourn for a while and then move on."

"I bet she wouldn't have."

"I know for a fact she would have," I replied. "Your mom knew about Carmen. She even suggested I look her up if the time ever came."

"She did not."

"She did."

"Is that why we moved here? Did you move us back here so you could hook up with your old girlfriend?" The anger was evident in his features.

I shook my head. "No. I came here because it was a good opportunity for my career. I had no idea if Carmen was even around this area or if she was married or what."

"Well, aren't you lucky?" he spat.

"Tripp, I don't know what is going to happen between Carmen and me, but I do know that if we do start dating seriously, then you will have to accept it."

"No, I don't, and don't even think of asking me to babysit for some stupid baby if you two have one."

I closed my eyes and hung my head. "What will you do if I decide to remarry one day and I do have another child?"

"I don't want anything to do with it or anyone you might marry."

"That's pretty cold, Tripp."

"I don't care," he retorted.

"I'm done with this conversation, Tripp. Why don't you head up to your room."

"Whatever," he scoffed and disappeared.

I had just sunk onto the couch and laid my head back when there was a knock at the door. It wasn't that late, but I wasn't expecting anyone either.

When I opened the door, I found Evan on the other side. "Hey, what are you doing here?"

He smirked. "I have come to give you some advice."

I held the door open. "Advice? Is Alaina not happy about something I'm doing at work?"

He laughed as he stepped in. "No, she thinks you are the cream in her coffee. I'm talking about my sister."

"Oh," I replied dryly as I shut the door. "You want a beer?"

"This conversation might require more than a beer, but we can start with that."

"That good, huh?"

He chuckled as he followed me into the house. "You buy this place?"

"God, no! I am renting until I can find a suitable place."

"No wonder there is nothing hung up," he commented as I pulled open the fridge and removed two beers.

"Let's sit outside. I can turn the fire pit on," I said as I handed one over to him and then twisted the cap off my bottle.

"It's a perfect night for that."

After we got settled, we chitchatted about the area and a few things that had changed since I was last here.

"There are a lot of things that are different and even more that are just the same," Evan said a few minutes later. "One of those things is Carmen."

"Has she changed or remained the same?"

He shrugged a shoulder. "She's changed a little bit, but she's still that driven woman you once knew."

"I can tell she is still driven. She has done well for herself."

He nodded as he swallowed. "She has, but she has also held herself back."

"How so?"

"By never getting involved with someone. She has dated some great guys, and ones that we all thought would be the one she would finally choose, but they never were."

"Are you saying that it's my fault?"

"No, I'm saying that my sister fell in love with you when she was a kid and never got over you. Either you two need to work this shit out together, or you need to tell her straight that there will never be a chance. Maybe she would have gotten over you if you had done that when you were younger."

It all came back to when we were sixteen and seventeen, and I did not officially break it off with her. "You would think that after so many years, she would have realized it was over."

"But is it? You two went out last night. You ended up in bed together. Is that being over?"

"Is there anyone who doesn't know we slept together?" I muttered.

"Probably, but that answer will likely be no by tomorrow."

"I am slowly remembering why I didn't like small-town living. In California, no one cared what you did. No one gossiped about you. You just came and went."

"Yeah, I see that. Sometimes I go with Alaina back to California, and I'm always happy to return."

"What do you suggest I do?"

"Personally, I think you need to figure out if there is a real chance for you and Carmen, and if not, you need to sit her down and tell her that. You have had a very different life, and she would understand if you told her it would never work. She might be upset, but she would deal with it."

"And if I want to see if there is something there?"

"Then you need to man up and realize a few things."

"Like what?"

"Like she hasn't been in a twenty-year relationship and never had a family. Family is important to her, and if you decide to build a life with her, she will love your kids as if they were hers, but she would expect you to make a few concessions."

"Meaning she would want to have a child."

"Or two—hell, maybe even three—but yes, she would want to have kids. If you aren't willing to consider that, then tell her now—in a nice way. Tell her that you are not in the least bit interested in having any more kids. Just don't play games with her."

"I'm not trying to play games, Evan. We had a great date last night. It was terrific, and I saw us doing much more of that together. Then we ended up in bed, and well, I guess I freaked out a little bit after I found out she wasn't on birth control."

"Would you be open to having more kids?"

I thought about that. "I honestly don't know. Emily and I decided that three was perfect, and we never considered more. If I had the chance to have more, I'm not sure how I would feel."

"Then right there is what you need to decide. If it's a no, tell Carmen straight up in a kind way. If you are open to it, I suggest you jump on it for the ride. She's worth it, man."

"I know she is."

"Then what are you waiting for? Some freaky sign saying it was meant to be?"

I blurted out a harsh laugh. "Maybe."

CHAPTER THIRTY-ONE

CARMEN

I sat in my tub, wanting it all to go away. What I wouldn't give to rewind time a few weeks and start over. I'd be cordial to Tim, maybe even have coffee with him again, but I would avoid going on a date, and I sure as hell wouldn't have had sex with the man.

I was also mortified that his son knew we had slept together. I sank under the water, wishing I could wash it all away. I had known from the beginning that Tripp would be the difficult one to deal with in terms of any relationship with Tim. I had hoped that the fragile relationship I had started with him concerning Missy would have helped us, but I was pretty sure I wouldn't hear from him again after today's incident.

After my bath, I climbed into bed and watched television until I was tired enough to sleep. I wanted nothing more than for this weekend to be in the past, and luckily, I could drift off without trouble.

BEFORE I WENT into the office Monday morning, I stopped by the hospital to check on Missy. She was doing much better and in a private room now. Her mother had returned to work now that she was improving, and I finally got to speak with Missy alone.

"You have no idea how glad I am that you are improving. How do you feel?"

"I constantly have a headache, and I'm always tired, but the world doesn't spin as much when I move—as long as I do it slowly."

"Concussions can take a while, Missy. I am sure they told you that."

"Yeah, they said I wouldn't be able to return to school this year, but my mom said they will pass me in all my classes, although I will have to do a little work from home at my own pace."

"I'm glad that school is working with you. They have protocols in place for this kind of thing."

"I'm glad. I can't imagine going to school right now."

"It's good you don't have to worry about it." I paused. "There is something that I am worried about."

"What is that?"

"You."

She frowned slightly. "But I'm getting better."

"I know you are, but your recovery will sometimes be long and difficult. I'm worried about how you are mentally with all of this."

"I haven't thought much about it."

"Have you thought of the accident?"

"Yeah, a little."

"How did you fall? Were you trying to jump in? Did you lose your balance? Or did something else happen?"

She stared at me for a few moments, and I waited patiently. She looked away and closed her eyes for a few seconds. Finally, she opened them and stared at the wall on the other side of the room. "I didn't fall. I jumped."

"Why?"

Her voice was a whisper when she spoke, but I heard every painful word perfectly. "Because I was hoping it would kill me."

"You wanted to die? At that very moment, you wanted to die?"

She nodded slowly, and a tear eased down her cheek.

"Do you still want to?"

"No."

"Are you sure?"

She nodded again and closed her eyes. The blue irises were bright with unshed tears when she opened them as she pled with me. "I don't want to die, Dr. Winston. I knew as I was blacking out that I was about to die, and I realized that I didn't want to. I don't want to. Can you help me? Can you help me fight this?"

"I can and I will, Missy. Can you tell me how much you had to drink that day?"

"A few beers, and I did a couple of shots."

"You know that the last time you tried to hurt yourself, you were drinking too."

"Yeah, I know."

"Growing up is difficult, and there are a lot of peer pressures, but are you aware that alcohol is a depressant?"

She shook her head.

"Well, it is, and when taken with your current medications, it can make you even more depressed."

"Is the beer why I wanted to kill myself?"

"You can't blame it all on the beer, but I will strongly caution you against drinking alcohol while you take your meds."

"But what if my friends give me a hard time for not drinking?"

"Peer pressure is difficult to deal with, but I suggest you tell people you can't drink because you take medication for a medical issue, and alcohol will make you really ill. A few other patients use that, and they have told me it works well with their friends. If one of your friends continues to pressure you, they aren't your friend."

"I can try that."

"I had one boy tell me that he decided he would be his friends' designated driver. Then he had another reason to be sober, plus he gets to take videos of his friends being stupid drunk. They never remember anything, but he does." I grinned at her, and she chuckled.

"I can try that too."

A thought crossed my mind. "Missy, did Tripp pressure you into drinking that day?"

She shook her head slowly. "No, he didn't want to drink, but I talked him into it." She grew quiet. "He didn't get into any trouble, did he?"

"No, not with the police if that's what you are asking. I think his father grounded him, but that was because he went out, not because he helped you. His father and I are very proud of him for stepping up the way he did and helping you."

"Have you talked to him?"

"I have. I have been texting Tripp to update him on your progress. He was very worried. Would you rather I don't do that?"

"No, that's okay." She grew quiet as she thought. "He hasn't come to visit me."

"That might be because he is grounded," I replied.

"Oh."

"I can message him later and tell him you asked about him. Maybe he can talk his father into letting him come visit."

"Would you?"

"Absolutely. In the meantime, let's talk a bit more, and then I will let you rest."

I pulled up the conversation with Tripp on my way out of the hospital.

I just saw Missy; she told me to say hello and that she would love to see you if you could visit.

I sent the message but knew he was in school and probably wouldn't respond immediately. I was surprised when he answered me as I crossed the parking lot.

Thanks. I appreciate the heads-up. Maybe you could talk to my dad and get him to let me.

I didn't particularly want to speak with Tim, but I wanted to help Tripp out, so I replied, *I'll see what I can do.*

Thanks, Dr. Winston, and sorry for being rude yesterday.

I stopped in my tracks. Now that I wasn't expecting. *I appreciate your apology and am sorry you had to hear that.*

He sent me a thumbs-up and nothing else. Well, at least that was a start.

Later that day, in between patients, I debated calling or texting Tim and took the coward's way out.

Hi, Tim. I wanted to let you know that Missy is doing better, and she asked to see Tripp. Do you think it would be possible for him to visit with her? I know he's grounded, but I think it would be helpful for both of the kids.

I read it like six times before I hit send. I didn't see a reply until after my next session, and it was short and to the point: *I'll see what I can do.*

I responded with a single word: *Thanks!*

That night I had to work late and didn't think much about Missy, Tripp, or Tim again. I had many other people who needed my attention more than them.

On Tuesday morning, I got a message from Evan asking me to come to dinner at his house. He said they wanted to discuss something with me, and I said yes because I was as curious as a cat.

Tuesday was another busy day, and I thought a few times

about reaching out to Tim to see if he would let Tripp see Missy, but I refrained from being a nag.

I arrived at my brother's a few minutes after six, and instead of heading out to the backyard where we typically hung out, Evan led me into the kitchen, where the scent of tomato sauce and garlic was ripe in the air.

"Yum, Italian. I haven't had good Italian in a long time."

"Good," Alaina said. "The gravy is a family recipe."

I chuckled. "I still can't get over how you call it gravy, and everyone else calls it sauce."

She grinned. "Americans are simple people."

"Very true." I accepted a glass of wine, and Alaina and I talked as she worked while Evan disappeared.

I didn't think much about it until he returned with Tim. I looked between them, then turned a raised brow toward Alaina. "Seriously? You let him do this again?"

"Wait!" Evan held his hand up. "I know you weren't aware that Tim was coming tonight, but he wanted to talk to you, and I figured that if Alaina and I were around, it could help from getting out of control."

"Evan, as much as I appreciate that, the last thing I need is you two in my business."

Evan cocked his head. "Versus the entire family being in your business?"

"Funny." I sighed. Perhaps it would be good to talk things out with Tim. Having a referee of sorts was probably wise. "Fine, I will talk to Tim."

Evan poured Tim a glass of wine, and I noticed Tim staring at mine as I took a sip. I rolled my eyes.

"Have a seat, Tim," Alaina said as she continued to stir the pot on the stove.

"Perhaps Carmen and I should speak alone."

Evan looked like he would object, but I put my hand up. "Just because you facilitated this does not mean you get a front-row seat to the drama. We will go out back."

Evan grinned and shrugged his shoulder, and I got off my stool and headed toward the back door, Tim on my heels. "There are a few blankets on the couch if it's cold, but you can turn the fire pit on."

"Thanks," I called out. Neither Tim nor I spoke until we were downstairs around the fire pit. He sat near me but not close enough to touch, and beside him was a little bag.

"I want to apologize again for what happened this weekend."

"What part are we talking about?"

"Any part you think warrants an apology."

I laughed. "There were so many; perhaps one apology will not be enough."

"Then I will get down on my knees and beg you to forgive me for anything I need to be forgiven for." He paused and then shifted off the cushion, getting to his knees.

"What are you doing?" He took my hand, and I had this crazy thought that he was about to propose. Panic began to claw through my stomach. "Tim, what the hell are you doing?"

"You better not be proposing to my sister!" My brother's voice boomed from the balcony. We both looked up and saw Alaina grab Evan's hand and tug him back into the house.

"Don't worry, I'm not proposing," he told me. "I want you to know that I am sorry that I never explained myself when I was younger. I hurt you a lot, and I realize that. I loved you, Carmen. I loved you so much, but I was young and stupid and needed to see other things. I should have explained that to you."

"You should have, Tim, and I appreciate you apologizing for that."

He squeezed my hand. "And I apologize for being an ass on Saturday. We were having such a great night, and I fucked that up." He paused, and I waited to see what he would say. I didn't particularly want to agree while he was apologizing.

"After we had sex, I guess I felt a little guilty. I know I didn't have a reason to, but after having only been with Emily for so many years—"

I covered our hands with my other one. "I understand that, Tim. There is no reason for you to apologize for that. I expected that."

"You did?"

I nodded. "I did. I know it wasn't easy to take that step, and while things didn't end well that night, I am glad you took that step with me." He winced as he shifted to his other knee. "Would you get off your knees, please?"

He laughed. "Thanks, I'm not as young as I used to be." He took a seat beside me. "I need to explain something to you."

"What?"

"Many years ago, I went through old boxes from my childhood with Emily. I came across a picture of you and me." He pulled a frame out of the bag beside him, and I gasped when I saw the picture of us that I had given him before he moved away.

"You showed this to your wife?"

"I did, and she wanted to know all about you. So I told her about you. About how incredibly patient and kind you were and how you laughed so much and loved life. I told her about your family and some things we used to do."

"What did she say about that?"

"She smiled and ate up every word. Then Emily told me that if something ever happened to her, I needed to look you up again."

I snorted. "No, she did not!"

"Yeah, she did. That day we also promised each other that if one of us died before the other, we would grieve and then move on."

"That was a good discussion," I replied, unsure what else to say.

Tim looked at his hand and fingered his wedding band. Then slowly pulled it off. "It's time for me to move on, Carmen."

I grabbed his hand. "Are you sure you want to do that? I mean, remove your ring. You don't have to."

"I do. I need to remove it to put the past in the past and build a future. A future with you, Carmen."

Could I dare to believe it? "And what about kids, Tim? I want kids of my own."

He cupped my cheek. "Then I hope you are pregnant right now because if you want us to have kids, then we will have kids."

32

CHAPTER THIRTY-TWO

TIM

Before Evan left, he suggested inviting Carmen and me over for dinner to talk. I said it was a bad idea, and he told me to let him know if I changed my mind.

I kept playing the conversation with Emily over in my mind, set my second beer bottle down, and went into the garage. I had to shift several boxes around but finally found the one I sought. The box held many of my childhood favorite items, including the picture of Carmen and me.

I cut through the tape and peeled back the corners, only to freeze when I saw the picture sitting atop the pile. I was pretty sure that had been tucked down deep in the box. I retrieved the frame and felt something on the back. Taped was an envelope with one word that was loving scrawled in Emily's handwriting. "Timmy."

A rush of grief filled me, and a soft groan left my lips as I stumbled back slightly. I took the picture and the note and sat on the step into the house from the garage. For a long time, I stared at the envelope, remembering other things she had written and how she had called me Timmy when she was being sweet, funny, or trying to get on my good side so I would do something for her. God, she had called me that a lot.

My hands shook slightly, and I inhaled deeply and released it in a calming manner before I opened the envelope and removed the paper from inside.

My eyes swam with tears as I unfolded it and read the letter she had written.

My dearest Timmy. I'd like to hope that you stumbled upon this while I'm still around. If so, put this back now! However, I think that might not be the case. If you are looking in this box again, you are searching for something—something to bring you back to a happier, easier time in life.

When you told me about all the goodies in this box, I noticed that your eyes sparkled and you laughed with each story, but no item in this box seemed to touch you the way this photograph did. I saw so much in you and understood you better as you spoke of Carmen.

I saw the love that you once felt for her and realized why you had been attracted to me. She sounds like a wonderful person, and I know we would have been friends if we had ever met. I also found it ironic that our features were so similar, but then again, I know you always had an attraction to blondes.

We discussed this, but I also know you so well, Timmy. You loved me more than I could have ever asked for, and you gave me an incredible life. One filled with family, joy, and romance. You gave me everything, Timmy, especially your heart.

You have always honored me with your faithfulness, selflessness, and your commitment to me and our family. You always did what was best for us, put your wishes aside, and never complained. I know you will continue to do that with our children too.

Now it's time for me to be unselfish and let you go—or better yet, tell you to let me go. Keep me in your heart and your memories but let me go and move on. Find someone to love and someone to build a life with. Fall in love! Get married! Have more children! You have so much love in your heart; don't let it grow stale or bitter. Find people to give it to.

Find Carmen. See if there is a future for you there. If she loved you even half the amount that I could tell you loved her, then there might be a chance, and if not her, then someone else.

Our children deserve for you to be happy, and they deserve a woman in their life who can guide and love them since I am not there. Find a woman who can love our children like they were her own.

I know you will always love me, and I hope you will keep my memory alive if I am gone. But live, Timothy Kohl! Live for us both and our children! Do all the things we always did and more! Do so much more!

All my love—Emily

By the time I reached the end, I could barely see through all the tears I was shedding. I put my head down on my arms and sobbed for a few moments, and then I wiped them away and reread it. Then one more time to make sure I had read it correctly.

I stopped in the bathroom on the way back inside and washed my face, then I climbed the steps to my son's room and knocked.

"Yeah?" he grumbled, and I opened the door to find him lying on the bed, watching television.

"Can I come in?"

He shrugged, not looking at me. I went to sit on the edge of his bed, and he glanced at me and then did a double take and frowned. "Have you been crying?"

I nodded. "Yeah, I have." I sniffed, and then I looked at the letter. "I told you that your mother and I talked about what we would do if one of us were gone. Your mother wanted to ensure I remembered my side of the bargain."

"What are you talking about?"

I told him what I had been doing and then held up the letter.

"She taped this to the back of the picture of Carmen and me." I held the letter out to him.

He sat up quickly. "That's from Mom?"

I nodded, and he snatched it from my hand, staring at the handwriting on the envelope like I had.

"I forgot what her handwriting looked like."

"Yeah, I did, too, until I saw it."

"Yeah," he said reverently. He lifted his eyes to mine. "Can I read it?"

"I want you to. I think it will help you understand."

He frowned as he unfolded the paper and leaned back to read the note. He blinked rapidly several times to dispel the moisture, but not before I noticed it.

When he finished, he stared at it with a perplexed look. "Did she really write this?"

"Do you think I made that up? I can't write like that or say such pretty things. That was all your mom, Tripp. I told you that we discussed it. This is what she wanted. She wanted us to move on."

"I guess," he said softly and handed the letter back to me.

"I love your mother dearly, Tripp, and one day you will understand how it feels not to have someone to share that part of your life with. Especially after you had that kind of love for so long and then it was torn from you. I'm ready to let someone else in. It's time that we all let someone else in."

"But does it have to be her? Dr. Winston?"

"Why not her?"

"I don't know."

"I'm not promising you anything, but I will tell you that I am going to start dating. Whether that is Carmen or another woman, I will start living that part of my life again."

"Okay, I get it."

I patted his leg and stood. "I appreciate that."

"And I appreciate you letting me read that. It was nice to see her handwriting again."

"I thought you might like that."

After I left his room, I returned to the kitchen and picked up my phone. I pulled up Evan's contact information and sent him a text: *Set up dinner. It's time for Carmen and me to settle this once and for all.*

TUESDAY EVENING, I showed up at the time Evan had requested, and I wasn't going to lie. I was nervous as hell as he opened the door.

"She's in the kitchen," he said as I entered.

"Does she know I'm coming?"

He shook his head and grinned. "Nope, but I don't think she will get as pissed as she did the last time."

"For both our sakes, I hope not."

I followed him into the kitchen, and while Carmen didn't appear enthusiastic about my appearance, she didn't burst from her stool, slap her brother, and run away—it was a start. Luckily, she agreed, and I was even more thankful when she suggested we talk alone. I wasn't entirely thrilled about the prospect of having this conversation in front of the owner of my company.

I apologized to Carmen and then told her how Emily and I had spoken of her before while showing her the picture I had kept.

"You showed this to your wife?"

I explained what I had said and how our conversation had evolved. I didn't tell Carmen about the letter Emily had left me, but then I looked at my hand. It was time. If I was going to commit to moving on, I needed to do it right here and now. Emily would understand.

"It's time for me to move on, Carmen."

Carmen grabbed my hand. "Are you sure you want to do that? I mean, remove your ring. You don't have to."

"I do. I need to remove it to put the past in the past and build a future. A future with you, Carmen."

"And what about kids, Tim? I want kids of my own." Her eyes looked so hopeful, making the next thing I said so easy.

"Then I hope you are pregnant right now because if you want us to have kids, then we will have kids."

She blinked and blinked again. "You aren't just saying that?"

"No, I'm not just saying that. I realized that I want to be with you, Carmen, and I want to give you everything you want as long as you are there for me and my children."

"Are you kidding me? Of course, I would be there for them. Haven't I already been there for them?"

"You have, and I appreciate it."

"What helped you decide that you were ready?"

I chuckled. "A voice from the past, but that's a discussion for another time. Right now, I'd like to kiss you and then go upstairs and have dinner because I'm starving. I haven't eaten since breakfast. I was too nervous."

"Nervous? About telling me this?"

"Yeah, I was afraid you would tell me no."

She took hold of my face. "Tim Kohl, I could never tell you no. I have wanted to be with you since I was fifteen, and that hasn't changed. I want us to make this work, build an incredible relationship, and have a happy family."

"I do too, Carmen."

"Good, then give me a kiss already."

CHAPTER THIRTY-THREE

CARMEN

C ould it work? Could Tim and I make this relationship work? I wasn't sure, but I knew that unless we tried, we'd never know.

I wanted it to work. I wanted it more than anything, and as Tim removed his wedding ring, I believed he did, too.

We climbed the steps arm in arm, and Evan was beaming as we stepped into the kitchen. "Are you guys good?"

Tim and I both chuckled. "Yes, we are good."

"And are you two officially a couple now?" Evan asked, looking hopeful.

"Are we?" I asked Tim, and he tugged me closer.

"Yes!" He kissed me quickly, and I grinned, looking back at my brother. He was typing on his phone.

"What are you doing?"

He ignored me and then grinned as he set his phone down. "Just letting everyone know it's official."

Alaina was shaking her head as she set a bowl of pasta on the table. "Your family just can't help themselves."

"No, they can't," I muttered as I heard my notifications go off on my phone. I decided to ignore them. "Who did you tell, by the way?"

"Um, everyone who needed to know."

Tim chuckled as he sat beside me at the table, and I said, "You know that our family gossips more than the entire sixth grade, right?"

"If we didn't, would we know what the others were doing?" Evan replied.

"No, we wouldn't."

AFTER DINNER, Tim walked me to my car and took my hands. "How would you like to have dinner with me again tomorrow night? I know just the place."

"You do, huh?"

"Yep, someplace I can guarantee you have never eaten before."

"Oh, that's gonna be hard."

"Hey, I found the winery, didn't I?"

I leaned forward and kissed him. "That you did."

He wrapped his arms around my waist. "Have dinner at my house with the kids."

I blinked a few times. "Are you sure you want me to do that? Do you think it's too soon?"

"I think the only person who might give us flak is Tripp, but he's either going to accept it or continue to make it difficult. Might as well try to get him on board sooner rather than later."

"All right, if you think that would be a good idea, I would love to have dinner at your house."

"Tomorrow at six-thirty?"

"I can do that."

"Good, I think it will be nice."

"I do too." Tim and I kissed goodbye, and then I headed

home, floating on cloud nine. It wasn't until I was home that I finally glanced at my phone to see a dozen messages from my siblings and the Youngs. Every single comment was positive and welcomed Tim into the family. I would have to show him the text messages tomorrow night.

I drifted off that night, feeling like I was finally on the right path for my future.

I PULLED up to his house and felt more nervous than I had in a long time. I shouldn't feel this way since I had already met all three of his kids, but tonight I was here for a different reason. I wasn't just a friend, but someone a little more.

Savannah opened the door as I approached it. "Hi, Dr. Winston!"

"Hello, Savannah. I already said you didn't have to call me that. You have my permission to call me Carmen."

"See, Dad! I told you." Savannah raised her voice so he would hear her as he came down the hallway.

"As long as she says it is all right." He winked at me. "Hi."

"Hi," I replied, looking nervously at him. Savannah giggled and raced down the hallway, and Tim leaned forward and took advantage of the privacy to kiss my lips quickly.

"Come on in. Dinner is almost ready."

"What are we having?"

"Tacos!" Savannah said from the kitchen as she carried plates to the table.

"Oh, I love tacos," I said and glanced around the kitchen to see Dean and Tripp both in the kitchen cooking. "They cook?"

"Yep, Dean is just starting to learn. Since Tripp has a job now, Dean will step up and help with cooking."

"Wow, that's impressive. Evan didn't learn to cook until—" I paused and cocked my head. "Well, let's just say he's delighted that Alaina cooks."

"Does Ethan cook?"

"Yeah, a little bit, but that's because Riley isn't all that domestic. If anyone wants to eat in that house, it's because Ethan cooks."

He chuckled. "Dean, Tripp, are you guys going to say hello?"

"Hi, Carmen," Dean said as he glanced my way and gave me a brief smile. Tripp was a little slower giving me his attention, but finally, he glanced my way.

"Hey." He immediately turned back to the pan of meat he was cooking, and Tim opened his mouth like he was going to say something, but I put my hand on his arm and shook my head, letting him know it was okay.

I watched the kids move around as they got dinner ready, and Tim poured me a glass of wine. I raised a brow when he handed it to me, and he shrugged. "Until we know."

While dinner was cooked, Tim and I sat in the living room and talked about work. It was only a few minutes until the food was on the table, and I stood, wondering which seat I should take.

Savannah pointed at the one beside her. "This is where my mom always sat. You can sit here."

The room went silent, and everyone looked at me and then Tim, but I focused on Tripp. "Tripp, where would you prefer that I sit?"

He was surprised I asked him. "Um, you can sit there. That's fine."

"Okay." I pulled the seat out and sat down before anyone could say anything else. While we ate, Savannah and Dean told me how busy they had been at school and sports.

During a lull, I asked Tripp, "Are you looking forward to starting your job tomorrow?"

He frowned slightly like he was surprised I knew. "Candy told me she hired you. You are going to be a big help there."

He relaxed. "Yeah, I am. This will be my first job."

"Does she know you cook?"

He shook his head. "No, I didn't tell her that."

"You should. Maybe after you get started, you can work in there if they get an opening in the kitchen."

He smirked. "I never thought about that. Do they get paid better in there?"

"I'm not sure of the exact salary, but it's decent, I know that."

"I'll mention it to her once I get used to the place."

After that, Tripp joined in on the conversation, and I started sharing stories of their father from when he was a kid. I talked about things involving other people, not just me. Most of the stories revolved around baseball or something he did with Wes Young or my brothers.

The kids asked lots of questions, and I felt like the tension had been removed by the time dinner was over. Savannah and Dean would accept me, and Tripp might take a little longer, but he would eventually come around.

After dinner, the kids were cleaning up the kitchen, and I took out my phone and sent Henley a message. Earlier, I had reached out to him to see if he was busy tonight. He was on duty but said he'd stop by if he wasn't busy.

"I hope you don't mind, but I invited someone over to speak with Tripp."

"Who?"

"Henley Young. I mentioned to Tripp that he was a paramedic and suggested he might want to speak with him."

"Thanks, Carmen, I appreciate that."

The two younger kids had just gone upstairs to shower and get ready for bed when there was a knock on the door, and Tim went to let Henley in. "It's good to see you. I appreciate you coming by," Tim said as they shook hands.

"Good to see you too, and I'm glad you two are together. I was getting tired of the group texts about the drama." He laughed. "Just kidding, I loved every minute of it."

"Let me go get Tripp," Tim said, disappearing up the steps as Henley entered.

"How are things going?"

"About as well as can be expected."

"Good, I'm glad to hear that." Before we could say anything else, Tim and Tripp were on the steps heading down. Tripp looked confused as he descended.

"Tripp, this is my good friend, Henley Young. I told you about him before. He's a paramedic."

"Oh yeah, cool."

Henley put his hand out and shook Tripp's. "I wanted to let you know that we talked about you at the firehouse."

"You have?"

"Yeah, see, we have this award that we give out to people who do heroic things, and my chief would like to give you that award."

"But what did I do?"

"You saved a young woman's life. You risked your own to pull her out of the water, and you gave her CPR. Did you, during that time, think about yourself?"

He shook his head. "No, all I could think about was getting to Missy and helping her."

"And did you stop and wonder if your actions were right?"

"No, I just did it. I learned CPR about a year ago. It was the first time I did it, but I didn't think about it."

"That's what a hero does, Tripp. They don't think about themselves, and they don't second-guess themselves. They do what they are trained to do in an emergency. That's why we would like to give you the award."

"Do you ever second-guess yourself?" Tripp asked him.

"All the time. That's natural, but you must rely on your

training and ability to work well under pressure. We have limited time to work sometimes, and we must go off our gut. There is always time afterward to wonder if what we did was right, but then we have to remind ourselves that we did what we did because that is what our training required us to do at that moment."

"Yeah, I can understand that."

"So, I understand you might be interested in becoming a paramedic, right?"

He glanced at me. "Yes, I am."

"That's cool. We have a program that was started a while ago for junior paramedics. They can get some advanced training to see if they would be interested in it. Sometimes we even allow them to go on a ride-along, but they must be seventeen and have parental permission."

"I'm only sixteen," he said.

"Well, you could join the junior paramedic team. They help us out at events like parades and fairs."

"That would be cool."

"So, will you accept the award?" Henley asked him.

Tripp glanced at his father. "Dad, can I?"

Tim grinned at him. "I think it would be great, Tripp. You deserve it."

"You do, Tripp," I added, and he grinned at me before turning to Henley.

"Then yes, I'd accept the award."

"Great! I'll get it all set up, and"—he reached into his back pocket and pulled out a few papers—"here are the forms to join the junior paramedic team. You can fill them out and give me a call. I put my number at the bottom. We can set up a time for you to come by the firehouse and get a tour."

"Sure! I'd love that." Tripp looked like he was on cloud nine.

Henley's radio squawked, and he pulled it out of its holder. "I gotta take off, but I'll talk to you guys later."

"Thanks, Henley. I appreciate you stopping over."

He quickly kissed my cheek. "See you later, Carmen. Bye, Tripp, Tim."

Tripp was grinning like a kid on Christmas. "Am I really going to get an award?"

"Looks like it," he said.

He threw his arms around his father and gave him a quick hug. "That's so cool. Do you think I can join the junior paramedic team?"

"We will have to see how much time it requires. You just got a job, remember, and you have school."

"Yeah, I know, but now I will need a car."

Tim sighed. "Yeah, I guess you will."

"I'm gonna go call Kyle!" He went to race from the room, but at the step, he paused and looked back. "Carmen, thanks for hooking me up with Henley. I appreciate that."

"You're welcome, Tripp."

He rushed up the steps two at a time, and Tim came to stand before me. "I think you might have just won him over."

I grinned at Tim, thinking he might just be right. Before I could say anything, though, Tim pulled me closer, his lips descending toward mine. "Come here, woman, I've been dying to do this all night."

CHAPTER THIRTY-FOUR

TIM

Three weeks later, we were all heading into the firehouse. Not just me and the kids, but Carmen and her entire family. The Youngs were all here too, and so were Missy and her mother. Missy wore dark glasses and moved slowly but appeared to be doing much better.

Carmen had taken Tripp to see her one afternoon while I was at work, and since then, he had been back to check on her a couple of times.

Carmen told me Missy was doing better and being very aggressive and receptive in her therapy. She didn't tell me the details, but that was none of my business. Carmen did tell me that Tripp's friendship was a massive help to Missy.

Speaking of friendship, the one that Carmen and I had grew by leaps and bounds daily. Most nights, she was at our house for dinner and even stepped in to help Dean cook a few new things when Tripp worked at the tavern.

We never slept together at my house, but at least twice a week, we went out on a date and always ended up at her house. Those were my favorite moments. Not just because of the sex but because it allowed Carmen and me to reach one another on a deeper level. A level that rivaled what I once had with Emily.

Occasionally, I would think about Emily, but I stopped feeling guilty. She had wanted me to be happy and find a new life. I had taken her advice.

While Carmen was not pregnant from our initial lovemaking, we weren't using anything. If she got pregnant, we were both prepared to do what needed to be done, and I hadn't admitted this to her, but I was looking forward to having another baby.

"Why is your whole family here?" Tripp asked Carmen as we got seated.

"Because you are part of the family, Tripp. When something good happens to one of the family, everyone is there to celebrate."

"But I'm not part of the family."

She eyed him carefully. "Well, that is up to you. If you don't want to be, you don't have to be, but I would like you to be, and I am pretty sure they all would too."

He glanced around the room but didn't reply. I had a feeling that he was a little overwhelmed by everything and didn't expect this many people to attend.

The award ceremony started, and it wasn't just one but several being given out. Tripp was the last one, and the fire chief who had met with us previously to speak with Tripp said beautiful things about him. I felt like I was going to burst with pride, and Carmen squeezed my hand, smiling as if she were sharing the pride with me.

Missy climbed on the stage before Tripp did and called him up. She was the one to give him the award plaque and thanked him for saving her life. I glanced at Carmen and saw her wipe under her eye. It was rare to see her show emotion. She was always so in control of her feelings. It meant the world to me that she was showing it now. I pulled her close and kissed her temple as we watched Tripp stand for photographs among the other award winners. I'd never seen my son beam like he was then.

After the ceremony, Carmen said we were having lunch at the tavern. When we arrived, we found it was closed to the public and decorated with banners and streamers to congratulate Tripp and the other winners.

Tripp was shocked at what they had done and floored that the entire fire department had come to the luncheon.

An extensive buffet was set up along one wall, and people quickly made their way to gather food. I was about to step into line when I felt a hand on my shoulder and turned to see Carmen's father.

"Mr. Winston, did you need something?"

"I think it is time that you called me, Richard, don't you think?"

"That would be nice."

"Do you have a moment? I want to speak with you in private."

"Of course," I replied, and we stepped out of line and into the bar, where it was quiet. "What can I help you with?"

"I won't beat around the bush, Tim. I want to know if you are serious about my daughter."

"Yes, Richard, I am very serious about your daughter."

"And you're not going to move away?"

"I have no plans on moving. I am happy here, and so are my kids."

He nodded. "You have nice kids."

"Thanks, Richard."

He paused for a moment. "I have another question for you, and it might be kind of personal, but well, hell, I thought I would ask."

"What is that?"

He looked uncomfortable as he shuffled his feet and glanced

around. "When did you know it was the right time to get involved with someone else?"

I almost laughed because that was the last thing I expected her father to ask me. "Emily and I had talked long ago and decided that we wanted the other one to be happy. We said we'd take the time to grieve, but then we would move on. I must admit the first time I was with Carmen, I felt a bit guilty, but then I reminded myself that I was alive, and Emily wasn't. I knew Emily would want me to be happy, which allowed me to move forward. Does that make sense?"

"Yeah, I suppose."

"I assume this is about Silvia."

"Yes, I have been thinking about taking the next step with her." He paused. "Us older people don't work as quickly as your generation does, but anyway, I just wasn't sure if I should feel guilty about it."

"I remember Mrs. Winston fondly, and I do not doubt that she would want you to feel loved and alive, Richard. I don't think she would fault you for wanting someone in your life or for wanting that physical connection that you share with someone you care about."

He studied me for a long moment. "Thank you. I think that makes me feel a little bit better."

"It's a touchy subject. I get it."

"I knew you would. That's why I asked you. I hope you don't mind."

"Not at all, Richard." I patted his back as we returned to the main dining room.

On the other side of the room, I saw Tripp standing off to the side, talking to Carmen, and my jaw dropped when he said something to her, and she opened her arms, and he stepped in to hug her. I blinked back the tears that had sprung forth, and I rushed to her side the moment he slipped away from Carmen.

"Did I just see you and Tripp hugging?"

She grinned. "Why yes, you did. Are you jealous?"

"No! What did you say to him to get him to do that?"

She chuckled. "I didn't say anything. He came over to thank me and asked if he could hug me."

"Wow," I replied.

"Yeah, wow is right." She grinned, looking very happy.

"I love you." I blurted the words, and she froze.

"You love me?"

"Yes, I do. I love how you make me feel. I love how you make my children feel. I love how devoted you are to your family and how devoted you will be to our family." I cupped her cheek. "I love you, Carmen Winston."

"I love you, too, Timothy Kohl. I always have, and I always will."

I kissed her right there, off to the side of the room, where everyone looking could see. There were a few comments about getting a room and a few hoots, but I didn't mind.

When I pulled back, I grinned at her. "I think we need some champagne to toast the occasion."

She tugged her bottom lip under her teeth. "Better make mine sparkling cider."

I froze. "What did you say?"

"I said, you better make mine sparkling cider."

"Are you—"

She nodded, her eyes sparkling brightly with excitement.

"How long have you known?"

"I found out this morning, but I didn't want to ruin the day for Tripp. I figured I would tell you tomorrow."

I pulled her tightly against me, whispering to her, "You're really pregnant?"

She nodded. "Yes, we are going to have a baby."

"Do you know how hard it is not to shout this to the whole room?"

She laughed and pulled back. "And that is why I didn't want

to tell you today. Don't take this day from Tripp. There will be enough time to share the news later."

I kissed her again. "I love you and want you to marry me."

"Whoa," she said, laughing. "Let's take this one step at a time. Don't go proposing just yet. We have time."

"Don't you want to marry me?"

She got into my face. "I have never wanted anything more in my life, but we have time, Tim. We have time."

"I learned a few years ago that time isn't guaranteed."

She looked sad. "No, it's not, but I don't want us to rush into this."

"It's not rushing if we both want it."

"I do want it. I want you and our baby and your kids. I don't think we have to commit to everything right now."

"Fine, I'll give you a week and then ask you."

She tossed back her head. "How about you give me a month, and if we still like each other after that, you can ask me."

"A month?"

"Yes, a month."

"Fine, I'll give you one month. It will give me time to go shopping."

She grinned and started to turn away. "Take Candy with you. She knows the one I already picked out."

I laughed as I watched her walk away. Then I let my eyes slip over the room. In here were all the people I cared about and those who cared about me and Carmen. They were family and my future.

Yes, Emily had been my wife and my life, but she wasn't here anymore. I knew without a doubt that she would approve. She would have welcomed this with open arms, and I smiled as a warm feeling filled me, and I went to enjoy my new future.

The End

SNEAK PEEK: CORAL

Enjoy the first chapter of Coral, Loving a Winston, Book 5

<u>Coral</u>

The last thing I wanted to be doing was sitting on an airplane flying to the other side of the country—especially with my entire family.

However, that was where I was, and despite feeling miserable, I was forcing myself to smile and laugh because that was what they expected of me.

Most people would be thrilled to be going on vacation, especially since we were traveling on a private plane and heading to an incredible house surrounded by some of the best skiing trails the United States had to offer—but I wasn't.

All I could think about was that by the time I returned home, I probably wouldn't even have anything left there for me. No one knew this, but my business was in trouble.

I had always known I wanted to be a business owner, but it wasn't until after college that I decided I wanted to own a coffee house. I went to school to study business and worked many odd jobs during those years. When I was working for ski patrol in the Poconos, I finally decided which direction to go. The day it opened, I had been flying high and thought all the hard work and calculated decisions would pay off.

I had even sourced the perfect coffee bean that I roasted myself. I loved roasting my coffee, but I should have thought twice about what machine I had bought. I invested almost ten grand in that machine to get professionally roasted beans, but that stupid thing was out of warranty and was constantly breaking down. They wanted another grand to extend the warranty a few years.

When I finally opened my doors, I assumed the worst was over, and now I could kick back and enjoy it. Granted, I knew I would still have to work hard, but getting all the pieces together was downright stressful. Unfortunately, I had been very wrong. The stress only continued, and it got more burdensome by the day. Inventory, employee issues, bills, and customers seemed to overwhelm me daily. It had been so difficult that I thought about giving up at least once a week.

Only our family never gave up, and I would never hear the end of it if I did. I could imagine my father shaking his head at me, his eyes sad as he realized I had not only wasted years but tens of thousands of dollars.

I didn't want to disappoint him, but I knew I would in the end. I glanced away from the window where I had been staring at the clouds and shifted my gaze around the plane's interior.

Not only would I disgrace my family by failing, but I would be doing it alone. All five of my siblings had fallen in love, married, and were moving forward with building their families. I didn't even have the time or energy to think about dating.

I'd had plenty of chances, as I'd been hit on many times at the café, but I'd turned down every single one because I had to focus on my business. I was determined to do everything possible to turn it around and make it profitable. I had to prove to them and myself that I could do it.

Every one of my siblings was thriving—not just in love but in their careers. Ethan was a sergeant and a detective; Evan was the head of his nursing department; Carmen owned a psychology practice; Candy was a structural engineer, and Cara was a helicopter pilot and flight medic. Plus, each of them had impressive spouses and children, too!

Even my father had found someone new to share his life with, but me? I was married to my coffee shop—and it was a relationship that was heading for divorce.

I sighed as I watched Carmen lean toward Tim and kiss him. They kept their heads together briefly and whispered before cracking up. Carmen glanced at me, and I wondered if I had been the butt of their joke.

It wouldn't surprise me. I always felt like I was on the outside looking in at my own family. I had felt that way most of my life, but recently, it had gotten worse.

Candy and Carmen would routinely come to the café for coffee, but I was always working, and they were always chatting away, laughing, and planning their lives. I would watch them sometimes, and pangs of jealousy would eat at my insides. If I approached them, they would try to pull me into the conversation, but I felt it was always half-hearted, and then I would get called away again, and they would resume their fun discussions.

Alaina, Evan's wife, slipped into the seat beside me. "You okay? You're very quiet."

"Yeah, I'm just exhausted." I laughed. "I worked extra hours to ensure everything was taken care of before I left."

She squeezed my hand. "You did, but now you can relax. Why don't you close your eyes and rest? We have about four hours before we land."

"Probably a good idea," I replied, and she slipped out of her seat and headed toward the back of the plane. I glanced around the sleek private plane again. Alaina owned it, and I had been on it one other time when she had flown us to a remote island for their wedding.

That was almost two years ago, the last time I had taken time off from my café. It had been the start of a nightmare I had tried to keep waking up from but couldn't seem to do.

I collected a set of headphones from the back pocket of the seat and plugged them into the plane's sound system. Using the controls on the back of the chair in front of me, I found a selection of music to listen to, and I closed my eyes and settled back.

I didn't want to be on vacation, but if I had to be, I would at least take advantage of the time to sleep—and ski. I couldn't wait to hit the slopes again.

My father woke me several hours later, and I blinked groggily as I tried to escape the stupor I had been in. I honestly hadn't slept quite that well in a long time, and I felt like I had a heavy dark cloud around me as I stretched in my seat. I cleared my throat. "Yeah, what's going on?"

"We are about to land. Look out the window." He pointed toward the small oval window, and I peered through the small opening at the majestic snow-covered mountain peaks in the distance. I smiled, feeling something positive for the first time since we left Pennsylvania.

"It's pretty," I remarked.

"Just think, tomorrow, you can be up there skiing down."

"Yeah, it will be nice to do that again."

"How long has it been?"

I shrugged. "I don't know. Maybe four or five years. I wonder if I'll even be able to do it anymore." It was probably longer than that, but I didn't want to admit it. I knew that I hadn't been skiing since I opened the café. Any time before that seemed decades ago.

He patted my arm. "I'm sure you can. You were always good at it. It won't take you long to be flying down the slopes."

I glanced at my father. "How do you know I was any good? You've never seen me ski."

He grinned. "I didn't have to see you to know you would be good. You've always excelled at everything you do."

I looked away from him quickly. "No, I don't."

He laughed. "Of course you do." He patted my arm. "I have to return to my seat. Silvia isn't a fan of landing."

He disappeared as everyone got situated back in their seats. Tim's son, Tripp, slipped into the seat beside me. Besides Tim's kids, I was the only one traveling single.

Ironically, this whole vacation idea had been a gift from my siblings. They wanted me to get away, relax, unwind, and have some fun. When I didn't seem thrilled by it and made no plans to use their gift, they turned it into a family vacation the week of Thanksgiving and guilted me into coming. How could I not come? Everyone would be here—except Cara and Bryan who had work obligations.

I watched the plane descend to the tarmac, and then we taxied to a private terminal off to the side of the airport in Reno. Originally, Alaina wanted us to fly right into Lake Tahoe, but the weather was too tumultuous for that, so we landed in the desert of nearby Nevada and would take rented SUVs into the Sierra Nevada Mountains that surrounded the lake.

I had been skiing in many places, but I had never been here, and although I wasn't excited to be on vacation with my entire family, I was starting to look forward to being on the slopes again. I looked forward to the crisp air, the wind on my face as I flew down.

I had done some research, too, and learned that the area we

were staying in was twenty minutes away from several different ski lifts and a host of trails.

While my siblings contributed to the trip, I knew Alaina and Evan had paid for most of it. There was no way we could have afforded the six thousand a night cost of the house we were renting alone. I would have been happy to stay at a hundred-dollar-a-night hotel, but Alaina wouldn't allow that.

When we landed, I turned airplane mode off on my phone and nervously waited for my notifications. The plane did have Wi-Fi, but no one would tell me the code. They all said I was on vacation and needed to unplug. They had no clue how difficult that was for me or how much I needed to stay in touch with things back at the café.

I had nine emails and three texts. The texts were from Monica, my assistant manager. The first one said: *Things are going well.* The second one stated: *The catering order was picked up with no problems,* and the third one read: *Things are still going well. Stop worrying and enjoy your vacation.*

I chuckled slightly; she knew me well. I quickly typed to her to say we had landed and I would now be available if she needed anything.

A few moments later, she told me to turn my phone back off and enjoy myself.

If only I could. I followed everyone out of the plane and assembled in the airport. It took a little while, but finally, we had our luggage, and Alaina, Evan, and Tim went to collect our rental cars.

"I wish Cara and Bryan were here," Candy said.

"I know," Carmen replied. "But she's due any day."

"You know, if you hadn't had a miscarriage, you wouldn't be here either," Candy said softly.

"Yes, I know," Carmen said sadly, then put her hand over her belly. "But this pregnancy will be better."

"I hope so," Candy replied before hugging Carmen.

I turned away from them. I had barely known that Carmen was pregnant the first time before she lost the baby. Most of my siblings had known much earlier but never thought to tell me. When she lost the baby a week later, I felt sorry for her but didn't feel as overwhelmed as most of my siblings, who were more attached to the idea. Unlike my family, I never thought of kids. It wasn't in my cards, so why even consider it?

However, Carmen did; five months later, she was pregnant again. I learned it early, but only because she switched to decaf coffee at the café. Now, she was only two months along, and while she had come on the trip, she had already said she wasn't skiing. I didn't blame her.

We split into three vehicles since there were fourteen of us. The five couples, and then Tim's three kids who had extensive skiing knowledge, plus me. The younger children had remained home with several of the Young family members to look after them.

We made a little train as we drove through Donner Pass, and the farther we traveled into the mountains, the more I began to relax. The first time we went around a curve and saw the lake surrounded by the beauty of the mountains, we had to pull over and get out.

We all stood along the guardrail and let our gazes wander from one side of the lake to the other. It was magnificent.

It took longer to get to our house than planned because we kept stopping and getting out to check out the scenery, but finally, we pulled down the driveway to a large house that sat directly beside the lake.

Everyone went into the house to check out the accommodation, but my feet led me to the water's edge, where I stared in wonder at the sight before me—not just the water but the mountains and the snow that surrounded the body of water. It was literally the most beautiful thing I had ever seen, and for the first time in a long time, I felt a peace descend over me as tears leaked from my eyes.

Coral, Book 5

What happens you overhear your family talking to the man you've fallen for?

Coral Winston has felt out of touch with her family since her mother passed away and threw everything she had into her coffee café. When her family forces her to vacation, they decide to come along for the fun.

Landan Lancaster is the oldest of the eight Lancaster children, and he's still trying to deal with walking away from his cheating bride the night before their wedding many months prior. When a large family comes to stay in the Lancaster guest house on the lake, he finds himself expectedly intrigued by the woman standing at the water's edge.

On the slopes of South Lake Tahoe, Landan realizes he has met his match in more ways than one, and Coral begins to feel as if she has finally found a place where she belongs. When she overhears a conversation between Landan and her family, Coral gets the wrong idea and flees without thinking. Unfortunately, she finds the café a mess and the cops waiting for her when she arrives home.

Can Coral overcome the issues facing her and find her way back to the beautiful mountains and water of Lake Tahoe, or will Landan lose her before he can ever call her his own?

LOVING A YOUNG SERIES

Wesley, Book 1

Traumatized by events of her past, Charlotte Bennett is not a fan of strangers. When she sees a man touching her daughter at the park, she reacts without listening. It's only later when her daughter is rushed to the hospital that she realizes how wrong she had been.

Doctor Wesley Young only wanted to help the tender-aged girl he witnessed fall, but when her mother attacks him at the park, he's left stunned. When the little girl arrives later in the emergency department, he comes face to face with the mother who makes more of an impression on him than the cut she left on his face.

Things heat up quick when Marisol is no longer his patient, but when things from the past are revealed, Wes isn't sure that Charlotte is the woman for him. Can Charlotte find a way to explain it all so that Wes will accept both her and her daughter before it's too late?

Henley, Book 2

Being a wedding planner is hard, especially when someone is

always trying to steal your business, and your family doesn't support you. However, Roxanne Novak is determined to keep her business afloat.

When Roxy's in a car accident hurrying to meet a potential bride, she's injured and scared, but paramedic Henley Young takes good care of her.

Henley loves his job and thrives on the adrenaline of helping people in need. Maybe that's why when he meets Roxy, he's inclined to help her with more than just medical care. Hooking her up with his older brother Wesley and his bride-to-be could be just what she needs. It might also be the start of something between Lee and the spunky little wedding planner.

When a position at a country club is offered to Roxy, she finds herself rethinking her entire business plan. Excited to start someplace new, Roxy and Henley begin making plans for the future. Just after she starts her new job, Roxy learns of Lee's past relationship, and everything she knew about him is questioned.

Can Roxy and Henley put the past to bed and move forward to something that might be more than what both of them had ever hoped for?

Huntley, Book 3
Daniella Knight works hard to create suspenseful and romantic tales, but after a violent interaction with a fan, she wants to hide from the world. When her house catches on fire, her and her protection dog, Tigger, are forced to rely on the help of strangers.

Huntley Young loves being in the thick of the action. Well, as long as that action has something to do with his job as a firefighter. When Huntley stops the homeowner from going back into the house, he has no clue, that he just placed himself firmly in the hero department.

As they get to know each other, Daniella's creative mind is always building on what is around her, and before she knows it, reality and fiction are hard to tell apart.

When danger strikes again, will Daniella be able to see what is right in front of her, or will her past trauma keep her safely inside her romantic fictional world?

Riley, Book 4

Riley is always the life of the party, and it's Ethan that is there to pick her up and keep her together. He knows her almost as well as she knows herself, and he knows she will never love him as he does her.

Now Ethan wants more out of life and love, but Riley denies her feelings and insists they are just friends with benefits. When a training opportunity comes up that will get Ethan out of town for months, he jumps on it. It's the only way to get over Riley and move on.

With Ethan gone and a new guy in her life, Riley finds herself dealing with several emotional issues without the help of her best friend. A family emergency has Ethan feeling lost without Riley there to lean on, but he refuses to go to her and seeks solace with another.

Will Riley make the right choices, and finally, admit how she feels, or will she find herself alone and falling further down the rabbit hole.

Kayley, Book 5

Independent Kayley Young is a real estate agent in New York and loves her life as a single woman. She's not one to get tied down, and she has no desire to have children.

Officer Cameron Sexton is new on the job, a veteran of the military, and proud of his dedication to the job. Unfortunately, he finds himself annoyed at his lackadaisical sergeant who should hang up his gun belt before getting someone hurt. When Cameron is dispatched to a burglary, he meets Kayley Young and is instantly attracted to her. Cameron has a feeling she reciprocates those feelings, except she's a little leery of the fact that he is ten years younger than her.

When Kayley's life starts taking a turn for the worse, she finds herself depending more on the attractive young man she has let into her bed for fun than she intended. Her original thought of enjoying the moment starts to last longer, but Kayley's not sure that dating a man ten years her junior is smart for the long haul. Especially with the rest of the changes that have happened in her life.

Can Kayley come to terms with the age difference, or will her family sway her away from the younger man?

Bradley, Book 6

Bradley Young is the eldest sibling of the Young family, and the only one who had previously been married. After losing his wife to cancer several years ago, he's used to caring for his two kids alone. The thought of dating is not something he's interested in, now with a busy construction business, and a family that always needs help.

Nolan Nickels needed a change, and with the help of her good friend, Kayley, she left New York and came to Millerstown to take a teaching position at the middle school. She has always been a huge tom boy and loves to fix things with her hands and play sports.

With a new house in her name, Nolan seeks out the perfect plan to get the house ready so she can bring her two daughters' home, but is her fixer-upper more than she bargained for? When Kayley finally gets Brad to stop by the house to check something, Brad finds himself more than intrigued with the spitfire, Nolan. Will he finally find the woman to spend his life with, or will she be put a halt on any type of future?

LOVING A WINSTON SERIES

The *Loving a Winston Series* is a five-book steamy romance series that spins off of the *Loving a Young Series*. Characters from both series will appear from book to book. Each book is a standalone romance with suspense and spicy romance scenes.

Cara, Book 1

What happens when the man you fall for is all wrong for you?

Cara Winston has always been a bit of a rebel and an adrenaline junkie. As a helicopter pilot and paramedic, she relies on that to do her job. When Cara and her team respond to a multi-vehicle accident involving motorcycles, she's expecting the worst. What Cara doesn't expect is to find herself intrigued by the blue eyes of a man wearing motorcycle gang colors.

Ryan Vigilante rides the road mostly on two wheels, not four. When several of the club members end up in an accident on the highway, Ryan never expects to see a future in the eyes of the intense female paramedic. The only problem is that she's way out of his league, and he knows that getting involved with her could only jeopardize her safety.

With Cara's family trying to keep them apart and Ryan's club breaking the law, Cara finds herself more of a rebel than usual. Will things work out for Cara and Ryan, or will Cara's law enforcement brother, Ethan, find a way to stop it for good?

Evan, Book 2

What happens when she's not really who you think she is?

EVAN WINSTON IS DEDICATED to his job as a registered nurse in the ICU department of the local hospital. He's one hundred percent focused on the needs of his patients and his family, or at least he usually is. That changes the day a woman visits one of his patients and turns his world upside down.

Laney Marshall wants nothing more than to help people who struggle—especially those women and children who are fighting to survive domestic violence situations. After losing someone close to her to an abusive man, she is determined to do everything in her power to help.

Unfortunately, Laney has people that don't want her to do that. In fact, they don't even like her in this town or even the state of Pennsylvania. They prefer her on the other side of the country, where they think she belongs, living the life planned for her.

Can Laney and Evan find a way to build a relationship while keeping others from getting involved, or will the revealed secrets be enough to end any chance of a future before it begins?

Candy, Book 3

What happens when your lustful heart wins over your intellectual mind?

WHEN CANDY'S SISTER, Cara, was dating outlaw biker member Ryan Vigilante, Candy paid little attention to Ryan's club buddy, Bollard. Sure, Bollard, who works behind the bar at the local tavern, was pleasing on the eyes and made a mean chocolate martini, but he was an outlaw, and that's not the kind of person Candy associates with.

Michael Bollard is out of the club now and hopes to purchase the tavern. He had never wanted more than his bikes and the club, but now, Mike has high hopes to build a future. A future that suddenly collides with sexy and intelligent Candy Winston in ways he could have never imagined.

Just when he thinks he might have this new future figured out, a stranger enters the bar with a surprise he never saw coming. Will that surprise send Candy running for higher ground, or will it cement her future in the tavern with Mike?

Carmen, Book 4

What happens when your first love returns to town—twenty years later?

CHILD PSYCHOLOGIST CARMEN WINSTON spends a lot of time at the schools, and when she comes across a man and the name of a new student, she mentally flashes back to a time of young love and dreamy hopes of the perfect future that never happened.

Tim Kohl lived in Millerstown for six years before his parents moved him across the country. He never expected to return or to bring three kids with him when he did. The last thing Tim expected to find in town is his high school sweetheart, who is still as beautiful as ever and still single after all this time.

When sparks fly, can these two put the past behind them and plan a future, or will the years apart separate them before they can figure it out?

Coral, Book 5

What happens you overhear your family talking to the man you've fallen for?

CORAL WINSTON HAS FELT out of touch with her family since her mother passed away and threw everything she had into her coffee café. When her family forces her to vacation, they decide to come along for the fun.

Landan Lancaster is the oldest of the eight Lancaster children, and he's still trying to deal with walking away from his cheating bride the night before their wedding many months prior. When a large family comes to stay in the Lancaster guest house on the lake, he finds himself expectedly intrigued by the woman standing at the water's edge.

On the slopes of South Lake Tahoe, Landan realizes he has met his match in more ways than one, and Coral begins to feel as if she has finally found a place where she belongs. When she overhears a conversation between Landan and her family, Coral gets the wrong idea and flees without thinking. Unfortunately, she finds the café a mess and the cops waiting for her when she arrives home.

Can Coral overcome the issues facing her and find her way back to the beautiful mountains and water of Lake Tahoe, or will Landan lose her before he can ever call her his own?

. . .

COMING IN 2025
The *Loving a Lancaster Series* will begin publishing in 2025 and spins off the *Loving a Winston Series*. This series is anticipated to be at least eight books long.

LOVING A LANCASTER SERIES

The Loving a Lancaster Series spins off of the Loving a Winston Series. In Coral's book, you are introduced to the Lancaster family while she is on vacation in Lake Tahoe. This series will consist of seven books, and stared with Leo.

Leo - Book 1

Leo Lancaster is coming home to Lake Tahoe. As a successful stockbroker and business owner, Leo has decided to open another office in Truckee and work out of that one instead of his Vegas office. Now, he must locate a house and get himself settled, and the last thing he expects to find on his return is love.

Heather McClain is a devoted mother of two teens, and a widow from Ohio. When her best friend encourages her to go on a girls trip to Lake Tahoe, she decides to take a break from the chaos at home and try to have fun. Only their antics are more than Heather bargained for.

Lucky for her, Leo is around to rescue her and the two of them quickly grow close, but is Heather ready to let go of her husband's memory and move forward into a relationship, or more importantly, are her children prepared to accept a new man into their mother's life when she surprises them with a trip to the lake?

Luna - Book 2

WHILE LUNA LANCASTER loves Lake Tahoe, she thrives in the outdoors near her home in Sedona, Arizona. When Luna's good friend, Sadie, plans a visit and decides to bring a guest, Luna is excited to show them the sights of the beautiful Red Rocks around her home.

Unfortunately, Luna's friend can't make it at the last minute, and Luna finds herself entertaining Trace Hampton alone. The chemistry between them sparks the moment they meet. The problem is that Luna thinks Trace and Sadie are a couple, and she does everything possible to hide her feelings and not act on them.

When Trace reveals that he is not involved with Sadie, Luna jumps at the chance to see what they could have, but when Sadie finds out, she's heartbroken that Luna stole the man she likes out from under her.

Will Luna save the friendship and lose the chance at a happily ever after with Trace?

Levi, Book 3

LEVI LANCASTER IS the youngest of the family, and while not as classy and outgoing as his older siblings, he works hard for his own HVAC company.

When a major snowstorm hits Lake Tahoe, Levi is enlisted to do a favor and finds himself quite taken with Diane Hampton. He's heard of her through his sister, Luna, and Luna's boyfriend, Trace, but he has never had the chance to meet them.

Diane loves her new life in Lake Tahoe, but she is not a fan of driving in the snow. When Levi comes to help her out, Diane may find herself finally ready to move on after the loss of her fiancée five years ago.

When a stranger arrives at the lake and tries to insert herself into Levi's life, Diane tries to figure out if the woman is after something, or just trying to find pieces of her past. Can Diane protect Levi or will he push her away when she is only trying to help?

Life is about to change for these two, but will it be for the better?

Still to come: Lance, Lily, Laney, and Lucas.

ABOUT THE AUTHOR

Stacy Eaton began her writing career in October of 2010 and, as each year goes by, she releases more and more novels. Stacy recently took an early retirement from law enforcement after over fifteen years of service, with her last three in investigations and crime scene investigation.

Stacy resides in southeastern Pennsylvania with her husband, who works in law enforcement, and her two dogs. She has a daughter in college and a son who is currently serving in the United States Navy.

Be sure to visit www.stacyeaton.com for updates and more information on her books.

Sign up for all the latest information on Stacy's Newsletter!

Join my Newsletter and get TWO Short Stories for FREE!

STACY'S OTHER BOOKS

Rise Again Warrior Series

The *Rise Again Warrior Series* is an intense and emotional journey through the lives of many service members, their families, and their friends. Focusing on the trials that they face after wartime is over, and they have returned home to a nation that sometimes seems to have forgotten what they were fighting for, and what all of these people sacrificed in the name of Honor & Duty. Books Include: Mission: Believe, Mission:Accept, Mission: Repair, and Mission: Courage

Loving a Young Series

The *Loving a Young Series* is a steamy romance series that consists of six books. While these books are all standalone romances, the characters will be seen across the series since this is a small-town romance series about siblings finding forever loves.

Books include: Wesley, Henley, Huntley, Riley, Kayley & Bradley

The Loving a Winston Series

The *Loving a Winston Series* is a five-book steamy romance series that spins off of the *Loving a Young Series*. Characters from both series will appear from book to book. Each book is a standalone romance with suspense, adult language and spicy romance scenes.

Books Include: Cara, Evan, Candy, Coral and Carmen.

The Loving a Lancaster Series

The *Loving a Lancaster Series* spins off of the *Loving a Winston Series* when Coral Winston meets Landon Lancaster in Lake Tahoe. Characters from previously series maybe show up in these books. Each book is a standalone romance, adult language and may contain spicy romances scenes.

Books includes: Leo, Luna, Levi, Lance, Laney, Lucas, and Lilly.

The Unexpected Series

The *Unexpected Series* is a steamy romance series where anything can happen and probably will. Each book in the series is a stand-alone happily ever after, or happy for now book. While they are stand-alone, the books are all centered around Safety Zone Security and the employees there. Characters from one book will continue throughout the rest of the series. Books Include: Unexpected Packages, Unexpected Arrivals, Unexpected Trouble, Unexpected Storms, Unexpected Desires, Unexpected Ties.

Paranormal Romance:

My Blood Runs Blue Series

My Blood Runs Blue Series is an adult Paranormal Action/Romance Series with vampires and is intended for mature audiences.

Books Include: My Blood Runs Blue, The Pulse of Blue Blood, Blue Blood for Life, Mixing the Blue Blood, Blue Bloods Final Destiny,

The Return of Blue Blood Series:

This series is 40 years in the future after My Blood Runs Blue. It is a very steamy series intended for mature audiences.

Books Included: Kristin: Blue Blood Returns, Hugh: Blue Blood Compelled, Zander: Blue Blood Reborn, Lena: Blue Blood Desired, Reckoning, Blue Blood Finale

Single Titles

Whether I'll Live or Die

You're Not Alone

Garda ~ Welcome to the Realm

Liveon ~ No Evil

Second Shield

Distorted Loyalty

Six Days of Memories

Second Shield II: The Return

Tempt Me Too

Finding the Strength

Finding Love in Special Places:

Stacy's Short Story Series

Sweet Romance about adult topics. Stories include: Finding Love on Christmas Vacation, Finding Love on the Summer Surf, Finding Love with Dear Santa, Finding Love with a Champagne Toast, Finding Love on the High Seas, Finding Love on a Dude Ranch, Finding Love at the Farmer's Market, Finding Love at the Coffee Shop

Heart of the Family Series

The *Heart of the Family* Series is a small-town steamy romance series that is best read in order. Books Include:

Mistletoe & Cocoa Kisses, Roses & Champagne Kisses, Orchids & Hurricane Kisses, Carnations & Hot Toddy Kisses,

Heal Me Series

Love Spicy Medical Romance? Check out the rest of the Heal Me Series for sexy romances that will warm your heart as they deal with life-altering medical and psychological issues. These books do contain language and open door sexual relations. While each book in the Heal Me Series is a stand-alone book, the characters cross between books and are best enjoyed by reading them in order. Books Include: Cured, Revived, Mended and Rescued.

The Celebration Series

The Celebration Series: Celebration Township is made for family, friends, falling in love, and don't forget celebrating the holidays. The first twelve books bring two people onto center stage as they overcome odds and figure out what their futures may hold. There is laughter, love, romance and even suspense when you join these couples as they each find a happily ever after over a holiday. The thirteenth book brings all twelve couples, and even a few special guests, into final focus as the first couple in Tangled in Tinsel prepares for their wedding one year after they met. Books Include: Tangled in Tinsel, Tears to Cheers, Heathens to Hearts, Rainbows Bring Riches, Sweet as Sugar, Making Mom Mad, Sparklers or Spankings, Raffles to Rattles, Flirting with Fireworks, Working Under Wheels, Masquerading at Midnight, Blessing & Beans, Velvet & Vows.

The Sometimes Series:

The Sometimes Series consists of three romances where the passion is a touch spicy and there is a hint of suspense is in the air. Sometimes You Win is a stand-alone story that ends with a Happy-for-Now ending. Sometimes you Lose, Book 2 of the series does end in a cliffhanger and Sometimes You Play the Game will finally give the couple a Happily Ever After. In all three books, you will find adult language and situations. Books Include: Sometimes You Win, Sometimes you Lose, Sometimes You Play The Game.

Pleasure Your Fantasies Series

The Pleasure Your Fantasies series is an ADULT Series with coarse language and intense sexual situations along with suspense. Books Include: Mistletoe Fantasies, Whispered Fantasies, Secret Fantasies, Conflicted Fantasies, Returning Fantasies, Arrested Fantasies, Discovered Fantasies, and Explosive Fantasies

List Updated 10/27/25